Blind Side of Love

By

Beth Rinyu

Blind Side of Love

Copyright © 2014 by Beth Rinyu

All rights reserved

Cover design and Cover photo by Lindee Robinson of Lindee Robinson Photography

Cover models: Models: Garrett A. Thierry & Megan A. George

Thank you so much to all of my awesome readers! Hope you love this story just as much as my others.

An extra special thank you to Judy and Tanya for triple checking for errors and making sure that it was in perfect condition for all of you!

Happy Reading xo

Also by Beth Rinyu

The Exception to the Rule

An Unplanned Lesson

An Unplanned Life

Drowning in Love

A Cry for Hope

A Will to Change

Part One

Becca

My life as I knew it began on the day I met Drew Bryant. He taught me that it was okay to not always be perfect, that it was okay to loosen up and have a little fun in life, and that it was okay to fall in love.

My life as I knew it ended on the day I met Drew Bryant. He taught me that giving my heart to someone completely was the most dangerous thing I could ever do, and that the perfect world I was living in didn't matter anymore without him in it.

But the most important lesson that he taught me? A broken heart turns into a reckless one, and what we feel inside that heart at one particular moment can set our destiny, making us a stronger person, a weaker person, or leading us into a darkness from which we can never escape.

Chapter 1

Becca

I was born with a silver spoon in my mouth, or so I've been told. But I didn't see it that way. Sure, I was lucky enough to have everything that I ever asked for. Instead of going to *Disney World* on family vacations, I went to places like Tahiti, Hawaii, and Australia. Unlike other kids, I didn't have to scrimp and save for a car; I was handed one, and not just any car; an Audi A5 Cabriolet Convertible. To some, that may seem a little extravagant but in the affluent Connecticut community that I grew up in, it was the norm. My dad was a very successful orthopedic surgeon who had worked hard to make that lifestyle a reality. I tried to repay him by being the "perfect daughter". I had just finished up my third year at Columbia University, studying pre-law with a 4.0 GPA. Yes, my life couldn't get any better. Unfortunately to some, I came with a prepackaged label of "Stuck Up Bitch" which was so far from the truth. I didn't date many guys. In fact, I was still a virgin at twenty-one years old. I didn't have time for any of it with keeping up with my studies. The guys that would ask me out and that I had turned down would have a few choice names to call me behind my back, but I never really paid attention. They were just battling with the sting of rejection and their own insecurities. The truth was that none of them interested me. To me, they were only looking for one thing; the one thing that I wasn't going to give away to just anyone. So I mainly kept to myself, keeping busy with classes and volunteering my time at a center for women and children of domestic violence. To the rest of the world, I may have been Becca Rose Keeton, spoiled rich girl, but to me I was just a normal twenty one year old girl whose family just happened to have money. I tried to remain as grounded as possible. Unlike most girls that I grew up with, I didn't look down on other people for

what they didn't have, I saw everyone equally.

I raised my head from my laptop when I heard a knock on my bedroom door. "Hey, Mom!" I said as she walked in and took a seat on my bed.

"Hey Sweetie. Can I just tell you how happy I am to have you back for the summer?"

"Me too, and I am super excited that Lynn Barrett wants me to meet with her on Monday when she gets back to spearhead one of the children's charities that she's trying to start up." Lynn Barrett's husband was another doctor in my father's practice. In addition to being co-workers, they were also very good friends with my parents. They were very well known in our community for all of their charity work. I grew up with their son, Ashton and although I admired his mother for all of the time that she had put into various charities, her son was a complete asshole.

"You absolutely amaze me, Becca!" My mother smiled and took my face in her hands. "You have such a bright future ahead of you. You're beautiful, talented, as smart as a whip, and have the biggest heart I know. If I wasn't your mother, I'd be a little jealous." We both began to giggle. "Now, if some of that could just rub off on your brother."

"He'll grow up, someday….maybe," I joked.

My brother, Jordan, and I couldn't be more opposite if we tried.

Physically, there was no doubt that we were brother and sister. We both had brown hair and the same crystal blue eyes. My mother would say that whenever she was missing the Caribbean she would just look into our eyes because they were the same color as the ocean. As much as I hated to admit it, Jordan was just like all those boys that I did my best to avoid back in High School. He thought he was God's gift to girls and even at seventeen I was beginning to see how he would manipulate them, and I hated it.

"Your father and I are going out for dinner when he gets home. What are your plans?"

"Krista asked me to go to this party with her." I didn't dare tell her that it was at Ashton's house or she would have been on the phone with his parents in a heartbeat. Even though I hated Ashton and could care less if he got into trouble, I didn't want to look like a tattle tale to everyone else. It was bad enough that I was already labeled as a goody good. My mother raised her eyebrow at me in disapproval. "What?" I asked.

"You're not going to be drinking and driving?"

"Mom! Seriously! I think you know me better than that!"

"I'm sorry, Honey. Yes, I do." She kissed me on the forehead, before getting up from my bed. "Have fun."

"Thanks, you too!"

We pulled into Ashton's driveway. His parents were away for the weekend and Ashton was taking full advantage of the opportunity. I normally didn't go to parties, but my best friend, Krista, begged me, and since I hadn't spent time with her in months with both of us being away at school, I couldn't say no. To say that Ashton Barrett wasn't one of my most favorite people was an understatement. He had always been relentless with asking me to go out with him, even though each time I would shoot him down. He was a total snob, jock, and womanizer all rolled into one.

All the girls fell at his feet, but I could see right through him. According to my mother, he had failed out of his last semester at Fairfield University because he was doing too much partying. There had always been rumors surrounding him regarding drug use, which only added to my aversion to him. It was wall to wall people when we walked through the double doors and into the marble tiled grand foyer. Half of the people I had never even seen before. My eyes instantly focused on the guy laughing away with Ashton. He was nice looking, no doubt. Normally, I wasn't instantly attracted to people based on physical characteristics alone but something about this dark haired stranger made me think differently for the moment. Even from across the room I could see his well-defined muscles in his arms and chest through his form fitting tee shirt, making me stop and stare a little longer.

"Hello! Earth to Becca," Krista said, waving her hand in front of my face.

"Oh, I'm sorry. What's up?" I asked, breaking myself from my trance.

"Were you just checking out that guy with Ashton?" Krista grinned.

"What? No!" I played it off as best as I could.

"Well, well, well, the beautiful ladies finally showed up, now all the rest of these bitches can go home!" Ashton said as he approached us with a red plastic cup in his hand. Ashton Barrett was by no means ugly on the outside. He was a pretty boy, who had been spoiled his whole life and took advantage of his parent's money. Any redeeming physical traits that he may have exhibited were immediately erased as soon as he opened his mouth. He moved closer to me and whispered in my ear: "So, beautiful girl, are you finally gonna give it up to me tonight?" I cringed at his warm breath that reeked of alcohol on my neck and pushed him away. He held his hands up in defense when two of his friends began to laugh at my reaction. "Well, you can't blame a guy for trying?" He tried playing it off like he wasn't bothered as he walked away, but I could tell that I had majorly bruised that huge ego of his.

Less than an hour into the party and I was ready to go home. This was so not my thing. I wasn't into drinking and acting like a complete idiot. I stood around, feeling out of place as I searched for Krista, who had disappeared. I was praying that she didn't go up in the bedroom with Jack VanNess, another one of Ashton's high school buddies. I noticed him flirting with her all night. He ranked right up there with Ashton as far as assholes went. Ashton stood on the landing of his double staircase and got everyone's attention. I could tell he was totally wasted as he swayed back and forth.

"I have something to say!" he shouted, getting everyone to quiet down somewhat and look up at him. "I just want to thank everyone for coming to what will be my first epic party of the summer."

"Go Ashton! You're the man!" a few kids shouted.

"Tonight we are privileged by a very special guest." His glassy eyes stared into mine. "The ice princess, dick tease, Becca Keeton has honored us by lowering herself to be here tonight. Some of you may remember her from high school. Well, college hasn't changed her much, she still has that same stick up her ass!" I felt my face heat up and was fairly certain that I was blushing when everyone began to laugh. *I hate him!* "So since she still won't give up any of that sweetness, which one of you ladies wants to join me in my bedroom and take care of my throbbing dick? No need to fight over me, ladies, I'll take more than one."

I felt the tears welling in my eyes as I pushed through the droves of people and out the front door. I needed to find Krista so I could go home, but there was no way in hell that I was going back into that house.

I walked down the driveway and leaned up against Krista's car, hoping that she would come out soon. I ran my hand through my hair and stared up at the starlit sky. As much as I loved being home, I missed school and being out of this pretentious town and all of the uppity people that came with it.

"Hey, are you okay?" I jumped at the voice that had snuck up behind me.

I wiped away the tear that was rolling down my face when I turned around to find the cute guy that Ashton had been talking to when we had first arrived, approaching me. "Oh yeah, I'm good." I smiled, trying to play it off. He smiled back and I got butterflies in my stomach upon noticing that he was even cuter closer up.

"So do you like looking up at the stars?"

"Yes, as a matter of fact I do!" I said in defense, not knowing if he was being sincere or making fun of me for it.

"No need to take offense, I just thought I was the only one that liked star gazing."

I let my guard down a little and gave him a slight smile. "In case you didn't hear Ashton's little speech, I'm Becca Keeton. The ice princess or dick tease, take your pick." I extended my hand to him.

"I'm Drew Bryant," he said, gently shaking my hand back.

"So, are you a friend of Ashton's?"

"Yeah, college buddies." I nodded and stared up into his deep blue eyes. "Why don't you come back inside?" he asked.

"Umm….no. I think I'll just wait out here for my friend."

He leaned up against the car and stood next to me. "So, Becca, tell me about yourself."

"Well, you already know that I'm a stuck up bitch."

He shook his head and smiled. "I don't believe one word of it."

"Well, that's very kind of you. But you're going to take my word over your buddy's?"

"I got a mind of my own. Plus, I'm really good at reading people and I can tell you're not."

"Well, thank you." *God, his personality is just as nice as his appearance.* Still, I kept my guard up. He could just be a really sweet talker who was hoping to get lucky. I didn't trust any of these guys, especially one that was good friends with Ashton. "So what's your story?" I asked.

"What do you mean?"

"I mean, you obviously go to Fairfield but where are you originally from?"

"California. What about you?" he asked with a smile.

"Born and raised in this uppity town my whole life; finally got away from it three years ago when I went off to college. Columbia. Pre-law."

He raised his eyebrows as if he were impressed. "So, how long have you known Ashton?"

I rolled my eyes. "Too long. His parent's and mine are really good friends. His dad and mine are both in the same medical practice. His parents are such nice people, I just can't believe they have a son like that." I placed my hand over my mouth to stop talking. "Oops sorry, don't mean to be talking about your buddy like that."

He shook his head and chuckled. "Nah, it's all good. So –"

"There you are!" Krista shouted, cutting Drew right off.

"Oh hey!" I smiled.

She looked at me and then at Drew. "Well, I was going to see if you were ready to leave, but if –"

"Nope, I'm ready!" I said without hesitation.

Although Drew seemed like a nice guy, I was still a little leery. Yes, he was a total cutie that unleashed the butterflies inside of me, but I was sure under that sweet boy next door exterior there was a hidden agenda somewhere that included: *Score with Becca Keeton*....and that was a line item that I wasn't allowing anyone associated with Ashton Barrett to ever check off.

Chapter 2

"Becca! How are you, Sweetheart?" Lynn Barrett said, pulling me into her and giving me a kiss on each side of my face.

"I'm well, thank you."

"Come on in and sit down." She led me into the formal living room and we both took a seat on the couch as her housekeeper brought in a tray containing a pitcher of iced tea and fresh fruit. "Your mother told me that you are doing wonderful in school. She's so proud of you." She smiled. "So let me tell you a little about this charity." She lifted up the pitcher and poured us each a glass.

"Thank you," I said, taking a sip.

"Well, here's what I was thinking: the name of the organization would be called *Tiny Tears* and it will help raise money for scholarships for children affected by child abuse."

"Wow, that's a really great cause. I love that idea."

"Well, I know that you have a lot of experience working in the women's shelter—not to mention your legal background will be a tremendous help."

"Oh Mrs. Barrett, I am nowhere near ready to give any legal advice but I would love to be part of this wonderful cause."

She placed her hand on my shoulder. "I'm so happy to hear that, dear! I'm getting together a spreadsheet with a checklist of all the things that need to be done to get this started, so why don't we meet again next week? Same place, same time?"

"Sounds perfect!"

"I also have another favor to ask?"

"Sure, what is it?"

"Well, you know that Edward and I do a lot with the local disaster relief charities." I nodded. I knew that she and Dr. Barrett were into a lot of charities; I just couldn't keep track of them. "Well, Saturday night we're having a formal dinner to raise some funds and holding a bachelorette type of auction. The winning bidder gets to have dinner and a dance with the bachelorette. I've got two girls lined up and was hoping that you would agree to be the third."

Even though I knew it was for a good cause I still couldn't help but feel like I was being sold into prostitution. But it was only dinner and one dance, how bad could it be? "Sure, count me in."

"Oh Becca, I'm so glad. Just between you and me, you are the prettiest one. I have a feeling you're going to be raising a lot of money for us." *Okay, now that just made me feel like a high class hooker.* I smiled, not knowing what else to do. "So tell me all about –"

"Hey, Mom, what's going on?" Ashton interrupted as he walked into the living room.

He gave me his shifty smile like he was looking at me without any clothes. I immediately crossed my legs to make sure I wasn't giving him a free show with the short skirt that I was wearing before shifting my eyes to Drew, who was standing right beside him. His eyes focused on mine and he gave me an adorable little smile, which made me involuntarily smile back even wider.

"Ashton Thomas Barrrett, I would like a word with you in

private," she said through clenched teeth as she got up from the couch. "I'll be right back, Becca," she shouted, leading Ashton up the stairs.

I raised my eyebrows and smiled. "Looks like someone's in trouble," I said to Drew, unable to hold back my laughter.

He smiled a cute boyish grin. "Yeah, it appears that way. So what are you doing here?" he asked.

"Oh, Ashton's mom asked me to help out with one of her charities. I love doing this stuff, especially when it's for a worthwhile cause."

"What's the cause?" he asked.

"Abused children. It's my passion, I volunteer at women and children's shelters at home and in the city when I'm in school. Mrs. Barrett runs so many different worthwhile charities, this will be really good experience for me if I ever want to start up one of my own someday."

He nodded, looking like he was deep in thought. "So, Becca, I wanted to ask you the other night. Did you want to go out some time?"

"Oh....umm." He totally caught me off guard with that question. He seemed like a great guy and he was absolutely adorable, but *he was friends with Ashton*, which caused him to lose a few points in my book. "Actually, I don't think so. I'm just really busy this summer and –"

"Sorry about that, Becca, my son and I had some business to discuss," Mrs. Barrett interrupted as she and Ashton came back down the steps.

I got up from the couch, wanting to get away from Ashton as quickly as possible. "No problem. I'll see you Saturday."

"Yes! And thank you so much. If you boys don't have any plans for Saturday, come to the *Oakwood Country Club* and you may be able to win dinner and a dance with Becca," Mrs. Barrett said to Ashton and Drew.

I looked down as I walked past them, but I could feel Ashton checking me out from head to toe. I briefly glanced in Drew's direction and gave him a quick smile before walking out the door, praying that Ashton didn't take her up on that offer. The last thing I wanted was to be stuck having dinner with him. Drew on the other hand...

The week flew by and I was keeping busy making up for lost time; hanging out with Krista, shopping with my mom, and trying to teach my younger brother some manners when it came to girls. I was hoping to spend some time with my dad, but he was so busy with work that our time together had been limited.

I let Krista drag me to another party that I didn't want to be at, but since it was on the beach at least I didn't feel like I was trapped in a fish bowl with a bunch of people that I didn't want to be with. About a half hour into it, things were finally beginning to look up when I spotted Drew. We exchanged quick glances and a few awkward smiles but nothing else. I actually couldn't believe that I was finding myself getting a little jealous when I happened to look over his way to find a pretty blonde hanging all over him. He immediately met my gaze when I was staring at the two of them a little longer than I should have. I turned my attention to Krista and her latest conquest, pretending that it didn't bother me, even though deep down inside for some unknown reason, it did. There was no denying that he was good looking and not in the pretty boy way that Ashton was. There was just something about him that made him stand out. It was the little things like the way his t-shirts hugged his broad chest and shoulders and the way he carried himself with confidence but without being over-cocky. Part of me was regretting turning him down for a date and the other part was telling me that I did the right thing. Even though he didn't exude arrogance, the way Ashton did, I was sure deep down inside he knew that he could probably have any girl he wanted.....just not this one. But the more I tried to convince myself of that, the more I kept thinking about him.

"Hey Becca!" I jumped and nearly spilled the beer I had been nursing the entire night all over myself. I pulled in my bottom lip to try and contain my smile at the site of Drew standing close enough to smell his delicious cologne.

"Oh, hey!" I said, trying to play it off nonchalantly as if he were any other guy and not one that I had been thinking about the entire night.

"So how come you're not looking up at the stars on this beautiful night?"

"Hmm....guess I really didn't think about it." I didn't want to tell him that I was too busy checking him out instead. My eyes finally broke their attention from him to the star filled sky. "It really is beautiful tonight." My nerves were getting the best of me and my stomach began to churn. I scanned the area for Krista, who, of course, was nowhere to be found. *I knew I should have taken my own car.*

"Looking for someone?" he asked.

"Umm....no. Well, yeah actually, my friend, Krista. I think she ditched me for that guy she was with and she was my ride home."

"I can take—"

"Drew, there you are!" The blonde that I had seen him with earlier exclaimed, throwing her arms around his neck. Once I saw her closer up, I recognized her as a girl that I had gone to high school with. I couldn't remember her name, but I knew that she was a year younger than me. Drew removed her arms from his neck and she glared at me as if I was the reason for it. "Hey, aren't you Becca Keeton?" she asked, as if I was some wanted convict or something, making me unsure how to answer.

"Yes. We went to school together, didn't we? But I'm sorry, I don't remember your name."

She let out a loud laugh. "Well, of course you wouldn't remember a low life like me. I mean, you were Miss Popular that all the boys wanted and could never have. Don't waste your time, Drew, because she's not going to give it to you either. Too bad you just turned down a sure thing for that." She shook her head and rolled her eyes before walking away in defeat.

"Okay, whatever," Drew said under his breath. His eyes met mine once again and we both began to laugh over the girl's sudden outburst.

"Don't know what I ever did to her, but oh well!" I let out a deep, exhausting breath.

"So, like I was saying before we were interrupted, I can give you a ride home if you need one."

I looked over the crowd of people one last time for Krista, knowing that it could be hours before I found her and that was *if* she hadn't left without me already. The last thing I felt like doing was standing around this party, feeling more awkward than I already did. "Umm, I really don't want you to leave on my account."

"Nah, that's okay; this party is kind of lame anyway."

"Oh, well, okay then."

His single dimpled smile made my knees go weak. I had never allowed this to happen with any guy. I was always in control of the way I felt, but Drew was just different.

"Hey Drew, where you going, my man!?" Ashton shouted as we were heading off the beach. I looked down at the ground, trying my best to avoid any eye contact with him; just the sound of his voice was enough to make me cringe.

"Oh, I'm pretty beat," Drew replied.

I finally looked up and wished I hadn't when my eyes locked with Ashton's. "Oh, say no more." Ashton sneered, never taking his icy blue eyes from mine.

"I'm just giving Becca a ride home and then heading home to bed. I'll talk to you tomorrow."

"Yeah, right! Whatever you say, bro!" His grin grew wider. "Have fun....*sleeping*." He chuckled loudly, looking at me one last time before walking away.

I shuddered just by his mere presence. I detested him with everything I had and the more I was around him, the stronger that feeling grew. "God, I cannot stand him," I whispered.

Drew and I made small talk during the short drive to my house and I found myself getting disheartened when we pulled into the driveway, not wanting the drive to end. I unclasped my seatbelt and had my hand on the door handle. The butterflies in my stomach were unleashed when I looked past his long dark lashes and into his eyes. "Well, thanks for the ride."

"Anytime."

He smiled and the butterflies now turned into a flock of birds. I cleared my throat and snapped out of it when I realized I was entranced in his smile a little longer than I should have been. I knew it was crazy to be thinking, but part of me was hoping that he would lean over the seat and kiss me. I gave him another quick smile and hurriedly opened the door, hoping that he wasn't able to read my thoughts.

"I guess I'll see ya around."

He nodded. I closed the door and walked up the driveway on shaky legs. I was trembling as I tried to get my key in the keyhole. *Becca, calm down! He's just a guy! He's just like the rest of them....nothing special,* I told myself as I tried to steady my hand. I was finally able to calm myself enough to manage to get the door open. Drew's car drove away as I closed the door behind me. I leaned my back up against the door and closed my eyes, unable to erase my smile as I imagined him in that snug fitting tee shirt, his beautiful one dimpled grin, and the way he came to my rescue and gave me a ride home tonight. No, he wasn't like the rest of them.....something somewhere deep inside of me was telling me there was something about him that was pretty darn special.

Chapter 3

I went up to my room after the shopping spree that my mother and I had just returned from and stood back, admiring the beautiful aquamarine, beaded halter gown that we had purchased for the benefit dinner. I had wanted something a little less extravagant and less costly but my mother insisted on this one after seeing me in it. Since she was paying for it, I had to do as she wished. But looking at it hanging on the back of my closet door, I was glad that she was so persistent. It was absolutely stunning.

"Aren't you glad I talked you into that one now?" my mother said as she came walking through my bedroom door as if she was reading my thoughts.

"It is really beautiful."

"Your father doesn't like this whole idea of this auction thing. He's afraid that some strange man is going to pick you and he'll have to get into a bidding war to get you out of it."

She and my father were so overprotective of me that sometimes it drove me crazy. They weren't used to me bringing guys around and even if I had, I knew that no guy would ever be good enough in their eyes. What they failed to realize was that I was an adult who could make her own decisions. Wise decisions. I hadn't let them down yet and I just wished they had a little more confidence in me.

"Mom, you and Daddy will be at this event; it's not like I'm going off to some strange place with some strange man. I am not three years old anymore. I am a grown woman."

"Becca, you are twenty one years old. Trust me; you're not a grown woman. You have no idea how many bad people there are in this world."

"Mom! Please, just have a little faith in me."

"I do, Becca. I just worry about you."

"Well, don't. I will be fine. I promise. When have you ever known me to not be able to handle any situation life throws at me?"

She shook her head and smiled. "I haven't. I know you're a smart girl. But you will always be my *little girl*, no matter how old you are." She wrapped her arms around me and hugged me.

I knew that I was lucky to have a mother and father that loved me and wanted to protect me as much as mine did. In turn, I wanted nothing more than to please them and make them proud of me. But every now and then I wondered just what it would be like to stop striving for perfection and live a little.

Sitting in the back of my father's car on the way to the benefit brought me right back to when I was twelve years old and going to my first school dance—at least that's how my parents made me feel. Lecturing me about what to do, what to say, how to act while stopping to take a few breaths and scolding my brother for his inappropriate comments that he was making. I would normally agree with my parents about his behavior, but for now he was creating a diversion which took the focus off me and I was grateful to him for that. I couldn't get out of the car fast enough when we pulled up to the valet. Jordan was right behind me, both of us wanting to get away from the fifteen minute lecture that we had each been subjected to on the way here.

"Jordan, walk in with your sister, please!" my father shouted as he and my mother were stopped by another couple and deep in conversation.

"You have no clue how lucky you are to be away from them!" Jordan said as he looped his arm in mine.

"Oh, Jordan, they're not that bad."

"Yeah, maybe not for you because you're the *perfect one!*"

I shook my head and laughed. "And you are their wild child that has thrown them for a loop."

"Damn straight, girl, you should try it sometime. It's pretty fun!" He smiled back.

We walked into the elaborate ballroom that was already filled with people. I scanned the area, wondering which one of these men would be my date for the night and immediately got a sick feeling in my stomach. I stretched my neck and whispered into Jordan's ear. "Hey, by any chance are you going to be bidding tonight?" I asked, giving him a pleading smile.

"Well, I would but Dad cut off my funds because of my last report card. Plus, I wouldn't want to interfere with fate."

"What do you mean?" I asked in confusion.

"Well, my future brother in law may be in the making tonight." He laughed.

I shook my head. "Nah, don't think so, Jordan."

As we made our way further inside, we were stopped every now and then by some of my father's coworkers and acquaintances that he had met over the years. Some of them I didn't know or didn't remember ever meeting, but they remembered my brother and me.

"Here, you want to do a shot of this to calm you down?" my brother asked, exposing the small bottle of vodka that was in his pocket.

My eyes widened. "Jordan Michael! Where did you get that?"

He laughed at my reaction, but I wasn't finding any humor in the situation at all. He was underage and could get in serious trouble if he got caught with that. "Did anyone ever tell you that you sound just like Mom? Calm down, Becca, believe it or not but this is the *normal* thing that kids our age do."

"You are not my age, Jordan. I am legal to drink, you are not!"

"Becca, Sweetheart!" Jordan looked relieved when he saw Lynn Barrett approaching us, seemingly knowing that he had just escaped one of my big sister lectures that he would painstakingly listen to every now and then. "You look absolutely stunning, as expected," she said, placing her hand on my shoulder and thoroughly inspecting me like a piece of meat. "Oh hello, Jordan, I'm so glad you were able to make it," she said, finally acknowledging my brother.

"Well, more like I was forced into it."

I rolled my eyes and shook my head. "Jordan, really?"

Mrs. Barrett waved her hand in the air, dismissing his comment. "Oh don't be embarrassed, Becca. Boys will be boys and my Ashton acts the same way when it comes to these functions."

Oh shit, Ashton! I had forgotten that she had told him about this function tonight and was praying that he wasn't here. I swallowed hard before asking the dreaded question. "Oh, is Ashton coming tonight?" I finally blurted out.

"Who knows? He never gives me a straight answer. I'm just waiting for everyone to get here and take a seat and we should be starting in about fifteen minutes," she said as she was whisked away.

I took a deep breath, noticing that Jordan was no longer standing beside me. *Great!* I always felt a little out of place in social situations. I was much more comfortable being by myself and not on display.

"Would you like a glass of wine?" A familiar voice finally broke me from my trance.

I could feel the smile forming on my face when I noticed Drew standing beside me, looking as handsome as ever in a gray, perfectly tailored suit. His short brown hair was perfectly tousled and his deep blue eyes were looking a little grayer tonight as they reflected off the colors in his tie.

"Um, no, I'll just have a club soda with lime."

"Okay, I'll be right back," he said before walking over to the bar. Panic began to set in when it finally dawned on me that if Drew was here, that meant Ashton was, too. My stomach began to churn as I scoured the area, once again looking for him.

"Here you go," Drew said, handing me the glass.

"Thank you," I said as I took a sip.

"Can I just say, you look beautiful?"

I could feel myself blushing. "Thank you," I whispered.

"Don't be ashamed to take a compliment, Becca."

"I'm...not." I felt my face become heated once again. "So is Ashton here?" I asked.

"Oh yeah, somewhere," he said, looking around at the crowd. I sighed heavily. "What's the matter?" he asked.

"It's just....well, I will die if I get stuck spending the rest of the night with him."

He let out a light hearted chuckle. "Boy, you really do hate him, don't you?"

"Well, hate is such a strong word—more like....I strongly dislike him or I despise him." I giggled as I looked into his eyes and was instantly overcome with a strange sense of calmness. Even though he was friends with Ashton, there was just something about him that put me at ease.

"Becca, there you are," my father said as he approached me, thoroughly eyeing up Drew in the process.

"Oh Drew, this is my father," I said.

Drew extended his hand to my father, who gave him an uneasy

look as they shook hands. "Nice to meet you, Dr. Keeton."

"You too. How do you and Becca know each other?" My father wasted no time jumping into his interrogation.

"I go to school with Ashton."

My father nodded, still giving a wary look. "Well, come sit at our table until they are ready to get this underway, Becca," my father said, taking my hand. I felt myself becoming a little annoyed by his actions. I was having a really nice time talking to Drew and then he had to come in and swoop me away. But I knew better than to argue; at least not here, anyway. Perhaps, I would say something once we got home.

I gave Drew an apologetic smile. "Thanks for the drink."

"Anytime." He smiled back as my dad led me away and through the crowd.

"Who was that boy?" my father asked.

"I don't know, Dad. Just a friend of Ashton's."

"Well, Lynn and Edward may be good friends of mine but I happen to know that Ashton gets into his fair share of trouble. You don't need to be associating yourself with anyone that is friends with him."

"Dad! Please! I'm not a little baby. I think I can form my own opinion of others quite well!"

"Becca, we're ready to start!" Mrs. Barrett interrupted.

Even though my stomach was in knots over the entire thing, I was still feeling relieved because I knew that my father and I were about to get into a major battle. She took my hand and led me up to the podium. I stood alongside of the other two girls, keeping my head down, totally tuning everyone and everything else out. God, I just wanted to get this over with, and I wanted to get it over with *without* spending the rest of the night with Ashton.

My ears finally perked up and my stomach dropped when I heard Mrs. Barrett say, "Our next bachelorette is studying pre-law at Columbia University. Besides being very smart, she is also very beautiful. Meet Becca Keeton." I walked over to the podium, feeling like my legs were about to give out. I hated being the center of attention, especially for something like this. My head was spinning through the loud applause of the crowd and the shrill whistle coming from Ashton, who was now front and center. "Okay, I will start the bidding at one hundred dollars," Mrs. Barrett said. As expected, Ashton was the first one to bid. Mrs. Barrett smiled at her son. "Okay, we have a bid for one hundred. Do I have one hundred and fifty?" *Oh God please somebody, anybody.....but Ashton.*

"One hundred and fifty," someone shouted from the back of the room. I tried to see where the voice was coming from, but it was impossible in the dimly lit crowd. Not that I cared; anyone would be better than Ashton.

Just as I was starting to gain some hope that I wouldn't be stuck spending the night with Ashton, he blurted out, "Two hundred," before Mrs. Barrett could even raise the bid.

"Okay, we have two hundred. Going once, going twice......" I took a deep breath, preparing myself for the next two hours of torture ahead.

"Five hundred." The voice from the back finally made his way up to the front and I couldn't help but smile when I saw the face behind it...Drew. Tonight he would, hopefully, be my date. But for the moment, he was my hero.

Chapter 4

Ashton shook his head and high fived Drew. "You win, bro! I ain't spending that kind of money on any chick unless I know she's gonna be puttin' out." There were a few gasps and a few laughs from the crowd. I felt my face turn completely red, but, judging by the look on Mrs. Barrett's face, I could tell that she was just a little more embarrassed than I was. She shot Ashton a dagger with her eyes before calling off the final bid to Drew.

Drew approached me and lifted my hand, placing a gentle kiss on it before taking it in his and walking off to our table. "Wow, well thank you. That was really generous of you," I said as we took a seat.

"Well, a good cause, a beautiful girl, it was a no brainer."

"Well, thank you. But I was actually thanking you for saving me from Ashton." My stomach flipped at the cute boyish grin that flashed across his face.

"Oh, come on now, he's not that bad." He chuckled.

"I guess it's just a matter of opinion." I sighed.

The waitress came over and took our order and I tried my best to stop Drew from ordering me a glass of wine but he wasn't paying me any mind. He stared at me intently after the waitress walked away. "So what kind of law did you want to get into, Becca?" he asked.

"Criminal."

He raised his eyebrow at me as if he were surprised. "Prosecuting or defending?"

"Oh, definitely prosecuting. It seems like so much fun putting the bad guys away." He looked away and nodded. "So how old are you?" I asked.

"Twenty two."

"And what are you studying in school?"

"Business. Not sure where I want to go with that yet, but I have a few ideas."

I nodded and smiled. "So how come you don't go back to California and spend time with your family over summer break?"

"Geez, you ask a lot of questions." He smirked.

"Well, isn't that what lawyers, or should I say 'wanna be' lawyers do?"

His smile deepened and so did his dimple in his left cheek. "You are so right. Actually, I really don't have any family in California anymore. My parents died in a car accident a year ago."

I covered my mouth with my hand. "Oh God. I am so sorry for prying like that. You should have just told me to mind my own business."

"It's okay. After they passed away, I decided to transfer out here last year mid-semester. I needed a change."

"Why here?"

"Well, my grandfather has a house on the sound that he left me after he passed away. I would come here every summer to visit growing up and I kind of liked it. So that's where I live, and I commute back and forth to school every day."

"Do you have any brothers or sisters?"

"Nope. What about you?"

"A younger brother," I said as the waitress brought us our wine.

He lifted his wine glass up. "Thanks for being my date tonight, Becca," he said as we clinked our wine glasses together.

We talked nonstop throughout dinner. He had come from a very wealthy family and when his mother and father passed away, he was pretty much set for life financially. My heart ached while listening to his story. Everyone in his life had been taken from him and he was basically on his own. "Well, I'm really sorry about your parents. It must be really tough to not have that support system in your life." He looked down at the table and nodded.

"So, you and your parents, are you close?"

I took a sip of my wine and nodded. "Yeah, my parents are great. Sometimes a little too overprotective, as you witnessed earlier. By the way, I'm very sorry for my dad's abruptness."

"No worries. It must be tough on a guy having a beauty of a daughter like you." I felt my face heating up once again over his compliment as I looked away. "Hey," he whispered, taking my hand across the table. I lifted my head, finally locking eyes with him. "You really need to learn how to take a compliment. A beautiful girl like you is going to be getting a lot of them in life so you may as well get used to it and just accept them with dignity."

A smile spread over my face. "Thank you," I managed to get out, feeling his warm hand in mine. As I stared into his eyes, I couldn't help but think, he wasn't like most guys my age, who had a limited attention span that only included sex and partying. There was definitely something about him that made him stand out from the others but I just couldn't put my finger on it.

"Becca." I was broken from my trance as I looked up to find my dad standing over the table. He looked down at Drew and our hands latched together before shooting me a look of displeasure. I removed my hand from Drew's and cleared my throat. "Your brother isn't feeling well so we have to get going."

"Well, Dad, I have to stay. I promised Mrs. Barrett—"

"I don't care what you promised her, your brother is sick and we are your transportation home."

"I can take you home, Becca," Drew chimed in.

I smiled at his suggestion. I wasn't ready to leave at all. Contrary to how I was feeling in the beginning of the night about this whole function, I was having a great time here with Drew. "No, that won't be necessary. Becca can just—"

"Dad, I am staying. I told Lynn that I would do this, and Drew has donated a good amount of money to this charity. I will see you later tonight." He glared at me in disbelief. Normally, I was always the obedient daughter who never went against my father's wishes, but tonight he wasn't going to win this battle. I raised my eyebrow at him. "I will be fine, Dad."

He shook his head and gave me a cautious look before turning his attention to Drew. "I'll be waiting up for her to make sure she gets home in one piece."

"Not a problem," Drew responded.

He sighed deeply before walking away and disappearing into the crowd. I shook my head in total irritation. "Again, I am so sorry," I apologized to Drew.

His smile widened. "No need to keep apologizing, Becca. Just forget all about it and let's have a great time." I smiled back and was overcome with a strong sense of pride. I had actually stood up to my dad, letting him know that my feelings were just as significant as his. I wasn't sure if it was the wine or Drew that gave me this newfound inner strength. Maybe it was just a little bit of both.

Chapter 5

Much to my dismay, the night was flying by. I had allowed Drew more than his allotted one dance that his bid had covered. It seemed like we were on the dance floor all night. I had lost count of our dances by the fourth one. Any skepticism that I had about him being like Ashton was washed away when Ashton tried cutting in on us and Drew wouldn't allow him, telling him he had to get his money's worth. I closed my eyes and leaned my head into his chest as he pulled me closer. I inhaled his cologne with its hints of cedar, spice, and musk and couldn't get enough of it. He smelled so good. So masculine. His muscular arms wrapped around me just felt so perfect. I wasn't feeling like my normal awkward self. For once in my life, I was relaxed and not worrying about what I was doing wrong or achieving more. I was content with the moment that I was in. The music ended but we were still swaying back and forth.

"Becca," he whispered in my ear.

"Hmm...." I didn't want to remove my head from his chest. I was so relaxed.

"The music stopped. I think that was the last dance of the

night."

"Who says we need music to dance? I want to make sure you get your money's worth." I looked up at him and smiled.

He gazed down at me and gave me a sexy grin that made my insides flip. "Whatever you say." I closed my eyes, ignoring all of the people walking past us to exit and the wait staff cleaning off the tables. For the moment, it was just Drew and I on the dance floor, dancing away to the most beautiful music that was playing in my head. "So, do you mind telling me what song we're dancing to so I can keep up with the rhythm?"

I looked up at him and giggled. "Hmm??....*Moonlight Serenade* by *Glenn Miller*." He looked at me strangely. "Don't judge! My dad always says I'm an old soul trapped in a young body. There's something about the forties era that's just so romantic, right down to the music."

"I'm not judging. I think it's great that you see things differently than most girls your age. It shows your character." I stayed in his arms for some time, moving back and forth, not worrying about the time or the fact that I probably had twenty missed calls from my dad. "Hey Becca, I think they're starting to shut off the lights."

"They just don't appreciate good music." I giggled, finally releasing myself from his embrace. I was hoping that he would ask me out again and that my rejection from his first invite wouldn't deter him. We walked outside into the warm early summer air and through the beautiful garden area. "So I was thinking, I had a really great time tonight and I was pretty dumb for turning you down the other day when you asked me to go out. So, if you want to ask me again....I'll more than likely say yes." I smiled.

He shook his head and laughed. "Well, I would love to, but seeing how you're so busy, I wouldn't want to keep you from all your work," he teased.

"Oh yeah, that. Well, I had some preconceived notions about you in my head because of who you're friends with, but I think you convinced me tonight that you are nothing like him."

He stopped walking and stared down at me. "Well, I guess I'll forgive you for having those notions. That comes with the territory of being a future lawyer. But I think my rejection from the other day would sting a lot less if *you* asked me out." He grinned.

"Oh, so you're going to make me grovel?"

"I cried for days after you turned me down," he teased.

We both busted out with laughter. "Oh poor baby! You should have asked Ashton for some tips on handling my rejection. Well, since I don't like to see grown men cry….." God, I felt so weird doing this, I'd *never* asked out a guy before.

"I'm feeling the tears starting to form, Becca….hurry," he joked.

"Do you want to go out with me sometime?" I blurted out.

"I'm sorry, I didn't quite catch that," he said with a devilish grin.

I shook my head and laughed. "Drew Bryant, would you do me the honor of going out with me sometime?"

"Oh, is that what you just asked? Well, I will on one condition."

"What's that?" I asked.

"I have to see if you're a good kisser first."

"Is that so?" I smiled.

"Yup; can't be wasting my time on a girl that doesn't know how to kiss."

"Well, you certainly don't waste any time, do you?" I raised my eyebrow at him.

"Not when I see something I like."

He raised his eyebrow back at me and I was gone. I felt my knees melting and my heart began beating faster. His head inched closer to mine as I closed my eyes, finally feeling the softness of his lips on mine and his tongue parting my mouth. I opened my mouth wider to allow him in as our tongues began to dance together in perfect unison, the same way that our bodies did on the dance floor just a short time ago. And just like our dance, I didn't want this most absolute perfect first kiss to end either. My insides awakened. Everything inside of me wanted him when he pulled me closer, moving his hands up my bare back. I couldn't help but wonder what it would feel like to have them all over the rest of my body. As our kiss ended, his hands had moved to both sides of my face while he stared down at me.

"Well, am I worthy?" I joked.

The corners of his mouth slowly turned up into a huge grin. "Yeah, you'll do."

He took my hand in his as we walked off to his car. My stomach was doing cartwheels. My lips still had his delicious taste all over them and my heart was opening wider than it had ever been in its entire life.

Chapter 6

Mrs. Barrett was keeping me busier than ever with the charity. I was running all over town, all over the state, and a few times even out of state and into New York to deliver information and pick up donations from the different benefactors. I was hoping that soon I would be getting in on the actual ins and outs and the day to day operations of how it all ran, which was my whole reason for getting involved in the first place. Drew and I had gone out on several dates and he always kept me company during all of my travels that Mrs. Barrett had me going on, which I was really grateful for. The benefactors that I would have to deliver to would range from everyday normal people to what seemed to be very powerful people just based on the size of their homes. Some of them had intimidating security guards that looked like they were plopped right out of an action hero movie. They would eye me up like I had no clothes on but they would back right down the minute they saw that I had a guy with me. I couldn't thank Drew enough for taking his time to come along with me. He normally took summer classes or would intern, but he wanted to take this summer before his senior year off completely. I felt a little guilty about making him feel like he had to be my babysitter, but he didn't see it that way and I was glad. I loved spending time with him. He was so easy to talk to about anything, things that I would normally find off limits with anyone else, even Krista. Not to mention that his kisses just got better and better, making me yearn for him more and more with each one. I didn't mention anything about Drew to my parents. I knew that my father would not be pleased with all of the time that I had been spending with him, and I was quite certain that he would have made no qualms about letting me know. So, I spared myself the lecture and kept quiet. Normally, I would heed to my father's warnings, but with this I wasn't. Drew made me feel like a grown woman, not a child. He respected me and didn't demand perfection from me like everyone else did. I could be myself completely with him. He didn't judge me for my imaginative thinking or my love of beautiful sunsets and star lit skies. He allowed the inner girl, the creative one, the dreamer, the one that I had suppressed deep inside of me for so long, to come out whenever I was with him. I didn't feel like Becca Keeton: Perfect student, perfect obedient daughter, and perfect role-model big sister. I felt like Becca Keeton: the girl that I *wished* I could be.

"So did you want to get something to eat?" Drew asked as we were on our way home from one of my runs.

"Sure, but how about if I cook you dinner at your place as a thank you for giving up all your free time these past few weeks and keeping me company?"

He smiled and my heart flipped. It seemed like he didn't have to do much of anything to have that effect on me and along with the butterflies that he set off in my stomach, I was also noticing the burning desire in other parts of my body. Parts that hadn't been explored by anyone, and every now and then I couldn't help but wonder if Drew would be the first one to get that special part of me.

"Sounds good to me, but I have nothing in my house to cook."

"Well, that's what they make grocery stores for, silly."

"I would have never known that." He grinned as I pulled into the food store that was right up the street from his house.

"Silly boy." I giggled, leaning over the console in my car and placing a kiss on his lips. He gazed at me and suddenly I wasn't hungry for food anymore. The only appetite I had was for him.

"Okay, if I tell you that you are a good cook as well as beautiful, are you going to get all embarrassed on me?" Drew asked, taking the last bite of his pasta.

"Nope! Thank you!" I said with a newfound confidence.

"You're getting much better at it, Becca."

I got up to start clearing the table, and he stood up and stopped me. "I'll get it later," he said, pouring us each a glass of wine before leading me outside. His grandfather's beach house was absolutely adorable. The rooms were soothing and decorated in calming pastel colors with light colored wood floors. Original art work hung on the walls, adding to the seaside feel. We walked out onto the large slate patio and took a seat together on the lounge chair. "Sun's getting ready to set." I smiled as we looked out at the water.

"It doesn't take much to please you, does it?"

I shook my head. "Guess I'm not like most girls."

"No, you are not," he said as he moved his head closer to me and pressed his lips on mine. My tongue was intertwined with his in an instant. My entire body ached for him from head to toe. My heart was beating faster and my breathing became heavier when he moved his hands up my shirt and began kissing my neck. "God, you are so fuckin' beautiful," he whispered in my ear as his hand reached under my bra and his fingers began to tease my hardened nipple. My hands wandered under his shorts and to the waistband of his boxers before sliding my fingers underneath to his rock hard erection. He let out a deep breath when I began to stroke him up and down. Just knowing that I was causing him to get this way turned me on completely, creating an unbearable pain of want for him. He gently rolled on top of me and glided his tongue down my neck. It wasn't a matter of me choosing who to give it away to now, it was a matter of needing to. I felt like my insides were going to combust. He moved my hair from my face and stared deeply into my eyes. "You have no clue what you do to me." Taking his face in my hands, I kissed him hard as I ran my hands up his shirt and caressed his back.

His hands slid under my shorts, tracing his finger over the top of my underwear. He stopped and looked down at me for approval. "I want you so bad," I whispered. His mouth was on mine once again. He was just about to remove my shorts when I cringed.

"Hey, dickhead, what's goin'on?" I knew that voice all too well and detested it more than I normally did at that particular moment. "Oh, sorry didn't know you were busy," Ashton said, giving me an obnoxious smirk. I looked at him and the trashy looking girl that was with him with pure disgust as she giggled away. "I saw your car in the driveway and when I knocked on the door and you didn't answer, I just figured you were out here." He turned his attention back to me and raised his eyebrow. "Sweet little innocent Becca, does your dear old daddy know that his precious little girl is putting on a display for all of Drew's neighbors?" I ran my hand through my hair and looked away, trying my best to not even acknowledge his vileness.

"Shut up, Ashton!" Drew said as he sat up.

"Calm down, bro. Maybe this will help a little," he said as he pulled out a bottle of vodka from the brown paper bag he was holding in his hand and a bagful of weed from his pocket.

"Ashton, put that shit away!" Drew demanded.

My eyes widened as I sat up and adjusted my shirt and shorts as best as I could. "I'm just going to head home," I said to Drew.

"Oh, come on Becca, don't leave on our account. Or is it because you're embarrassed by what we walked in on? Well, don't be. Kayla just sucked me off on the way over; blew my whole load in her mouth and she's not embarrassed. She just swallowed it down like a good girl. Right, Kayla?"

"That's right, Baby," the girl said while wrapping her arms

around his neck and sticking her tongue down his throat.

I closed my eyes and shuddered in disgust, keeping my head down as I walked inside with Drew right behind me. "I'm sorry, Becca. Look, I could get rid of them if you want."

"No, that's okay. I really need to get going home. I have an early tennis match with my dad in the morning."

"Well, thanks for making me dinner. It was really good."

"You're welcome," I responded, giving him a halfhearted smile.

He pulled me into him and rested his forehead on mine. "Are you sure you don't want to stay?"

"No, that's okay, really."

He gently pressed his lips on my head. "I'll call ya tomorrow?"

"Sounds good," I whispered.

He walked me to my car and waited until I got in before walking back up the driveway and into the house. God, how I hated Ashton Barrett, not only for being the normal obnoxious jerk that he always was, but for interrupting what could have been happening between Drew and I right now. I pulled down my visor and looked in the lighted mirror at my swollen lips from kissing and my brush burned cheeks from rubbing up against the razor stubble on Drew's face. *Damn that Ashton Barrett.* Just because he could never have the one thing from me that he always wanted, he had to go and ruin it for everyone else.

Chapter 7

"Well, I see you haven't lost your edge after being away at school," my father said as we sat down to breakfast after our tennis match at the country club.

"See that, Dad, all of those tennis lessons really did pay off." I grinned, taking a sip of my orange juice.

He smiled back. "That's my girl, successful at everything she does. I couldn't get your brother to pick up a racket if I paid him."

"Well, Jordan just marches to the beat of a different drummer.

"Yeah, I suppose," he said, shaking his head in disappointment. Even though I had become so busy with this charity and with Drew over the past few weeks and hadn't been home much, I *did* know that my brother had been grounded for getting drunk the night of the benefit.

"Dad, it's just a phase. He'll snap out of it." I tried my best to reassure him.

"I sure hope so." He sighed. "So, what's going on with my princess? I feel like I haven't talked to you in ages."

"Well, I feel like I'm working a fulltime job with this charity.

Mrs. Barrett is keeping me busy being her gopher. I was really hoping that she would have enough faith in me to help her run the whole thing."

"Well, give it some time. Everybody has to start somewhere. I'm sure she'll see what a great worker you are and eventually hand the reigns over to you."

I shrugged. "Yeah, I hope so."

"So have you and Krista been making up for lost time? You're never home anymore."

I didn't want to lie to him and tell him 'yes' when the truth was, Krista and I hadn't hung out in well over two weeks. But I didn't feel like getting the evil eye and a lecture about all of the time that I had been spending with Drew either. Since I wanted to continue the enjoyable morning that we had been having, I just nodded in agreement. The waitress had just brought us our food when I instantly lost my appetite upon seeing Ashton and his father entering the restaurant. I was hoping that they wouldn't notice us, but as luck would have it....

"Jeff, does Gail know about this beautiful girl that you're having breakfast with this morning?" Dr. Barrett joked as he approached our table with Ashton right behind him, looking completely hung over.

I gave an uneasy smile. "How are you doing, Becca?" Dr. Barrett asked, leaning down and giving me a kiss on the cheek.

"I'm well, thank you," I replied, lifting my head for one brief moment before staring back at the table, not wanting to make eye contact with Ashton.

"Are you guys here for breakfast?" my father asked.

"Yes, we're grabbing a bite to eat before our nine o'clock tee time."

"Well, grab a seat," my father said.

My stomach instantly began to churn as Ashton and his dad took the two empty seats at our table. "Becca just got done ripping me apart on the tennis court," my father said, taking a sip of his coffee. "Becca, eat your eggs," my dad demanded, as I moved my potatoes around on the plate.

"I'm not that hungry." I stared out the window at the golf course as my dad and Dr. Barrett began to talk about work.

"So Becca!" I was in such a trance that Dr. Barrett's voice made me jump.

I turned my head from the window and looked in his direction. "Yes?"

"Lynn tells me you are a tremendous help with this new charity," Dr. Barrett said.

"Yes, it's really—"

"Becca was just saying she wants to get involved more in the operation of the whole thing. I told her to give it time. Everyone's got to start somewhere." My dad took over as usual, never letting me speak for myself.

"Oh Becca, sorry about that. My wife can be a little bit of a control freak," Dr. Barrett said.

"Geez, Becca, you really are a busy girl, aren't you? How do you find time for it all?" Ashton asked, finally breaking his silence.

I was expressionless as I glared into his eyes, wanting to knock that obnoxious smirk right off his face. "It's called applying yourself, Son; you should try it sometime," Dr. Barrett said.

"Well, you certainly are *applying yourself* to Drew. I hardly ever get to hang out with my buddy anymore." He raised his eyebrow at me and smiled, and I instantly felt my father's eyes burning into me. I pursed my lips and shook my head at him.

"Who's Drew? That boy from the benefit?" my father asked. I nodded. "I didn't know that the two of you were seeing each other."

I shook my head. "It's really not a big deal."

"Oh, and I apologize for interrupting your romantic dinner last night," Ashton added, making the situation even worse.

My father stared at me a little longer before clearing his throat and completely changing the topic of conversation to golf. I managed to get two forkfuls of cold eggs down my throat while they were talking before pushing my plate away and excusing myself to use the ladies room. As I walked off, I could feel Ashton's perverted eyes burning into my back.

The text that had come through from Drew as I was finishing up and washing my hands lifted my mood a bit.

Drew: **Good morning, gorgeous.**

A smile instantly spread across my face.

Me: **THANK YOU and good morning to you, too.**

As I was walking out the door, his reply came through.

Drew: **I trained you well. You're becoming a pro at accepting those compliments**.

I was giggling as I read his message, walking right into Ashton who was headed into the men's room. He gripped the bottom of my elbow and I instantly pulled away.

"Better tell lover boy no texting and walking," he smirked. I didn't respond as usual and began to walk off. The less conversation that I had with him the better. "Hey Becca, I was hoping that you would allow me to be your first, but if you'd rather have Drew break you in, I'm cool with that, too."

I stopped dead in my tracks and turned around to face him. "Not if you were the last guy on Earth. You make my skin crawl, Ashton Barrett."

"Well, I'm sure Daddy's skin would be crawling, too, if he knew what his sweet little innocent princess was doing last night."

"God, I hate you!" I said before walking away.

"Get in line with most of the women in my life, Becca. They all hate me, but they all keep coming back for more!" he shouted.

My father was just signing the credit card receipt when I walked back to the table. I didn't even bother sitting back down, hoping that he would get the hint that I wanted to leave. Not that the car ride home was going to be any more enjoyable. I knew I was going to be lectured about Drew, big time.

I was so happy when my father finally stood up. I said my goodbyes to Dr. Barrett, hoping to get out of there before Ashton returned. "Dad, I'll wait for you at the car," I said when he and Dr. Barrett started up a whole new conversation about their surgery schedule for the week.

"Okay, I'll be right there," he replied, tossing his car keys at me.

I was almost out the door when I heard Ashton shout, "See ya, Becca! Don't do anything I wouldn't do!" I walked as fast as I could out to the car and flopped myself into the passenger's seat. I pulled my phone from my purse and texted Drew back

Me: **You're a very good teacher and you're pretty cute, too**.

I smiled as I hit the send button.

Drew: **Thank you and I know on both statements......see, Becca, that's how it's done.**

I wiped away the grin that was plastered across my face and put my phone away when I saw my dad approaching the car.

"Are you feeling okay? You didn't eat much." my dad asked as he got into the car.

"Yeah, I'm fine. Just lost my appetite, I guess."

He backed out of the parking spot and waited until we were on the main road before the interrogation began. "So, what's going on with this Drew kid?"

"What do you mean?"

"Well, apparently you've been spending a lot of time with him. I would just like to know a little more about him."

"He's just a really nice guy."

"A really nice guy who is probably only after one thing."

"Geez, Dad, really?"

"Becca, come on; you're a beautiful girl. Guys your age only have one thing on their mind."

"Well, he's not like most guys my age."

"Oh Becca, don't let him fool you, they're all the same. I was that age at one time, you know?" I sighed heavily and looked out the window, hoping that he was done with his rant. "Your mother has talked to you about birth control, hasn't she?"

"Oh Dad, I am NOT having this conversation with you!"

"Becca, why are you getting so embarrassed? Not that I want to think that you are doing such things, but if you are ever faced with that I want to know that you are protected and won't be ruining your life by getting pregnant."

"Dad, I am twenty one years old and a senior in college. I think I know all about birth control and the birds and the bees by now." He was looking at me questionably. "And no, I'm not saying that I *have* done those things that require birth control….oh my God, I just cannot talk about this to you."

"Becca, I'm a doctor and it's a fact of life. You really don't need to get embarrassed discussing these things."

"Fine, if you must know….I've been on the pill since I was seventeen." He raised his eyebrow in alarm. "Mom and the doctor decided that would be the best route for me to take, to help with some problems I was having with…..well, you know the thing that comes after a sentence." I felt my face instantly turn red, but if it would get him off the subject and put his mind at ease then it was all worth it.

He sighed in relief and concentrated deeply on the road before speaking again. "So when can I pencil you in for our next tennis match?"

That little bit of humiliation worked like a charm; he had gone completely off topic. I knew I may have won this battle with him, but something told me that the war was just beginning.

Chapter 8

After much convincing, I had let Drew talk me into going to a party on the beach. I really didn't want to attend, mainly because I knew exactly who would be there. But I put my desire to hang out with Drew over my hatred for Ashton. Plus, I knew Krista would be there as well and since she had been on me about not spending any time together since I came home, I figured this would be a good opportunity. Even though I knew she would more than likely get drunk off her ass and end up leaving with whatever guy was paying her the most attention. She and I were complete opposites and sometimes....actually a lot of times, I found myself wondering how our friendship had lasted since kindergarten. We arrived at the party and for the first time ever I didn't feel like a total outcast as long as I had Drew's hand in mine.

"Hey Dickwad, Becca allowed you to come out tonight?" Ashton shouted.

"Just ignore him," Drew said.

"Always do!" I smiled.

"Here you go!" Ashton said to Drew as he filled up a plastic cup from the keg of beer.

"What about you, Becca? Are we going to be daring and walk on the wild side tonight?" Ashton asked. I rolled my eyes and didn't respond. "Do you always have to be such an uppity bitch?"

Drew was just about to intervene before I cut him off. "I'm only an uppity bitch to people I hate, so if the shoe fits...."

"Damn, you got told!" one of his friends that was standing alongside of him shouted.

His signature obnoxious smirk was now replaced by an angry glare. I stared right back, not backing down to him. "Told you about all the women that hate me the other day, Becca. It's actually an honor."

"Yeah, keep telling yourself that," I muttered under my breath.

"There's my girly girl," Krista said, planting a huge kiss on my cheek. I could tell that she already had a little too much to drink.

"You mind doing that again, but on the lips this time and throw in a little tongue while you're at it?" Ashton asked.

"You are such a pervert, Ashton." Krista giggled as she playfully slapped him on the arm.

"You want to find out how big of one I can be?" He raised his eyebrow at her.

She smiled and raised her eyebrow back. "Just, maybe I might."

Oh God no, Krista! Are you insane? Now I was going to have to play babysitter to her all night and make sure that she didn't leave the party with Ashton and do something that she would thoroughly regret in the morning. Her eyes focused on Drew. "So are you the guy that's been hogging up my BFF since she has gotten home?"

"Guilty." Drew grinned. "But it's her fault."

"Hey, how's it my fault?" I asked.

"Because if you weren't so damn gorgeous, I wouldn't want to spend all this time with you."

"Awwwww…..that is so sweet," Krista said, holding her hand over her heart. She wrapped her arm around me. "She *is* absolutely gorgeous. She's my beautiful bestest friend in the whole wide world, so you better be good to her….or else." Krista giggled.

"Let the fun begin!" Ashton shouted as he pulled out a joint.

I shook my head and rolled my eyes. "Come on, let's go for a walk," Drew said. I looked around for Krista, but she had disappeared into the crowd, doing her social butterfly thing, no doubt. We took a walk along the water, finally taking a seat in the sand when we were far enough from the crowd. The full moon shined above the rippling waves. "That moon is beautiful tonight," I said.

"Yeah, it is," Drew said, throwing a rock into the water.

"I prefer half-moons, though."

He looked at me and began to chuckle. "And why is that?" he asked.

I shrugged. "There's just something about it, you know… kind of like it's looking for its other half to make it whole but still beautiful just the same….I know I'm weird."

He kissed me softly on the cheek. "Nah, you're not weird, you just think outside the box. I like that." His eyes widened for a brief second. "Hey, I forgot about something."

"What?" I asked as I watched him pull out his phone from his pocket. He stood up and grabbed my hand, pulling me up as *Moonlight Serenade* played through the speakers of his phone.

"I thought this would be better than listening to it in your head."

I wrapped my arms around his neck, unable to wipe the smile from my face as we swayed back and forth under the star filled sky.

"Much better," I said, standing on my tiptoes and planting a gentle kiss on his lips. He moved his hands to the small of my back and pulled me closer. I rested my head on his chest, breathing in the familiar scent of his cologne that I had grown so fond of. I had never felt so at ease, so free, and most of all so happy in my whole life.

After Drew and I finished our dance, shared a few long hot kisses, and got ourselves almost to the point of ripping each other's clothes off right there on the beach, we decided to head back to the party. The crowd had died down and I scanned the area. I didn't see Ashton or Krista and I immediately scolded myself for being a bad friend and leaving her. I only hoped that she wasn't *that* drunk and didn't leave with Ashton. My attention was turned to the group of people gathered around as someone screamed, "Fight!" As I moved closer, I watched three guys run off, leaving the guy that they had just pummeled laying on the ground in the fetal position. Once I got a better look, I realized that it was my brother.

"Oh my God, Jordan!" I shouted, pushing my way through the crowd. I was shaking as I bent down to help him up.

"Becca, I don't know what happened. I went to go get a drink and the next thing I knew these three kids were jumping him," my brother's friend, Jason, said.

Tears immediately gushed from my eyes when I saw his bloody face.

"Becca, what's going on?" Drew asked, finally catching up with me.

"My brother….these three guys just–" I couldn't even get the words out; all I could do was cry. Drew bent down on the other side of me and helped my brother up while his friend grabbed onto his other arm, helping him balance. "I have to get him home," I said to Drew.

He nodded and helped my brother to his car.

"Jordan, what are you even doing here? You're grounded." Of course I knew what he was doing there; my parents had gone to visit friends of theirs in Boston for the weekend which meant my brother took it upon himself to unground himself.

"Becca, can you please spare me the lecture right now?"

"Can you at least tell me what happened?"

"Really, I don't know."

"How do you not know?"

"Ashton was leaving the party with Krista. He gave me this envelope and told me this guy was coming to pick it up and to make sure I got the money from him and he would give me a cut. Well, *three* guys ended up showing up, took the envelope after they jumped me from behind and never gave me the money. Now Ashton is going to be pissed."

"Oh, fuck Ashton!"

My brother's bruised eyes widened at my uncharacteristic language.

Drew was silent for the most part before finally chiming in. "What was in the envelope?" he asked.

"What do you think?" my brother replied.

"What?" I asked, totally naïve as to what they were talking about.

"Oxycodone, Becca," my brother replied.

My jaw dropped and I covered my mouth. "Oh my God, Jordan, what the hell is wrong with you!? I'm going to kill Ashton for getting you involved in this!"

"Becca, just calm down. Don't make the situation any worse!" Jordan said.

"Oh, it's gonna get worse, especially when Mom and Dad find out about this!"

"They're not gonna find out!"

"Oh yes they—"

"Becca, just let it go," Drew said.

"What? Are you crazy? No, I'm not gonna let this go! Don't you see what those animals did to my little brother? Not to mention that your dirt bag friend has him pedaling pills for his benefit. Did you know about this, too?"

He took his eyes off the road for a brief second and looked at me in surprise. "Becca, just because I hang out with Ashton from time to time it doesn't mean I know everything or am in on everything he does, and I really wish you'd stop lumping me in with him like that."

"I'm sorry; I'm just really upset right now."

"And you should be, but before you go making it any worse just calm down and try to think rationally." He looked in his rearview mirror at my brother. "Jordan, you do know that was a bonehead move tonight, don't you? You could have seriously screwed up the rest of your life if you got caught doing that. Not to mention you're lucky that those guys only used their fists and not guns."

"Yeah, I do now, that's for sure."

I turned around and stared at him. My stomach hurt just looking at his banged up face. "I can't believe how stupid you are! Now how are you going to explain that mess on your face to Mom and Dad?"

"Just let me worry about that. I promise, Becca, I learned my lesson."

I turned around, hoping that he had and that I wasn't going to regret not telling my parents.

Chapter 9

Once we arrived home, I helped my brother clean up his face and got him some Tylenol. "I'm going to bed, I'm beat. Thanks Becca."

"Jordan, just promise me that you will never be that stupid again."

He nodded. "I promise."

"And stay the hell away from Ashton Barrett!"

"I will." He leaned down and gave me a kiss on the cheek. "Good night, Becca. Love you."

"Love you, too," I replied while hugging him tightly. No matter how big and stupid he was, he would always be my little brother who I would protect with everything I had.

I walked back downstairs and into the family room where Drew was sitting on the couch waiting for me. "Thanks for calming me down. If you hadn't been there, my parents would have been on their way home, ready to kill my brother," I said while taking a seat next to him.

"No problem, Becca."

"I just hope that he's learned his lesson." I sighed.

"You're a good big sister." Drew smiled.

"Thanks," I said, leaning my head on his shoulder.

"I should get going so you can get some sleep."

I lifted my head and looked at him with disappointment. "Well, I'm not very tired after all of that excitement." He kissed me on my head and my insides began to tingle for him once again. I was finding that it didn't take much for this to happen whenever he was around.

"Okay, I just didn't want to keep you from getting your rest. Want to watch a movie or something?" he asked.

I shook my head and stared into his eyes before standing up and taking his hand. He looked at me strangely as I pulled him off the couch. I led him up the stairs to my bedroom and closed the door behind us, knowing that I was breaking the number one rule in my house: *no boys in the bedroom*. That rule was never challenged, because I had never brought a boy home before. Since my parents were away until Sunday and my brother was probably already passed out in his room, which was all the way down the hall, I knew I was safe.

We took a seat on my bed and my lips instantly found their way to his. He grabbed the back of my hair, pulling me closer and kissing me harder while he lifted my shirt over my head. He removed my bra before laying me down on my bed.

"Drew, this is my first time," I whispered, a little ashamed to admit it.

His eyes widened as he gently swept his hand along my face. "Are you sure you want—" I nodded before he could even get the words out. I had never wanted anything more in my entire life. He kissed me again, this time a little gentler, moving his lips to my breast and tenderly taking it into his mouth. I arched my back and ran my hands through his hair, feeling my insides becoming awakened. He looked up at me and smiled before moving his lips back up to my neck. "Becca, are you sure that you want to do this?"

"Yes! I want you, Drew. I want you to be my first."

His lips trailed down my stomach as he unbuttoned my shorts, slipping them off along with my underwear. I took a deep breath when I felt him moving his way further down. I gasped as he began to work magic on my body with his tongue. Krista always talked about oral sex and how wonderful it was and I always thought that she was exaggerating. I realized now that she wasn't. I ran my hands through his hair, lifting my hips in excitement. He gently placed his finger inside of me and I took a deep breath. He looked up at me, gauging my reaction. I tried desperately to hide the pain on my face but failed miserably. He moved back up and took me in his arms.

"Becca, maybe we should just wait. I don't even have anything on me."

"I'm on the pill. Please, Drew, I really want to do this....with you."

He looked at me with hesitation before I grabbed his face and kissed him deeply. I lifted his shirt over his head and unbuttoned his shorts, staring at his perfect chest, his perfect arms, and perfect abs. Everything about him was flawlessness. I ran my hands down his bare back, feeling the buildup of desire and need for him reaching its breaking point. He was breathing heavily as he removed his shorts and boxers. My stomach fluttered with apprehension and anticipation when I saw him standing over top of me, naked. His fingers trailed back down to the spot that was yearning for him. He gently moved them around while he kissed me, which was only adding to my excitement and desire for him. After a few minutes of his pleasurable torture, I couldn't take anymore; I needed to feel him inside of me. I looked up at him and arched my back as he gently eased into me, letting out a light groan of pleasure. I held my breath and bit my lip to try and halt the discomfort. I knew that this would happen the first time so I wasn't concerned and I completely trusted Drew. I buried my face in his shoulder to try and hide my pained expression. I didn't want him to know that it hurt. I didn't want him to stop. I wanted to get past this point of pain so I could start experiencing the pleasure.

"Are you okay?" he asked. I nodded. He kissed me hard as he began to move in and out of me and my insides felt like they were tearing apart. I closed my eyes tightly, hoping that the hurt would finally subside. He slowed down a bit and brushed his lips against mine. My discomfort was finally diminishing as I raised my hips to meet him. I ran my hands up and down his back and felt his heart beating against mine. "You are so beautiful," he whispered, pushing my hair from my face and staring into my eyes. "Are you sure this is okay for you?"

I swallowed hard and nodded. "Yes, it's perfect," I replied. This was so surreal to me. I had always imagined my first time and what it would be like. I was scared to death about giving something so special away to just anyone, but with Drew it just seemed so natural. He was so caring and gentle with me that I knew he was the right one.

His breathing was becoming heavier and I knew that he was trying his hardest to hold back for me. "I want you to…" I whispered in his ear.

He lifted his head from my shoulder and looked down at me. "But—"

I couldn't help but smile. He was so giving and compassionate where most guys would have taken that as an open invitation. I ran my hands through his hair and planted a gentle kiss on his lips. "I think you and I both know it's not going to happen for me the first time. But we still have lots of time this summer to make sure it does."

He looked at me and smiled before moving quicker, taking my body by surprise in a good way. I was finally getting into a rhythm with him when he buried his face into my shoulder. "Oh my God, Becca, you feel so fuckin' good," he whispered just as I felt the warmth of him inside of me.

I smiled as he tried to catch his breath. I loved knowing that my body had the power to make him feel that way. He kissed me on the lips and pulled me on top of him. "Thank you for allowing my first time to be with you," I said.

"Becca, you are amazing, you know that?" I shrugged my shoulders and looked away. He took my face and moved my head so I was looking at him. "Are you forgetting our lessons? You're supposed to respond with, 'Well, yes Drew, I know I'm amazing at everything I do.'"

I giggled and kissed him on the lips. "Well, are you as good at teaching lessons in the bedroom as you are at self-confidence lessons?" I asked.

"Hmmm.....maybe. Would you like to sign up for that class, too?" he teased.

"Oh definitely!" I replied, placing a gentle kiss on his chest.

I wrapped my arms around him and hugged him tightly, suddenly feeling myself becoming sleepy. After a while, I lifted my head and noticed that he was sound asleep. I smiled as I watched his chest rise and fall. Not only did I have a boy in my bedroom, but I had just had sex with him in my bed. I was breaking all the rules and it felt good.

Chapter 10

I awoke the next morning in Drew's arms and even though I was still the same girl, I felt like a new one. I had given Drew a very special part of me that I was saving for someone just as special and I didn't regret if for one second. "Good morning," I whispered in his ear.

"Morning," he responded. He kissed me on the top of my head and then got up to dress.

"Hey, where are you going?" I asked as I sat up, covering my bare chest with the sheet.

"Umm....I don't think it's a good idea if your brother knows that I spent the night here."

I looked at the clock and giggled. "It's only seven a.m.; my brother won't be up for at least another four hours."

He stood up and pulled up his shorts. "I got some stuff I have to do this morning," he said, sounding a little off his game.

I bit my lip, slowly regretting what had happened last night between us. Was this his way of getting what he was after and leaving? Or maybe I was really so bad in bed that once was enough for him. "Can I at least make you some coffee?" I asked, throwing on my shorts and tank top that were on the floor.

"No, I really need—" he stopped himself upon seeing the tears in my eyes. "Hey, what's the matter?" he asked, grabbing my waist and pulling me into him.

I shook my head, trying my hardest to play it off. "Nothing."

He tilted my chin so I was looking into his eyes. "Hey, I know what you're thinking and you couldn't be more wrong. I forgot I told a buddy of mine I'd help him move this morning and I'm supposed to be there in twenty minutes." I felt a little relieved but at the same time a little too clingy. I didn't want him to think that just because we slept together, that I felt like I owned him. I grabbed my phone from my nightstand to check the text message that had just come in from Mrs. Barrett before walking him to the door. "You are one incredible girl; you know that, Becca?" he said, taking my face in his hands.

A smile inched across my face. "Yeah, I do."

He smiled back. "That a girl! I'll see you later?"

"Sounds good. Mrs. Barrett just sent me a text asking me to deliver a welcome package to Long Island this afternoon. Once I'm done with that, I have no other plans, so just call me when you're done."

His smile disappeared in an instant. "What time are you doing that?" he asked.

"I don't know whenever I shower and get myself together. She didn't give a specific time, she just said this afternoon."

"Well, I'll go with you."

I furrowed my brows in confusion. "I thought you just said you have to help—"

He shook his head, looking a little nervous. "I'll be done by this afternoon. I don't want you driving all that way by yourself."

I shook my head and laughed. "Drew, I've driven further than that by myself."

"Yeah, well, why should you go by yourself when I can go with you? I'll drive. You have the address? I'll plug it into my GPS so we'll be all ready to go." I pulled out my phone and pulled up her text. I rattled off the address while he put it in his phone. "Meet me at my house at two?" he asked.

"Yeah, that sounds good," I responded, giving him an uneasy look while still trying to figure out why he was so hell bent on coming with me.

"See ya later, gorgeous." He gave me a soft kiss on the lips and my insides melted.

"See ya!" I stood in the doorway, unable to wipe the smile from my face as I watched him drive away. I shut the door behind me and jumped when I saw Jordan standing at the bottom of the steps.

"Oh my God, you scared me!" I said, placing my hand over my heart. "What are you doing up so early?"

"I don't know. I just wasn't tired, I guess. Don't worry, your secret's safe with me." He smiled.

I tried my hardest to not seem embarrassed as I moved closer to his eye, hoping by some miracle that it healed overnight. Unfortunately, it looked even worse. "Oh Jordan, I can't stand looking at it," I said.

"It looks worse than it feels."

"So do you want to go to breakfast? My treat?" I asked.

He smiled. "Sounds good to me."

"Okay, I'll be ready in twenty minutes."

I headed into my bedroom to gather my clothes before getting in the shower. I sat down on my bed for a minute, picking up the pillow that Drew had slept on, hugging it tightly and breathing in deeply. As I closed my eyes, I replayed last night over in my head. My insides tingled once again, remembering how good it felt to have his lips and hands all over my body. He was so gentle and caring, putting me at total ease. I was still a little sore but it was a good kind of sore; it was a beautiful reminder of what Drew and I had shared last night. I took in one last breath before heading into the shower.

Jordan and I finished up breakfast and spent the early part of the afternoon sitting by the pool. I was actually enjoying myself with him. Outside of his stupid mistake that he had made last night, he really did seem to be growing up. I looked at the time on my phone, realizing that it was already after one and I still had to stop by Lynn Barrett's to pick up the welcome packet and get to Drew's by two. I was praying to God that Ashton wasn't home when I went there. I seriously didn't know if I would be able to hold back, telling him where to go. He had called Jordan when we were at breakfast to find out what happened. I tried grabbing the phone from him to tell him off, but Jordan wouldn't let me. I was hoping that he heard the few choice words that I called him as Jordan talked louder to block me out.

"Hey, I have to go run some errands for this charity today. Are you going to be okay here by yourself?"

"Becca, do you think I'm still four years old?"

"I know you're not, but you will always be my baby brother."

"I'll be fine. Lindsay is coming over to keep me company." He smiled.

"Wow, I'm impressed. You're still with her?" I asked, knowing that he had been seeing her for a few months now, which was a record for him.

"Yeah, I really like her a lot."

I smiled. "Well, good, just don't do anything to screw it up, like what you did last night."

"I know, Becca. Really, I mean it.....it WILL NOT happen again."

I got up from the lounge chair and kissed him on the cheek. "Behave! I told Mom and Dad that I had everything under control when they called this morning. Don't make me out to be a liar!"

"I won't," he said, shifting his sunglasses back to his eyes. "See ya later, Becca."

"See ya!"

I walked through the house and out the front door, and before I knew it I had already picked up the package from Lynn and was pulling into Drew's driveway. I couldn't wipe the smile from my face when he opened the door. His muscles rippled through his form fitting tee shirt, making me yearn to feel his hands all over my body again.

"Hey you!" I smiled. He closed the door behind me and I threw my arms around his neck, kissing him hard.

He took my face in his hands. "Gorgeous girl. You're making me crazy coming over here in your short little skirt and smelling good enough to eat. But we have to be somewhere, remember? And, if we start this now, we won't be going anywhere for the rest of the night."

"Fine." I stuck out my bottom lip and pretended to pout.

He took my hand in his and we walked out the door to his car. I clicked my seat belt and he placed his hand on my bare thigh. "Ready?" he asked.

I was more than ready. But what I was ready for didn't involve driving anyplace.

BLIND SIDE OF LOVE

Chapter 11

We arrived back at Drew's house a little after six. I was really glad that he was so persistent on coming with me. We hit major construction that took us on a ton of detours that I knew I would have surely gotten lost going through. The benefactor's home that I went to today was the nicest one I had been to yet. You could fit about four of my houses, which many people referred to as mini mansions, into this one. I found myself picking my jaw up from the ground several times even before I had entered, just at the array of high end cars parked in the horse shoe driveway, ranging from *Porsches* to *Lamborghinis*.

I sat outside on Drew's patio, staring out at the sound while he showered. I became mesmerized by an older man who had been tossing a stick into the water and his German Shepherd who relentlessly kept going back into the water to retrieve it. I quickly went out to my car and took out my sketching pad and my pencils before walking out onto the beach and taking a seat in the sand. The dog had now taken a break and was sitting side by side with his master as the two of them stared out at the water. I sat behind them and began to sketch them sitting there quietly. By the time I finished, I was actually impressed with the ability of the two of them who had sat so still while I drew them up, almost as if they knew they were being my muse. I was even more impressed with the way the drawing had come out, capturing the moment to a tee.

"Hey, whatchya doin'?" Drew asked as he walked out onto the beach, bending down to my level. His eyes widened as he looked at the picture and then up at the man and his dog, who were still sitting in the same position. "Becca, did you draw this?" he asked. I nodded and smiled. "This is awesome!"

"Thanks. I just drew it up really quick. I love witnessing moments that seep into my heart, they make the best pictures. And this one was one of them. I just had to draw it out."

"Do you draw a lot?"

"I used to. I love sketching and working with charcoals, but my favorite is pastels. I never knew how many different colors were in a sunset. Unfortunately, I don't have time to do it much with school."

"Did you ever think of pursuing this as a career?"

I laughed. "Yeah, for about a minute. Until my dad lectured me and told me that no daughter of his was going to be a starving artist. So I kind of traded in my art stuff for law books." I sighed deeply, wishing that I had had the courage to stand up to my dad and tell him what I really wanted to do with my life. "But every now and then, I sneak some in. It's good for my soul."

"Well, you should do it more often, especially if it's something that makes you happy. Not to mention that you have a true talent."

"Well, thanks. You're the first person that ever encouraged me to keep drawing. My parents always say it's just the weird creative side of me coming out and creativity gets you nowhere in life."

"That's not true, Becca. Don't ever let that side of you fade away, that's what makes you different."

Just when I thought that I couldn't like him anymore than I already did, he would do or say something that would make my heart leap from my chest. He just seemed to *get me* on so many different levels. He allowed me to be the girl that I truly wanted to be without being chastised for it.

I ripped the sketch from by book when I saw the man getting up. "Excuse me," I said as I stood up and approached him. "I hope you don't mind, but while you and your dog were taking a little rest, I drew this up. I thought that maybe you would want to have it." I noticed that he was looking past me, making me feel a little uneasy, before it finally dawned on me, he was blind and this was his seeing-eye dog. "Oh my God, I'm so sorry," I whispered.

"Don't be." He smiled. "I *can* see it, you know?"

"You can? How?" I asked.

"In my mind and in my heart. You'd be surprised by the beautiful pictures I have stored in there." I placed the picture in his hands and he bent down to show the dog. "What do you think Sampson, is this a good picture of us?" The dog barked loudly. "Well, Sampson seems to love it and since he's my eyes, I love it, too. Would you just mind doing me a favor and sign the bottom for me if you haven't done so already? That way I can say that I have an original when you become famous."

I laughed at that outrageous thought, but obeyed his wishes, signing and dating it for him. "I'm Becca Keeton, by the way," I said, placing my hand in his.

"I'm Luke Thompson," he replied while shaking my hand. "Thank you so much for this. I'm going to have my wife get a frame so we can hang it over the mantle where all of my favorite pictures are displayed."

A smile came from deep inside my stomach. I had truly made someone happy with something that I created and even though I knew that he couldn't see it with his eyes, he had shown me that he could feel it in his heart which meant more to me than anything. "It was a pleasure meeting you, Miss Keeton, and I will be sure to remember the name to make sure that no one gets their hands on my original when you become famous."

"Well, I think the chances of that happening are slim to none, so for now just enjoy the picture."

"Oh, never say never, child. I could tell you're a very creative person, just by your voice. You're beautiful on the inside and out. You put your heart into everything that you do and give all of yourself to those you care about."

I smiled at this observation. "Well, I'd like to believe that's true."

"Oh it is. I've been blind my whole life. I use my other senses to make up for what my eyes lack. I don't see beauty like most people do. I feel it. It's more than just the physical makings of a person, it's what's inside. If you ask me, everyone should be blind before they could see. People would view the world much differently."

"That sounds like a really good thought, Mr. Thompson."

He smiled and nodded before grabbing onto his dog's leash. "Ready, Sampson?" The dog looked up at him, leading him on his way as I stood there silently, watching them walk away.

Drew came up behind me, wrapping his arms around my waist and kissing my neck. "You know, everything that man said about you was true. And, I was very impressed with the way that you handled his compliments."

I leaned my head back into his chest. "Did you ever feel like certain people come into your life for a reason, even if it's only for a few minutes and you never see them again?"

"I guess I never thought about it," he said, planting another gentle kiss on my neck. I turned around to face him, placing my arms around him.

"Well, I do, and that man just now, he came into my life for some reason tonight. I don't know why, but I just feel it."

He pressed his forehead up against mine. "Maybe it was just to reinforce the lessons that I've already taught you. That even a blind man can see just how beautiful you are."

"Well, thank you." I stood on my tiptoes and planted a gentle kiss on his lips.

"I think you may have graduated from my school of confidence, Becca."

"Oh good, does that mean that we can get started on the next lesson that we discussed last night?"

The smile on his face made me want to rip my clothes and his off right there and prove to him that I could be an A plus student. "I believe that class is in session right now."

I giggled as he scooped me up in his arms and carried me off the beach and back to his house, finally placing me down on his bed. I couldn't get my lips on his fast enough. He held his hands up and laughed. "Wow, an over enthusiastic student, I like that."

"Well, I can't help it if I've got a little crush on my teacher."

"Geez, you're not even giving me time to think of what today's lesson is going to be."

"Oh I know!" I grinned.

"What's your suggestion, Becca?"

"An oral presentation." I giggled.

His eyes widened and his smile deepened. "Becca! What happened to that sweet little innocent girl?"

"She's still here, just a little more confident."

Drew and I had our first lesson that night and it was the best class I had ever taken. My nerves from last night had completely diminished and it was nothing short of wonderful. By the time it was over, Drew had made sure that I had achieved something for the very first time that I had only heard about. And as with any good teacher, he assured that it completely lived up to my expectations, making me want to show up for class every day so I could experience it over and over.

Chapter 12

The big red 2:47 on the clock came into focus as I raised my head from Drew's chest and opened my tired eyes. "Shit," I whispered. I tried to quietly reach for my phone from the nightstand to see if my brother had tried calling me, or worse yet, my parents.

"Hey, what are you doing?" Drew asked in a sleepy voice.

"I'm just checking to see if my brother tried calling. I should really get going," I said, breathing a sigh of relief upon seeing no missed calls or text messages. He pulled me back down and hugged me. My stomach flipped, feeling his naked body pressing up against mine.

"Stay, Becca. It's the middle of the night. Your brother is probably sleeping." A million things raced through my mind....*What if my parents came home early? What if Jordan was doing something stupid like he did last night and I wasn't there to stop him?* Every single thought that was going through my head quickly diminished when I felt Drew's lips on my bare back. I turned around, forgetting about all of my responsibilities and not even caring if it meant paying the price with my parents later on.

At that moment, the only thing that mattered was Drew and making love to him once again.

Drew was still lying in bed, staring at me as I dressed once we woke up later that morning. "What are you looking at?" I smirked as I pulled my shirt over my head.

"One gorgeous woman!" He smiled back.

"Why thank you Mr. Bryant, I know I am." I giggled.

"Yeah, you aced that class. And after last night, you aced the second one, too."

"Well, I'll keep attending the second one if you don't mind. You know, for extra credit?"

"Sounds good to me."

I leaned down to kiss him on the cheek and he pulled me on top of him. "I know I said this before but I just have to say it again, you are one amazing and gorgeous girl."

I hugged him tightly. "Well, thank you, but I have to really get going," I said with reluctance.

"Well, you better get while you still can," he teased. I stood up and he was right behind me, pulling on his shorts. "Does she have you going anywhere this week?" he asked as he walked me to the door.

I rolled my eyes. This whole charity was really starting to get to me. It definitely wasn't what I signed on for. "Who knows, I'm sure she'll text me if she does."

"I'll call ya later," he said just as his doorbell rang. He looked out the window and gave me an uneasy look.

"What's the matter?"

"It's your favorite person."

My stomach clenched not only because I wanted to haul off and punch Ashton right in the face over the situation that he had put my brother in, but also because I was fairly certain that even he was smart enough to put the pieces together and figure out that I had spent the night here. I took a deep breath before Drew opened the door.

The familiar arrogant smirk that he always had plastered across his face was the first thing I saw. He looked me over. "Well, well, well, sweet little Becca! Does Daddy know where you spent the night?"

"Don't even talk to me, you dirt bag."

"Damn and here I thought that once you got fucked you would get the stick out of your ass!"

"You are nothing but an asshole, Ashton Barrett, plain and simple. Stay the hell away from me and stay the hell away from my brother."

"Well, I will say you've gotten a little more spunk in you since Drew's been boinkin' you."

"Ashton, just shut the fuck up!" Drew chimed in.

"I get it, bro. You don't want me pissing off your piece of ass and I respect that, but maybe you should tell her to lighten up a little so we could all get along."

"I will *never* get along with you and I will *never* be friends with you, so I don't have to lighten up."

"Suit yourself, Becca. I didn't come here to talk to you, anyway. I came to see Drew." He raised his eyebrow at me before turning his attention to Drew. "A bunch of us *guys* are going kayaking today and maybe doing a little par-taying after. You in?" Drew looked at me almost like he was asking my permission. Unfortunately, Ashton picked up on it right away as well. "Oh my God, are you fuckin' serious?" Ashton shouted. "She has you that whipped already?"

I did my best to ignore him, but at the same time I didn't want Drew to feel as if he had to ask for my approval to go. Even though I couldn't help but wonder in the back of my mind, what girls would be at this party afterward. I wrapped my arms around Drew's neck and kissed him deeply, acting as if Ashton wasn't even standing two feet away. "Have fun today and call me later," I said.

"See ya, gorgeous," he said, giving me a quick kiss on the cheek.

It took everything in me to keep walking out the door and not smack Ashton across the face when he shouted, "Oh my God, I think I'm gonna throw up!"

I hopped into my car and pulled my phone from my purse to call my brother. "Great!" I said, upon noticing that the battery had gone dead. Reality was finally sinking in and I was praying that he had behaved himself last night, especially after I promised my parents that I would keep a close eye on him this weekend.

My stomach dropped when I pulled into the driveway and saw my father's car. They weren't supposed to be back until tonight. I felt myself instantly breaking out in a sweat as I tried to come up with an excuse as to where I spent the night. My legs were trembling as I walked up the driveway and in the front door.

"Becca! Is that you?" my mother shouted from the family room.

I slowly inched my way closer. "Yeah, what's going—" my jaw dropped when I saw my mother walking around the living room, tossing beer bottles into a garbage bag. "What….what happened?" I asked.

"I don't know, Becca. Why don't you tell us?" my father asked as he came walking down the steps.

"I-I…..had to do some work on the charity yesterday for Lynn and then Krista and I went back to her house and watched a few movies and I ended up falling asleep."

"Don't lie to me, Becca!" my father shouted. "I called Krista looking for you and she said she had no clue where you were. You were with that boy, weren't you?" I looked at him and nodded. "Well, while you were out having fun last night, your brother decided to throw a party with God knows how many kids getting drunk off their asses and trashing the house."

"He promised me that he—"

"He promised you! Are you that stupid, Becca? You know

better than to believe that!"

"Look, Dad, I'm sorry if Jordan can't be trusted to be left alone in the house at seventeen years old. But I shouldn't have to be his babysitter that makes sure that he behaves himself all the time. Maybe you need to take up whatever issues he's having with him and not me. I'm sick of being lectured over his mistakes!" I shouted, surprising myself a little. I never raised my voice to my dad.

"Who do you think you are speaking to in that tone?" He inched closer to me. "What, do you think you can talk to your father anyway you want now because you're out whoring around with that boy?"

My heart dropped over his words. "Jeff, that's enough!" my mother shouted. Tears filled my eyes and I could see his eyes filling with emotion as well as I stared into them. He glared at me one last time before walking into his study and slamming the door.

After I helped my mother clean up, I decided to swallow my pride and make amends with my father. "Hey," I said as I knocked lightly on his study door. He barely lifted his head as I placed the cup of coffee on his desk. I took a seat and looked around at all of my artwork hanging on the walls, some of it dating back to when I was three years old. "So, when did you want to reschedule our tennis match?"

"I don't know right now, Becca. I'm really busy with work."

My eyes filled with tears. "I'm still the same girl, Daddy. I'm still your Becca."
He had a pained expression as he looked into my eyes. "My Becca never lied. She never made stupid mistakes."

"I didn't make a stupid mistake, Dad. What are you talking about?"

"Sleeping with the first guy that gives you any attention."

"That's not true, Dad! I'm a twenty one year old woman. Most girls my age have been having sex since they were sixteen, so how dare you say that to me!"

"You're not like most girls, Becca! You have the whole world at your fingertips and you're throwing it away over a guy."

"How am I throwing my life away over a guy? Because I like him and I enjoy spending time with him? How is that throwing my life away?"

"The next thing you know, you'll be talking about marriage and then having kids and then that's it!"

"Dad, just calm down. Drew and I have only been dating for three weeks, we are not that serious."

"But you're serious enough to be having sex with him?" He looked at me with sheer disappointment.

I looked down at the ground and shook my head. "Dad, he's just diff–"

He put his hand up to stop me. "I don't have time for this right now, Becca, I have to finish up here," he said, putting his head back down into his paperwork.

I swallowed hard, trying my hardest to halt my tears. "I'm sorry for not being here for Jordan last night," I whispered as I got up from the chair and exited his study. My father and I never fought. I was constantly living up to his high expectations of me. And although I *was* sorry for letting him down with my brother, I would never be sorry for sleeping with Drew.... and for that, I would never apologize.

Chapter 13

I kept to myself the rest of the day, going out of my way to help my mother around the house before spending a few hours by the pool. My father stayed locked in his study for the afternoon and my brother was still passed out in bed while I took the brunt of his punishment.

"You need some help with that?" I asked my mother as I walked into the kitchen and saw her peeling potatoes for dinner.

"Sure, if you're up to it; grab a knife and start slicing some carrots." She looked up at me and smiled. I smiled back, happy to see that she wasn't giving me the silent treatment as well. I took a seat at the counter stool next to her and wasted no time dicing up the carrots.

"So how was Boston?" I asked.

"Oh you know, hectic as usual, but it was nice to see Lorraine and John again."

I nodded and took a deep breath. "Mom, I'm really sorry for not being here last night. I really thought that Jordan was being sincere."

"That's okay, Becca, it's not your fault. Your father has to learn that your brother is seventeen years old and has to start bearing the brunt of his mistakes, instead of blaming everyone else for them." She put down the potato that she was peeling and looked at me. "But I am a little hurt that you didn't share with me just how serious you were becoming with this guy. I mean, your father and I haven't even met him."

"Daddy did meet him the night of the benefit."

"Becca, you know what I mean; we would like to have met him for longer than a minute."

"I'm sorry. I just didn't think Daddy would be very welcoming."

She looked at me and smiled. "Becca, this is all so new to him. You've never had any serious interest in boys before."

"Well, I would love for you guys to get to know him, but I just don't want him feeling uncomfortable."

"You let me take care of your father and I will make sure that doesn't happen."

"Okay," I whispered as I began chopping once again.

"Becca?"

"Yeah," I replied, looking up from my carrots.

"You are still on the pill, right?"

I felt my face turning red. I hated talking about these things with anyone, especially my parents. "Yes, I am."

She nodded. "Well, did you have any questions about....you know?"

I shook my head. "No, Mom, I'm good."

"Okay." She smiled.

"So what's for dinner?" I asked, trying to break up the awkwardness of the moment.

"London Broil on the grill, mashed potatoes, and fresh vegetables."

"Oh, can I make my special mashed potatoes?" I asked.

"Sure, knock yourself out," she replied. My brother strolled into the kitchen and my mother and I both lifted our heads from our chopping and peeling. He opened the refrigerator door to get a drink, looking like he was half dead. "I better go start that grill," my mother said as she got up and exited the kitchen.

"Becca?"

"What?!" I raised my voice in annoyance.

"I'm sorry if you had to take a lot of crap because of me."

"What else is new, Jordan? I'm always getting yelled at for *your* mistakes. If you can't be responsible and trusted, that's not my problem. You promised me yesterday that you wouldn't do anything."

"I know I did and I'm sorry, but Lindsay came over and then her brother and then a few of his friends and then it just kept going from there."

"And it never once dawned on you to tell these kids to leave?" He looked at me blankly and shrugged his shoulders. "Whatever, Jordan, I just don't even care anymore."

"Ready to start those potatoes?" my mother asked as she walked back in, still totally ignoring my brother. He stood in the kitchen for a little while longer before walking out and heading back up the stairs.

My father finally came out of his study when it was time to sit down to dinner. Jordan came downstairs looking somewhat human after taking a shower and I began to wonder what excuse he had given my parents over his black eye. "These potatoes came out delicious, Becca," my mother said in an effort to break up the silence.

"Thank you," I whispered as I took a sip of my water.

"So, Jeff, I was telling Becca that we would really like to get to know this boy that she's been seeing a little better." I felt my food instantly churning in my stomach. Why did she have to bring this subject up now? My father continued eating, never lifting his head from his plate. "So, I was thinking next weekend we can have a little barbeque. What do you think?" He finally looked up from his food and glared at her. "Maybe I'll invite a few other people over so he doesn't feel awkward," she continued on, completely ignoring my father's look of warning. "Becca, ask him if he's free next Saturday night." I instantly lost my appetite, just judging by the look on my dad's face I knew that he wasn't going to give Drew a fair shot and I didn't want Drew to have to feel uncomfortable because of it. My only positive in it was that I still had a whole week for my dad to cool down and my mother to work on him, so maybe by Saturday he would at least be a little cordial. I sighed deeply and nodded.

"So Jordan, are you up for some golf with me, Edward, and Ashton tomorrow morning?" my father asked my brother as if nothing ever happened last night.

My brother quickly nodded, knowing that this was his way of escaping further punishment. Tears filled my eyes. I stared at my father, who was making sure that he avoided eye contact with me. My brother was the one that had trashed the house. My brother was the one that was underage drinking with all of his friends. My brother was the one that let him down time and time again. Yet, I was the one getting the silent treatment from him all because I *finally* had a guy in my life.

I got up from the table to clear my plate. "Becca, where are you going? You didn't even touch your food," my mother said.

"I lost my appetite," I said, rinsing off my plate as my father's eyes finally locked with mine before he looked away without saying a word.

I walked out of the kitchen and upstairs to my bedroom, throwing myself down on my bed. As I checked my messages, there was a missed call from Krista and a text from Lynn Barrett, letting me know that she needed me to run back to Long Island tomorrow morning. I hadn't heard from Drew since I had left his house that morning which was only adding to my anxiety, especially since I knew who he was with. I grabbed my phone to call Krista back, hoping that would help me temporarily forget Drew's silence.

"Hey, chickie. What's going on?" she answered.

"Not much."

"I hope I didn't get you in trouble with your dad this morning. I was half asleep when he called."

"It's okay."

"Well, where were you?" There was a brief moment of silence. "Really, Becca, you're going to hold out on me?"

"I ended up falling asleep over at Drew's," I blurted out.

She gasped and giggled. "Becca? Were you finally being a naughty girl?"

Leave it to Krista to make me smile when I didn't think it was possible. "No," I said half-heartedly.

"Liar!" She laughed. "Well, I can't say I blame you, girl, he is a total hottie! I saw him today without a shirt ......wow!"

The smile that was on my face instantly disappeared. "When did you see him today?" I asked.

"Ashton had a little beach party when he and the guys got done kayaking. He asked me to come and then got totally wasted, so I left. You know he's so hot but he's always drunk or high and that's such a turn-off." *That was his biggest turnoff to her*? If you asked me, everything about Ashton Barrett was a turnoff but I wasn't going to go there with her right now.

"So what other girls were there?"

Krista picked up on my insecurities right away.

"No one worthwhile. Just all of Ashton's little groupies that fall at his feet." *Great, just what I wanted to hear.* I knew that all of those girls that Ashton associated with had sex with guys like it

78

was nothing. "Don't worry, Drew was behaving himself," she said with a hint of sarcasm to her voice. I pretended to be into the rest of the conversation but my thoughts were totally consumed by Drew and what he was doing, who he was with, and if he was missing me as much as I was missing him.

Chapter 14

The sun streaming through my bedroom window and the birds singing their morning tune would normally be enough to put a smile on my face first thing in the morning. But as I picked up my phone and saw the text that had come through from Drew last night, after I had fallen asleep, I was fairly certain that I was grinning from ear to ear:

Sorry for not calling you earlier. My battery died and I had to wait till I got home to charge it. I missed your gorgeous face all day. Talk to you tomorrow.

I loved the butterflies that I got in my stomach whenever I got a text from him, heard his voice, or felt his touch. This was all so new to me. I had never been under the spell of a guy like this before. I just wished that my dad would come around and be happy for me so I could enjoy the feelings I was having without feeling guilty.

I got up, showered, and dressed. I called Lynn as I chugged a cup of coffee down and was on my way out the door to pick up her deliveries for the day. My phone began to ring as I was backing out of the driveway. A smile instantly shrouded my face when I saw that it was Drew.

"Hey!" I answered, switching it to speaker.

"What's goin' on, gorgeous?" he asked, still sounding half asleep.

"Oh, just on my way to play gopher to Mrs. Barrett for the day!"

"Where are you going?" His voice suddenly perked up.

"I have to go back to Long Island to the place that we went to the other day. She forgot to give him a few of the donor forms, and she needs the original signatures by today."

"Well, give me twenty minutes to shower and I'll go with you."

"Drew, you really don't have to waste your time."

"Becca, just be at my house in twenty."

"Okay," I replied before hanging up. I hated taking up all of his time, making him feel like he had to go with me, but I had to admit, I was looking forward to seeing him and spending time with him today.

After I swung by Lynn's to pick up the envelope, I stopped to get my extra dose of caffeine as well as a cup of coffee for Drew. "Get it while it's hot!" I teased as he opened the door while pulling his tee shirt over his head. Suddenly, I wasn't sure if I was referring to the coffee or him.

He took both cups of coffee from my hands and placed them on the table. "Come here you!"

He pulled me into him and placed a gentle kiss on my lips, leaving my heart screaming for more. He must have immediately sensed how I was feeling as his lips came down on mine once again, kissing me with a lot more vigor. I wanted him to take me in his bedroom and make love to me. I didn't care about the errands that I had to run for Lynn. I didn't care about the fact that my dad was pissed off at me. I didn't care about anything else that was going on in my life when I was with him.

"Is it too early for class?" I smiled up at him.

"Are you trying to bribe the teacher?"

I giggled. "Not at all."

He lifted me off the ground and carried me over to the couch. His hands were up my shirt and unhooking my bra in an instant. I pulled him closer, needing to feel his body close to mine while inhaling the intoxicating scent of his shower gel. "Oh, Baby, I want you so bad right now. You have no clue what you do to me, do you?" My insides were throbbing for him and I wanted to ask him that same question. His voice sounded different…. smoother, almost like he had a sexy southern accent. I shook my head, unable to answer. *Why the hell did he have to sound so damn sexy?* His hands were slowly making their way to the button on my shorts when my phone beeped with a text message. Even though I didn't want to stop to check it, I knew that I better. If it were my parents and something had happened, I would never hear the end of it. "Can you just hold that thought for one second?" I giggled.

"You're killin' me, Becca!"

I kissed him softly on the cheek before grabbing my phone from my purse to find a text from Lynn Barrett:

Wasn't sure what time you were going to Mr. Simms, but can you please make it a priority? He's going away on business and leaving at two. I need those forms and he needs that packet before he goes.

"Here's an idea, why don't you go and drop the stuff off yourself, Lynn?" I said into my phone just before throwing it back into my purse.

"What's the matter?" Drew asked.

I rolled my eyes. "Oh I have to be there by two because the stupid guy has to leave! You know, I'm about ready to tell her to forget this whole thing. I didn't sign up to be her errand girl and now I have to input a ton of names and addresses of the donor's into a spreadsheet by Wednesday." I sighed heavily. "I guess I shouldn't be complaining, at least she's trusting me a little bit more."

He sat up and moved my hair from my face. "Come on, let's get going. We'll finish up this lesson later."

"Fine! She's starting to get to me, just like her son!"

He shook his head and let out a lighthearted chuckle. "Really?"

"Okay, maybe not that bad." I smiled back, taking his hand as he pulled me off the couch and we headed on our way.

Two hours later, and we were pulling up to the elaborate mansion that we were at just the other day. We walked up the driveway and waited for a response after ringing the doorbell. "Wow, could you just imagine living in a place like this?" I asked.

"Not bad," he joked. We were greeted by a very intimidating looking man all dressed in black. He even towered over Drew, who was well over six feet tall. His personality seemed just as daunting as his appearance. I watched in confusion as he immediately patted Drew down. "I'm cool, bro," Drew replied. I held my breath as he began to pat me down, wondering what the heck he was searching for. I was getting a nervous feeling in my stomach and I was so thankful that Drew was there with me. I grabbed onto Drew's hand tightly as the man led us into the sitting area.

"Mr. Simms will be with you shortly," he said in a very deep voice.

"Drew, what the heck was that all about?" I whispered, still gripping tightly to his hand.

He shrugged it off as if it were no big deal. "Probably just making sure we're not planning on robbing the place because you're so scary looking," he joked. I could tell that he was playing it off to try and put me at ease.

"Ah, Miss Keeton, how are you?" a short, dark haired man dressed in what looked to be a very expensive suit said as he entered the sitting area. "I'm Carlos Simms, it's a pleasure to meet you." He took my free hand in his, lifted it up to his lips, and kissed it. "And are you the lucky guy that gets to call this beautiful lady his girlfriend?" he asked Drew.

"Yes, I am," Drew responded. I bit my lip to hold back the smile over hearing him declare that.

"You are a very lucky man," Mr. Simms said, eyeing me up and making me feel very uncomfortable. "Please have a seat." He pointed to the posh leather couch. I hesitantly sat down, still gripping tightly to Drew's hand. "Can I get either one of you a drink?" he asked.

"Umm no, I just had to drop this envelope off to you." I could hear my voice cracking with uneasiness.

"Yes, of course. Well, let me get those papers and you can be on your way."

I nodded and looked away as his eyes burned into me once again. There was something about this guy that I didn't like at all.

"I just want to get out of here," I whispered to Drew.

"Okay, just get the papers and we'll be on our way."

I immediately stood up as he re-entered the room. "Here you go, Miss Keeton." He grabbed my hands as he placed the envelope in them and stared into my eyes. "You are a very beautiful girl. Have you ever considered modeling?" he asked, still grasping tightly to my hands.

I could feel my face burning. My nerves were getting the best of me. "Umm, no I haven't. Thank you for the forms, Mr. Simms. We really need to be on our way." I quickly removed my hand from his and wrapped my arm around Drew as his eyes moved from me to Drew.

"You are a *very* lucky man," he said to Drew as he looked down at my arm wrapped tightly around him.

"Thank you, sir. I know I am." Drew stared back at him as if they were having a standoff. Mr. Simms was finally the first one to look away.

"If you ever decide that you want to give modeling a try, Miss Keeton, I have a few connections in the field that would kill to have a beauty like you working for them." He shot Drew another quick gaze.

"Come on, Becca, let's get going," Drew said. He didn't have to tell me twice, I was practically running out the door.

84

"It was nice meeting both of you," Mr. Simms shouted as we exited. "You make sure you take care of that beautiful woman and be good to her or someone else will scoop her up in a heartbeat."

Drew stopped in the doorway and turned around to face Mr. Simms once again. I wished that he hadn't. I just wanted to get out of there. "Oh you don't have to worry about that ever happening, Mr. Simms." I had my head down, staring at the ground before finally looking up at Drew, who was glaring at Mr. Simms. I could feel myself trembling. *Was he crazy?* This guy had a whole security team that I was sure were armed. Not to mention the fact that something about him seemed a little off. I knew that Drew was only trying to be noble and stand up for me, but it really wasn't necessary. The best thing that he could do for me at the moment was get us out of that house.....quick!

Chapter 15

My hands were trembling as I turned the key in the ignition. "Hey, are you okay to drive?" Drew asked.

I nodded. I just wanted to get as far away from the property as possible. "That guy just freaked me out. I don't know, I'm really good at reading people and there was something weird about him and then you had to go and challenge him."

He began to chuckle. "I didn't challenge him. I was just trying to get him to ease up with flirting with you. You're my girl and no one else can have you." He placed his hand on my leg. I took my eyes off the road for one brief second and gave him a smile. "That's better," he said, smiling back.

"Hey, I forgot to ask you, what are you doing Saturday night?"

"Nothing that I know of."

"Well, my mom is having a little barbeque and she would like for you to come so she can get to know you better. If you don't want to, I totally understand."

"Yeah, that sounds good," he said without hesitation.

"Okay, great." I went on to tell him what had happened with my brother, making sure I left out the part about my parents knowing that we had sex. I didn't want him to feel awkward when he came over Saturday night, even though my dad would probably go out of his way to make sure that he did.

"Hey, I want to show you one of my happy places," I said once we had gotten closer to home. I pulled off down the familiar long dirt road and into the little makeshift dirt parking lot. We got out of the car and I took his hand, walking through the wooded area until we finally reached the old abandoned stable that was still standing.

"Wow this is making me ecstatic," he teased.

I playfully smacked him on the arm. "Keep walking, wise guy!" We trekked through another wooded area before coming to the beautiful crystal clear lake. A smile instantly stretched across my face while I was remembering all of the happy memories this place held. I took a seat on a hollowed out log while Drew looked around and out at the water before sitting down next to me.

"This is really beautiful. Betchya you can catch some good fish out there," Drew said.

"Chestnut and I would come here once a week."

"Who's Chestnut?" he asked.

"He was my horse that I used to have when I was younger. He was a beautiful Arabian. I used to ride him in competitions. He lived in that stable back there. Back when Mr. Roberts owned this property. I would come here once a week for my riding lessons. The last twenty minutes were free time, so Chestnut and I would sneak out to this lake. I would capture pretty pictures in my mind, whether it was the beautiful autumn leaves or the Blue Heron that would come here each year to nest. Each week this lake gave me a new image to store inside my head and then when I would get home I would draw it out on paper."

He looked at me and smiled. "Do you still have all the drawings?"

"Yup, I do. My favorite one was the one I drew of Chestnut. I have that one hanging in my room and will keep it forever."

"What happened to him?"

I could feel the tears welling in my eyes. I couldn't believe that after eleven years I still got so emotional over that darn horse. "I was riding him one day and he got spooked and I fell off him and broke my arm. He didn't mean to do it, but my dad didn't see it that way. He sold him right away. Didn't even let me say goodbye or anything." I wiped the teardrop that was flowing down my face. "I begged him to let me keep him, but he told me it was too dangerous. He didn't care that I loved that horse more than anything. Just told me I would get over it." I sighed heavily and looked out at the water. "He always made my feelings seem so insignificant. Still does."

"Have you ridden since?" he asked.

I shook my head. "I think my parents actually brainwashed me somehow into being scared to death to ever ride a horse again. I tried doing it a few years ago and I just couldn't."

"Well, you know the only way to face your fears is to climb back up on that horse again."

"Yeah, I know. Maybe someday I will." I looked at him and smiled. "Thanks for coming with me today and for listening to me reminisce."

"Anytime." His face came closer to mine until our lips were finally touching. The only sound that could be heard was the water gently lapping and trees blowing in the warm breeze. I jumped when my phone began beeping with a text message from my pocket.

"Your phone has the worst possible timing ever," Drew joked.

I giggled and pulled it from my pocket to find a text from Krista:

Do you care to meet Brad and me for a quick bite to eat?

I looked at the time on my phone and was shocked to see that it was almost six. "Hey, do you feel like meeting my friend Krista and whoever Brad is for dinner?"

He shrugged his shoulders and was a little hesitant before

answering, "Yeah, that's fine. I guess."

I texted her back and we decided on the place and time.

"Ready?" I asked Drew.

"Yup," he responded, getting up first and taking my hand and pulling me up.

I looked out at the water one last time and smiled before looking into Drew's eyes. "Can I tell you a little secret?"

"What's that?" he asked.

"I liked being here with you just as much as Chestnut and I got lots of pictures in my mind to put on paper."

"Oh yeah?" he smiled. I looked up at him and smiled back. "Is one of those pictures this?" He took my face in his hands and kissed me. It was his best kiss yet. I wasn't sure if it was because I was feeling it with every ounce of my being as I tried to capture the moment forever, or if it was really *that good*.

"I don't need to paint a picture to remember that, Drew. Some things don't need to be displayed to see them clearly. Some things are best seen if we just close our eyes and look inside our hearts.... and that kiss will remain in mine for the rest of my life."

Chapter 16

"Over here!" Krista shouted as we made our way into the crowded restaurant. Krista planted a kiss on my cheek once we finally reached her. She looked at Drew as if she was surprised to see him. "Oh, hey Drew," she said quickly, looking away and then down at the ground.

"What's up?" he responded.

"They said about a fifteen minute wait. Of course that was about twenty minutes ago," she said as she rolled her eyes. I looked up at the big muscle head guy standing beside her, waiting for an introduction. "Oh, Becca and Drew, this is Brad."

"Sup?" he said with a wave of his hand.

Sup? What the heck? Where did she find these guys? I could tell right away that what he had in brawn he certainly lacked in brains. Krista acted as if he weren't even standing there, jumping into conversation right away with Drew, asking him a million questions about Ashton. Just hearing that name suddenly made Mr. Muscles seem a lot more likable. I was so happy when we were finally seated, hoping to now get Krista off the dreadful topic of Ashton.

"So Brad, how did you and Krista meet?" I asked.

Krista interjected right away almost as if she were embarrassed for him to speak. "At Kendall Layne's party."

I was trying to think up more conversation with him just as Drew excused himself, walking outside to take the call that was coming through on his phone.

"I gotta use the men's room," Brad finally spoke. Krista slid out of the booth to let him out. I watched as he walked away before turning my attention back to Krista.

"Okay, what's up with Muscles Mcgee?" I teased.

She shrugged her shoulders and smiled. "I don't know; he's kind of cute, don't you think?"

"Krista, he has the personality of a rock."

We both began to giggle. "Sweetie, his personality doesn't matter in the bedroom. As long as he knows how to use *it* the right way, then I'm fine with that!"

"Oh my God, is that all you think of?"

"Look who's talking. I think you and Mr. Hottie out there have been gettin' pretty busy by the sounds of it."

I turned around and looked out the window at Drew, who was still talking on his phone. "I seriously think I'm addicted to him. Oh my God, Krista, everything you told me about sex was true and even better with him."

She busted out with laughter. "See what you've been missing all these years! That's because you're still in the new phase; everything is perfect when you just start dating someone. Then once the newness wears off, it just becomes dull." I looked straight ahead. Maybe that was true but I couldn't ever imagine anything with Drew being dull. "You'll see once you get back to school and start experimenting with other guys." I furrowed my brows at her. I didn't want to be with any other guys. I just wanted Drew. "Oh come on, Becca, you don't seriously think that he's going to be the first and last guy that you ever sleep with, do you?"

"Well, I don't know. You never know."

"Sorry about that," Drew said as he came back to the table.

I smiled up at him. "No problem."

A wry smile stretched across Krista's face. "So was that Ashton? What's he up to tonight?" Krista asked.

"Nope it wasn't, and I have no clue," Drew replied. He seemed to be short with Krista since we arrived and I didn't know why.

"How do you have no clue what he's up to? The two of you are buddies," Krista said.

Drew shook his head and rolled his eyes. "Y'all think I keep up to date on his schedule or something."

Krista and I both stared at him at the same time and began to laugh. "What's so funny?" he asked.

"Y'all?" Krista giggled. "I thought Becca said that you were from California?"

"Oh, yeah well, my grandfather was from down south so I picked it up from him," he said as he nervously cleared his throat.

"I think you sound cute with your little southern drawl," I said, squeezing his hand under the table.

We all looked up when Brad returned. Drew and I did our best to make conversation with him throughout dinner while Krista continued to ignore him. He really wasn't a bad guy, just totally not my type, but then again neither was Ashton and Krista seemed to be pining away for him, big time.

After dinner, Drew and I went back to his place and it suddenly dawned on me that I hadn't checked in with my mother all day. I decided to shoot her a quick text, telling her that I was having dinner with Krista. She didn't need to know that I had already had dinner with her and was now at Drew's. I was feeling a little relieved when I saw her text back, letting me know that she and my father were out to dinner with friends. At least now I knew that my dad wouldn't be holding a grudge toward me for not showing up for dinner tonight. "Are you getting sick of me yet?" I teased Drew as we sat in the lounge chair in each other's arms, looking up at the sky.

He kissed me on top of my head. "How could I ever get sick of a beautiful face like yours?"

I looked up at him and smiled before placing a gentle kiss on his lips. "How many stars do you think are up in that sky tonight?"

"Lots," he replied. "Are you cold?" he asked as I shivered.

"A little." He got up and went inside, coming back out with a blanket. "All better?" he asked while covering us both up.

"Much." I snuggled closer to him and breathed in his cologne.

I looked up at the star filled sky again and smiled, creating another perfect painting to store in my mind. As he rested his lips on my head, I thought about what Krista had said earlier about what we had fading away once the newness wore off and I was back at school. It was a thought that scared me half to death. I had never been more content than when I was in his arms and even though it was the first time that I had ever been feeling this way for a guy, I knew that there was something different about him. I hugged him tighter and closed my eyes, still seeing all those beautiful stars in my mind. I didn't want to think about going back to school and leaving him in a few months. I didn't want to think that maybe Krista was right and this was just the effects of being with someone new. All that I could think of for the moment was how at ease I felt when I was with him and if what we had together was truly meant to be, then time, distance, and nothing else would ever be able to separate us. As long as we could both look up at the night sky and see the same stars, the same moon, and the same beauty in it all.....we would always be together.

Chapter 17

The week flew by and before I knew it, Saturday had arrived along with my mother's barbeque. My father was talking to me once again, but I could still sense disappointment each time he looked at me. I was happy that I didn't have to do anymore running around for Mrs. Barrett all week, instead I spent two days buried behind my laptop, inputting the benefactor information into a spreadsheet. Drew helped to input a lot of them as well when he saw that my eyes were going cross from it. I made sure that I rewarded him for all of his hard work, which actually was more of a compensation for both of us. I was finding that I couldn't get enough of him and it was scaring me. Besides my parents, I never felt like I *needed* anyone in my life. But I was finding that I wanted to spend every waking minute with him. I wasn't sure if it was normal to be feeling this way or if it was borderline obsession. But I never thought about it when I was with him, I just knew that he was the only person that I wanted to be with and I would blow off anything or anyone for him.

I tried my best to keep myself busy while waiting for Drew to arrive. I was a bundle of nerves, so afraid that my father was going to do or say something to make him feel uncomfortable. My heart dropped when I heard the doorbell ring, nearly falling over my own feet to answer it. I couldn't wipe the smile from my face when I did. I had just seen him last night, but to me it seemed like it had been years. I threw my arms around his neck and snuck in a sexy little kiss, knowing that all of the other guests were already outside and this would probably be the only chance that we had to be alone for the rest of the night.

"Hey there, my handsome guy!"

"Hey!" He smiled, sweeping his hand across my face. I took his hand and led him through the house and out onto the patio. My mother turned her attention to Drew and me when she saw us walk out the door. My father was deep in conversation with Dr. Barrett and didn't even notice, of which I was kind of grateful.

"Well hello!" my mother exclaimed as she approached us, finally getting the attention of my father who turned around to see whom she was addressing.

"Mom, this is Drew," I said.

"It's so nice to meet you, Drew."

"You too, Mrs. Keeton."

My stomach dropped when I saw my father approaching us while eyeing up Drew questionably. "Drew, you remember my dad, right?" I asked, finally pulling it together to form a coherent sentence. The look on my mother's face almost matched the anxious one that I was sure was plastered all over mine.

"How are you, Dr. Keeton?" Drew extended his hand to my father.

"I'm well, thank you," my father replied, shaking his hand back. I started to let out a little sigh of relief and was so grateful when Mrs. Barrett came over to help break up the tension.

"Drew! It's so nice to see you, Honey," she said, placing a kiss on his cheek. "Now if you could only get my Ashton to find a nice sweet girl like Becca, I'd be a very happy mom!" Drew smiled and looked down at the ground. "I told Ashton that you were going to be here tonight, so hopefully he will come by."

I sighed a little louder than I probably should have at that thought and I was hoping that Mrs. Barrett didn't realize why.

"So Drew, when are you headed back to school?" my father asked.

"My classes start up again at the end of August."

"Becca will be going back at the end of July," my father said.

I furrowed my brows in confusion. "What!? No I'm not. I'll be going back at the end of August as well!"

"Oh, I just assumed that you were going to be volunteering for the summer outreach program again."

"No, not this year. I need a break this summer, my course load in the fall is jam packed." I grabbed Drew's hand and stared into my father's eyes.

"Drew, come and get something to eat," my mother said, trying to break up the tension between my father and me. My father finally gave up on his intimidation tactic and went back to talking to Dr. Barrett.

"Why don't you go sit down and I'll make you a plate?" I whispered in Drew's ear.

He smiled at me and pushed my hair behind my ear. "I'm actually not very hungry yet, but thank you for being so sweet."

"Do you two ever get tired of gazing in each other's eyes?" Krista teased as she approached us.

"Hey you! No Mr. Muscles tonight?" I joked as I gave her a kiss on the cheek.

"Ah, no more Mr. Muscles ever again," she said, waving her hand in the air. I shook my head and giggled, not at all surprised. Krista never kept the same guy around for very long.

My brother immediately appeared out of nowhere when he saw Krista. He had always had a secret little crush on her and now he was becoming a little more open about it. She, of course, would play along with him and flirt back just to tease him. "Hey Krista. Hey Drew," my brother said. He didn't care that his girlfriend,

Lindsay was standing right next to him as he began to check out Krista from head to toe. His eyes finally met mine and I shook my head in disapproval at him. I could tell that Lindsay had just witnessed his recent eyeball assault on Krista and was feeling really bad about it.

"Oh, Lindsay, this is Drew," I said, trying to distract her from what had just happened. I grabbed my brother's arm and pulled him aside as Lindsay was talking to Drew. "Quit being rude to her!" I said in a loud whisper. He rolled his eyes at me and took Lindsay's hand, looking a little defeated.

"Let the party begin!" I didn't want to turn around at the voice I heard approaching. The hairs on my arm that were standing at attention already confirmed who it was. If that wasn't enough, the smile that was stretched across Krista's face was a guarantee. I finally looked up from the ground and was staring into Ashton's cold blue eyes. I hated the way he looked at me, making me feel like I was the only one around even though we were surrounded by a ton of other people. He made me feel dirty, uncomfortable, and most of all, nauseous when I looked at him. "So Becca, do Mommy and Daddy approve of the guy that popped your cherry?" I glared at him in disgust, becoming even angrier when I saw Krista giggling.

"Shut the fuck up, Ashton!" Drew said.

"Calm down, it was *a joke,* bro!" Ashton said, holding his hands up in defense. "You're still in for paint ballin' tomorrow, right?" Ashton asked Drew as his eyes shifted over to me to catch my reaction.

"Yeah, just let me know what time," Drew replied half-heartedly.

"Ashton, you came!" Mrs. Barrett exclaimed.

He nodded. "Hey Mom, I need you to spot me a few hundred for tomorrow."

She shook her head in disgust. "Honestly, Ashton, you really need to get a job for the summer." She was just about to walk away before stopping dead in her tracks and turning back around. "Oh

Becca, a new benefactor just called. I'm going to need you to drop off their welcome packet tomorrow. I'll text you the address when I get home."

"No problem," I said, taking a deep breath while trying my best to hide my frustration.

"What time are you doing that?" Drew asked with concern.

I shrugged my shoulders. "No clue, guess it just depends on where she has me going or how long it's going to take to get there. And here I thought I was done with being errand girl. Oh well!" I sighed.

"I'll go with you," he said.

"You don't have to come. Go do your paintballing thing. I will be fine."

"No. I want to go. I don't want you going by yourself."

"Drew, really, it's okay."

"Becca, I'm going with you."

I felt a little bit of satisfaction, knowing that he was choosing me over Ashton but at the same time I didn't want him missing out on something that he wanted to do because of me. "Are you sure?"

"Positive." He pushed a strand of hair behind my ear and kissed me on the head. I closed my eyes and smiled, only to open them again to find my father glaring at me from across the backyard. I looked away before wrapping my arm around Drew and pulling him closer.

Once I saw that Drew was deep in conversation with my brother and Lindsay, I decided to run inside and use the bathroom. As I got closer to the powder room off the kitchen, I heard voices coming from behind the closed door. There was no doubt that the familiar giggles were Krista's. When I heard the male's voice, I felt the bile rising in my throat.

"Yeah, right there Baby, oh fuck yeah."

Anger soon replaced my queasiness. I would expect nothing less from Ashton; it was Krista that I was irritated with. I used the upstairs bathroom, still in shock that Krista actually stooped that low and that she had the nerve to do it in my parent's house. As I walked back outside, I noticed that the downstairs bathroom was now unoccupied. I had a huge knot in my stomach when I saw Ashton and Krista standing next to Drew, laughing away. I couldn't even look at them. I pulled away when Krista went to touch me.

"What's up with you?" she slurred. Her eyes were glassy and in that instant I knew that the two of them were doing more than just having sex in that bathroom.

"Oh nothing is wrong with me, but obviously you're as high as a kite," I snapped.

"Geez Becca, why don't you say it a little louder? I don't think everyone heard that!" she snapped back.

"The two of you make me sick. Have you resorted to having sex with low lifes in exchange for drugs? And if that wasn't bad enough, you had to do it right in my parents' house."

Her jaw dropped. Krista and I never fought in all the years we had been friends. We always had the perfect relationship. "You know what, Becca? I always defended you to everyone that said you were nothing but an uptight, stuck up bitch. But the more I'm around you, the more I'm finding it's the truth!"

Ashton chuckled, enjoying every minute of it.

"Becca, just come on," Drew said, placing his hand on my arm, trying his best to pull me away.

"Yeah, Becca, better do what he says since you're attached to him at the hip, just because he's the first guy to ever fuck you! Hey Drew, did you know that Becca thinks that you are her first and last? Stupid little naïve girl. Better watch out. She may go all psycho on you if you try and break up with her." I stared at Krista in disbelief. It was as if I didn't even know who she was. We had been there for each other for *everything.* We always had each other's back, and now it was as if we were complete strangers.

"Leave now!" I shouted. I could feel the tears filling my eyes.

"Gladly!" she screamed, finally getting my mother's attention.

"Girls, what's going on over here?" my mother asked as she came rushing over, looking at each of us with concern.

"Nothing. I was just leaving," Krista said in a huff. "Ashton, can you give me a ride home?" Even though she had pissed me off beyond words, I knew that neither one of them were in any condition to drive.

"Drew, could you give her a ride?" I asked.

He nodded.

"Oh no Becca, that's okay, I wouldn't want to inconvenience your boyfriend by taking time away from you to drive me home," she slurred.

My mother looked both her and Ashton over. "Krista, either let Drew drive you home or you're leaving me with no choice but to call your parents. Neither you, nor Ashton are in any condition to drive like this," she said, keeping her voice down in an effort to not draw attention from the other guests.

"Whatever!" she shouted as she and Ashton staggered off.

"Drew, would you mind driving Ashton home as well? His parents had to leave to go to another party," my mother said.

"Yeah, no problem."

Krista turned back around and pointed her finger at me. "You and I -" She furiously grabbed the chain around her neck and ripped it off, throwing it in my face. "We are no longer friends."

Tears filled my eyes when I looked down at the ground to find the other half of the best friend charm that we each had worn since we were eight years old. My mother placed her hand on my shoulder, trying to comfort me as Krista stormed out of the backyard. I bent down to pick it up as tears rolled down my face. It was all so surreal to me. It was as if she had turned into this person that I didn't even know almost overnight. Or had I really been that wrapped up in my own little world that I failed to recognize that my best friend was fading away? My biggest fear today was getting into it with my father over Drew. I was prepared for it and had my battle gear on. Never in a million years did I imagine that Krista would be the reason that I would need to break out that shield around my heart.

Chapter 18

Two weeks had passed and I had finally broke down and called Krista. She, of course, didn't answer but I still left her a voice mail, apologizing for what had happened, even though I didn't believe that one was warranted on my end. I was worried about her. The Krista that *I thought* I knew was always a party girl but I never thought that she would turn to drugs. Again, Ashton was involved the same way he had gotten my brother involved. I hated that Drew still remained friends with him, but I knew I had no right to tell him who he could hang out with. I was so grateful to him over these past few weeks. Not only was he helping me out with all of the charity stuff that Mrs. Barrett was piling on me, but he was also a sounding board, listening to me vent over my frustration with Krista.

I didn't want to open my eyes. I was feeling so relaxed with the warm sun beating down on me, but when I felt Drew's cold lips on my bare back I couldn't resist. He dried himself off before sitting down on the beach blanket next to me. "Oh my God, that water must be freezing," I said.

"Nah, you get used to it. I have to do something to cool off from looking at you in that sexy bikini." I sat up and kissed him on the lips. "That's not helping my cause, you know."

"Sorry." I smirked. "I really should get home and take a shower." My parents were out of town for a wedding for a few days and had made my brother go with them after the last incident, leaving the house all to me for three days. I was happy that Mrs. Barrett didn't have anything planned for me within the next couple of days. I felt like I needed a mental break from everything. "Did you want to come over later on?"

"Ah shit, I told Ashton and a couple of the other guys that I'd hang out with them tonight."

I tried my hardest to hide my disappointment. "Oh, okay."

"Don't make any plans for tomorrow. I've got something special planned."

I couldn't hold back my smile. "What is it?"

"It's a surprise."

"Oh, I like surprises!" I said as I threw my cover up on over my bathing suit. I stood up and slipped on my flip flops, grabbing my beach bag.

"Why are you leaving so soon?"

"Because I *need* to get in the shower; I'm sweaty, sandy, and covered in sun block."

"Sounds pretty sexy, if you ask me." He raised his eyebrow, standing up and pressing his forehead against mine.

"Mr. Bryant, I do believe we already had our lesson this morning."

I couldn't resist grazing his salty lips. His hands moved down my back, pulling me into him and kissing me harder before taking my hand and leading me off the beach and into his house. His lips were on mine the minute we walked inside. He pushed me up against the wall and immediately removed my bathing suit bottoms. He eased his fingers inside of me as our tongues moved in unison. My insides began to throb for him once again.

"Becca, you fuckin' make me crazy. I never wanted anyone as

much as I want you."

He pulled down his swim trunks, wrapping my leg around his waist and bracing my back against the wall. I immediately felt the fullness of him inside of me. It was so perfect and so familiar now. We were becoming more and more comfortable with each other's bodies, learning each other's likes and needs, making each time better than the last. He moved in and out of me as I ran my hands through his hair.

I screamed out his name, feeling all of my emotions coming to the surface. He bit his lip, smiled, and began to move quicker and harder. I could feel his erection growing inside of me just before he let out a loud groan, releasing himself into me. He removed my leg from around his waist and was trying to catch his breath. I caressed his face and looked up at him and smiled.

"I can't get enough of you," he whispered in my ear.

His voice had that sexy smoothness once again, making my entire body tingle. He bent down and kissed me, taking my breath away. I pressed my forehead against his as our hearts pounded in unison.

"I'll see ya tomorrow." He nodded and placed another gentle kiss on my lips.

My stomach was doing cartwheels the entire drive home as I thought about what had just happened. I knew that I didn't have anyone else to compare to, but I didn't think that it could get any more intense than what Drew and I had shared. My body was still feeling like it was having aftershocks.

I arrived home and jumped in the shower. I was planning on spending the rest of the afternoon on the couch with a good book, until I got out of the shower and saw that Mrs. Barrett was calling. I rolled my eyes while trying to decide if I wanted to answer her and finally picking it up on the last ring.

"Hey, Mrs. Barrett," I answered.

"Hi Becca. I really hate to ask you this on such short notice, but Carlos Simms has more paperwork that I need by tomorrow morning." She caught me totally off guard as I tried to think of an

BLIND SIDE OF LOVE

excuse. "I would go pick it up myself, but Edward and I have a benefit that we need to attend tonight. If I don't have this paperwork by tomorrow, we will lose out on applying for a grant that can be used to fund more scholarships." I thought about the last time I was at Mr. Simms' house and how uncomfortable he made me feel and that was with Drew there. My stomach dropped, thinking about going by myself. "You'll be in and out. He's away on business and left the papers with his housekeeper."

"Okay," I finally relented. I wasn't looking forward to the long drive, but I could handle it as long as I knew that I wouldn't have to be dealing with Mr. Simms. I threw on a pair of shorts and a tank top, pulling my wet hair back into a ponytail and was on my way.

The warm sun and light breeze as I drove with the top down allowed me some much needed time to clear my head. I had so much on my mind this past week between Krista, my dad, and most of all, what was going to become of Drew and me once we went back to school. I tried my best to convince myself that I would be okay and I could handle it if our relationship had to end, but each time I was with him, I was starting to doubt that. I pulled into the horseshoe driveway of Mr. Simms' mansion, feeling a lot less tense this time, knowing that he wouldn't be there.

A tall woman dressed in a traditional maid's uniform answered the door with Mr. Simms' intimidating security guard standing right behind her. "Hi, Mr. Simms has an envelope that I'm picking up for Lynn Barrett," I said.

"Oh yes, please come in." She opened the door further and I hesitantly stepped inside as the security guard remained stone face. She led me into the living room and my stomach dropped when I saw Mr. Simms and two other men seated on the couch. My legs immediately began to tremble and I wanted to just run out.

"Oh Miss Keeton, such a pleasure to see you again," Mr. Simms said. "Gentlemen, this is the beautiful Miss Keeton." The two men got up from the couch and looked me over before each shaking my hand and introducing themselves.

"Please have a seat," Mr. Simms said, motioning toward the

couch.

"Umm, no thank you. I really have to run. My boyfriend is waiting for me," I lied.

"Oh, is he in the car?"

I wanted to say yes so badly but I was fairly certain that he had security cameras all over and would know that I was lying. "No, he's at home."

"Well, please just have a seat while I go get the papers."

I hesitantly sat down in the only open area on the couch, inching as far away as possible from the man sitting next to me. "I don't bite." He chuckled. I could feel my face heating up. I began to break out in an instant sweat, wishing that Drew was there with me, wishing that I had never agreed to come. A strange sense of relief washed over me when Mr. Simms walked back in the room with the envelope in his hand. As much as he freaked me out, these two other men were even creepier.

"Miss Keeton, my friend Kenneth here is the one that has the modeling connections," Mr. Simms said, gesturing to the older man sitting beside me. "She's a natural. Don't you agree, Kenneth?"

The man moved closer to me, choking me out with his strong cologne. "She certainly is, but she needs to relax a little bit more." I cringed and immediately stood up when I felt his warm breath on my neck and his hand moving up my bare thigh. Panic began to set in as a million scenarios began to play over in my head. My heart began to race. The only person that knew I was here was Mrs. Barrett. I should have told Drew but I didn't want him feeling like he had to cancel his plans to come with me. "Easy, beautiful, I didn't mean to scare you."

I looked away.

"Miss Keeton, please excuse Mr. Dainbridge. He sometimes forgets his manners around beautiful women," Mr. Simms said, placing the envelope in my hand.

I swallowed hard, not saying a word, walking out of that house as fast as my legs would allow. I controlled my trembling body long enough to pull out of the driveway and get far enough away from the house before pulling off on the side of the road to pull it together. How could I have been so stupid to go there today, especially by myself? I felt like such a fool. I wanted to call Drew so badly and just hear his voice to help put me at ease but I stopped myself. I needed to stop being so dependent on him. I calmed myself down as best as I could, trying not to think about what could have happened. I turned up the radio and let the warm breeze blow through my hair as I headed home, vowing to never return to that place again.

Chapter 19

My nerves were finally settling down, hours after arriving home from Mr. Simms' as I stood on the patio putting the last details on my painting. I stood back and admired it sitting on the easel. Just the feel of the paint brush in my hand and the smell of the paints put my mind at total ease. This was where my heart was and I scolded myself for not allowing myself to do it more often. The beautiful star filled sky and glowing half-moon was the perfect canvas. I wondered what Drew was doing and if he was thinking about me the same way I was thinking about him. My thoughts began to drift once again to what was going to become of our relationship once we both became wrapped up again with school. I sighed deeply, trying to think positive. I knew that I was willing to make it work no matter what. We would only be an hour away and I could come home as much as possible on the weekends and Drew could come and visit me in the city whenever he had free time. I knew that if we both wanted it badly enough it was definitely doable. I only hoped that he was feeling the same way that I was. The sweet smell of honeysuckle wafted through the warm summer breeze while the crickets sang their familiar lullaby. I closed my eyes, taking it all in and wishing that Drew was with me right now and wondering if he was noticing just how beautiful the stars were tonight as well. As I opened my eyes, an idea struck me. I carefully took my painting off the easel and laid it out to dry before getting to work on my next masterpiece.

My eyes shot open to the sound of my ringing phone. Seeing Drew's name on my caller ID first thing in the morning was a nice way to start the day.

"Hey," I answered, feeling the smile instantly stretch across my face.

"Morning, gorgeous girl. Are you ready for your surprise?"

I lifted my head from my pillow to look at the time. "It's only seven a.m.," I laughed.

"The earlier the better."

"Okay, I just need to take a quick shower and get some caffeine," I replied, sitting up in my bed and stretching my body.

"No need to take a shower; you're going to be getting pretty dirty and we can stop for coffee. Just get dressed and I'll be there to get you in twenty.....oh, and wear jeans."

I hung up the phone, not liking the sound of that. What the heck could he possibly have planned that was going to get us dirty? Still, I was up for any adventure as long as it was with him. I had just finished dressing when I heard the doorbell ringing. I ran down the stairs two at a time, feeling that familiar yearning in my body when I opened the door and saw Drew standing in the doorway with his overgrown stubble on his face, and his rock hard chest molding to his tee shirt. I threw my arms around his neck and kissed him with vigor.

"Wow, that's a nice greeting!" he teased.

"Why thank you, Mr. Bryant," I teased back. I took his hand and he led me out to his car. "So where are we going?" I asked.

"To get you some coffee."

"After that, silly."

"I don't give away my surprises," he said, wrapping his seatbelt around him.

The euphoria I was feeling quickly washed away when I saw Mrs. Barrett's name on my caller ID. Being with Drew had totally erased my memory of yesterday. I took a deep breath before answering. Drew looked over at me, seemingly sensing my uneasiness.

"Good Morning, Mrs. Barrett," I answered.

"Good Morning, Becca. Thank you so much for dropping off that envelope to my house yesterday. I really appreciate it. I'm going to need you to deliver some more forms to Mr. Simms sometime next week."

"I'm sorry Mrs. Barrett, but you're going to have to find someone else to do it. I was put in a very uncomfortable situation yesterday while I was there and I will not be making anymore deliveries or pickups to his house." I could feel Drew's eyes burning into me.

"Oh I'm sorry, Becca. What happened?"

"I really don't care to discuss it. I just won't be going there anymore."

"Okay, sure. I hope this doesn't mean you're not going to be helping out anymore."

"No, I can still help out."

"Okay, good. Oh and I wanted to thank you for all of your hard work on that spreadsheet. It looks great."

"You're welcome."

We said our goodbyes and hung up.

"What was that all about?" Drew asked as we pulled into the parking lot to the coffee shop.

"Mrs. Barrett was in a bind yesterday and needed me to pick up

110

some papers from Mr. Simms."

"Damn it, Becca! Why did you go there by yourself?" I could tell by the tone of his voice and the way that he had banged on the steering wheel that he wasn't happy.

"I - I don't know. She said he was away on business and that I would just have to get the envelope from his maid. But when I got there, he was there along with two other men that creeped me out even more than him."

"What happened?"

"Nothing really." I tried downplaying it.

"Becca, tell me!" he demanded.

I sighed heavily. "The one guy was his friend that supposedly had the modeling connections. He just got really close to me and just touched –me."

"Where the fuck did he touch you?" he shouted. The fury in his voice made me jump.

"Drew, calm down! He just put his hand on my leg, that's all. I got up and got out of there as fast as I could. I'm perfectly fine!" I said, caressing the side of his face and trying to put his mind at ease.

"DO NOT ever go there again! Do you hear me?" His voice was still on edge.

"I'm not planning on it." I kissed him softly on the cheek. "Now can we forget about it and just get some coffee? By the looks of it, someone is a little cranky and could use some caffeine," I teased, trying to put his worries to rest.

"I was in a good mood until you told me that," he said as we got out of the car. I hated seeing him so upset but at the same time it made me happy to know that he was genuinely concerned over me. He took my hand in his just before we got ready to walk into the coffee shop. "Just promise me that you will let me go with you to any more of these places she has you going." His tone was much softer.

I nodded. "Promise."

He kissed me softly on my lips and gripped my hand tighter. "Come on, Gorgeous, let's get you some coffee."

Chapter 20

"Umm....should I be scared?" I asked Drew as we pulled down a long dirt driveway.

"Yup, forgot to mention I'm wanted in three states for murder." He laughed.

As we finally came to the end, I focused on the sign *Blackwell Stables.* I shook my head and my stomach began to churn. "Oh no, Drew, I'm not ready for this."

"Come on Becca, you can do it."

"Drew, I'm – "

He placed his hand on mine. "Just try....for me? If you don't feel comfortable then you can get right off. But at least try. This is something that you used to love to do, don't be scared."

"Fine...." I sighed deeply.

We got out of the car and I slowly made my way to the stable. "Come on Becca, you can do it," Drew teased, pulling on my hand and forcing me to walk faster.

"Hey there!" We were greeted by a grey haired man and his

Border Collie. "You must be Drew?" the man said, extending his hand.

"Yup, I am," Drew answered, shaking his hand back.

"Norm Blackwell, it's a pleasure to meet you."

"This is Becca," Drew said, introducing me to the man.

"Ah, Becca. I understand that you used to ride?"

I nodded. "Used to…I haven't in a long time."

"Well, I think I have the perfect horse for you." We walked through the stable, finally coming to a stop at the pen of a beautiful black horse with white flecks throughout its coat. Even though I was nervous, I couldn't help but smile. "It's a Snowflake Appaloosa," I said.

"A girl that knows her horses. I like that!" Mr. Blackwell smiled.

"I was always told that this breed is nasty," I said, finally breaking myself from my fixation of staring at the magnificent creature standing before me.

Mr. Blackwell crinkled his eyebrows, looking a little insulted. "Now, who told you that? Ginny is just as nice as can be. They are actually a great breed, especially for new riders, it takes a lot to spook them." I took a deep breath and looked into the horse's eyes. "What do you think? You want to give her a chance?"

"I guess," I said with a shrug of my shoulders. The butterflies erupted as he began to saddle her up.

"You're going to be fine," Drew whispered in my ear. We followed him as he led her out of the pen, stopping her next to a beautiful Mustang that was already saddled and ready to go.

"The hardest part is getting back on for the first time, Becca. Once you do that, you'll be riding like a pro again." I took a deep breath and moved closer. I grabbed onto her mane and stood shoulder to shoulder before placing my foot in the stirrup, lifting myself up and swinging my right leg over her back. I breathed a sigh of relief when she stood quietly and didn't step out while I mounted her. Mr. Blackwell smiled. "See how it all comes back to you? Just like riding a bike." I could feel my legs trembling as I held tightly to the reigns. "Remember, Becca, she can sense if you're nervous. Just take a deep breath and relax."

I nodded, trying my best to do just that.

"Okay, Drew, since you're an expert, you get one of my best. This is Blaze."

My eyes widened. Drew was actually going to ride the beautiful Mustang standing next to me. He had never even mentioned that he had ridden before to me.

"Drew, I didn't know that you've ridden before!" I was thoroughly impressed with his ability to mount the horse, who was nowhere near as calm as mine.

"Just a little." He smirked.

"Okay, before I send you two on your way, take a couple laps around, Becca. I want to make sure that you and Ginny are a good fit," Mr. Blackwell said.

Drew gave me a look of reassurance before I gently pulled on the reigns and Ginny began trotting slowly around the penned in area. My nerves started subsiding before we were even halfway through the first lap and by the time we were done with the second, I couldn't wipe the smile from my face. And just like my artwork, I was silently scolding myself for not doing something that I loved so much, sooner. Mr. Blackwell and Drew were grinning from ear to ear as I reached them.

"I think the two of you make a good pair," Mr. Blackwell said, looking at me and then Ginny. "I'll see you guys in an hour," he said as he headed back into the stable.

"Ready?" Drew asked.

I nodded, unable to wipe the smile from my face. The horses walked off to the open field. I could tell right away that Drew had ridden quite a few times just in the way he was handling his horse, who seemed a little less tame than others I had been around. "So how come you never told me that you've ridden before?" I asked.

He shrugged his shoulders. "I don't know. I didn't think it was a big deal." He smiled over at me.

By the time we were halfway into our ride, I was totally relaxed. I couldn't believe that I had allowed myself to be scared of doing this for all those years. The warm morning sun beating on my neck and the calmness of the horse beneath me radiated into me. "Thank you so much for making me overcome my fears. This is just so much fun, Drew."

"I knew you could do it. You can't let fear hold you back. Just because something bad happened once it doesn't mean it's going to happen again. Some of the best moments are those that we never imagined ourselves in again. Don't ever let anything prevent you from what you want to do. If you want it bad enough, it's always obtainable no matter what obstacles are in your way. Sometimes, those road blocks make it much more gratifying when you do finally reach that goal."

I nodded, hoping that he would apply that same logic to us when it came to our relationship. He had opened my eyes so much in just the short time that I had known him. I was not only experiencing new and exciting things with him, but he allowed me to open that part of my heart that had been closed for so long. That part that I kept all of the stuff that I enjoyed doing so much tucked away in, so I could focus on being the perfect daughter and perfect student. Drew helped me realize that I could be as many things as I wanted to be. I could paint beautiful pictures, ride horses, and be absolutely caught up in him, while still being a good daughter and student. We may have joked around about his lessons that he was teaching me with my confidence and in the bedroom, but he truly was the best teacher I had ever known in teaching me one of the most important things in life....happiness.

Chapter 21

After our ride, Drew and I went out to breakfast before he dropped me back off at home. We had made plans to hang out at my house for dinner and a movie, and I found myself counting the hours until I could see him again. The warm sunshine was so relaxing, drying me off from the laps that I just swam in the pool while lulling me to sleep as I lay in the lounge chair. I jumped and quickly sat up, feeling the presence of someone standing over me.

"Oh my God, Ashton, what the hell are you doing here?" I said, holding my hand over my heart which was beating at warp speed.

His signature Cheshire cat grin stretched across his face. "Maybe you should tell your dad to install a better security system on the gate; wouldn't want anyone coming in and stealing his precious Becca, now would he?" He didn't try to hide that he was checking out every inch of my body as I sat there in my bikini. I grabbed the towel from the back of my chair and wrapped myself in it. "Don't cover up on my account, Becca."

"What do you want?" I snapped.

"I was looking for Jordan."

"He's not here, and what do you want with my brother anyway? I told you before, stay the hell away from him!"

"Oh you are so intimidating, Becca! I better do what you say. I wouldn't want you to kick my ass." He smirked.

I swung my legs over the chair and glared up into the bright sunshine at him. "I'm telling you right now, if this has anything to do with the shit that you had him involved with that night at the party, I will tell your parents."

"Oh no! Please don't tell my mom and dad! I'm so scared!" He mocked.

"Just leave, Ashton!"

He stared at me one last time and started to walk away. "Hey Becca," he turned back around and shouted. "Maybe you should stop spending so much time turning up your nose at me and worry about what your boyfriend is doing instead. But that's okay; when he dumps you for another hot piece of ass, you know where to find me. I'll gladly take sloppy seconds."

I shook my head. I didn't want him to know that he had just struck a major chord. *What the heck did he mean by that?* Drew and I were spending almost all of our time together. If there was *something* or *someone* else, I think I would have sensed it. I watched him walk out the gate and breathed a sigh of relief when I heard his car start up. The happiness that I was feeling from the morning had suddenly vanished all within three minutes of being around Ashton. My brother and Drew were now in the forefront of my mind. If Jordan had lied to me and was still involved with Ashton then I had no choice but to tell my parents. I knew he would hate me for it, but it was for his own good. I headed inside to take a shower, trying my best to prevent that seed that Ashton had planted in my head about Drew from growing. Unfortunately, the harder I tried, the faster it was taking root.

118

I couldn't control my laughter as I tried my best to teach Drew to use chopsticks while we ate our Chinese takeout. I didn't bother telling him anything about my little visit from Ashton earlier in the day. We were having such a great time and I didn't want any talk of that bringing us down. After thinking it over, I surmised that he was more than likely lying to drum up trouble anyway. The sun was just beginning to set as we sat out on the patio.

"Finally giving up?" I teased as he picked up his fork and began eating his rice.

"I surrender." He laughed. "I will never master the art of using chopsticks."

"Hey, what happened to your pep talk from earlier about never giving up on something you really want?"

"Yeah, well, eating with chopsticks isn't exactly one of my life long goals," he joked.

"I really had a great time this morning. Thank you so much for making me get back up on that horse again."

"No problem." His smile unleashed the butterflies, making it impossible for me to resist leaning over the table and planting a gentle kiss on his cheek.

"Hey, I got a little present for you."

"Oh, yeah?" He smiled.

"Not that, silly….well, yeah, that too," I corrected myself. "But that comes later," I teased, getting up from the table and kissing him once again before heading inside to get the paintings. "Close your eyes," I shouted as I walked back outside. "Okay you can open them." I stood in front of him holding up both paintings of my version of a starry night.

His eyes widened in amazement. "Wow, Becca, did you do those?" I nodded and smiled. "They are awesome."

"Thanks! I tried to replicate each of them to a tee, right down to the amount of stars. Do you notice the one difference?" I asked.

He examined them both closely. "The moon?"

I nodded. "Yup, one is a first quarter moon and the other is a third quarter." He raised his eyebrows at me. "Yeah, I know I'm a bit of an Astrology geek. But I did one painting for you and one for me. That way when we go back to school we can each have our paintings and know that we're looking up at the same star filled sky. I can be the first quarter and you can be the third quarter and together we can be the full moon." My heart sank to my knees when the smile that was on his face instantly disappeared and he looked down at the ground. *Oh God I was so stupid! It was too soon to be getting into this deep psychological stuff with him. He clearly wasn't ready for it.* The last thing I wanted was for him to think I was getting too needy and scare him away. "I'm – I'm sorry. I didn't mean to-"

"No, Becca, it's okay." He finally looked up at me again and I wasn't quite sure if it was pain or surprise that I was seeing in his eyes. "Thank you. It's really a great painting," he whispered. He stood up and kissed me on the forehead before hugging me tightly, still seeming a little unsettled.

"I didn't mean to seem like-" He placed his finger over my lips to stop me from talking, gently tilting my chin up to his and placing his lips on mine. I pulled him closer and moved my hands up and down his back as our tongues began to dance.

"Do you want to go for a swim?" I asked, pressing my forehead against his.

"I didn't bring my bathing suit."

"Who said anything about bathing suits?"

I bit my lip and stared up at him, lifting my shirt over my head. The wary look that was on his face just moments ago was now replaced with a sexy grin. I reached down and unbuttoned his shorts, blocking out any of the doubts that were racing through my mind. I didn't want to think about what Ashton had said earlier. I didn't want to think about the look on Drew's face when I had given him that painting. All I wanted to think about was being in his arms while feeling him inside of me and creating another perfect moment.

Chapter 22

Drew spent the night and was up and out early. I rushed around making sure that everything was spotless for when my parents came home. I had just gotten done vacuuming when I heard the front door open.

"Hey guys! How was the wedding?" I asked. My brother looked at me and went storming up the steps. I could tell right away that he had been fighting with my parents. "What's his problem?"

"Becca, why didn't you tell us that your brother was involved with drugs?" my father asked.

"What?"

"Don't play dumb, Becca! He told us that you knew."

"That I knew what?" I raised my voice in anger. Once again I was bearing the brunt of something my brother did.

"I found a baggie filled with Vicodin in his bag," my father said.

"Okay, and how is that my fault?" I asked.

"He said that you knew that Ashton Barrett was giving them to him."

"Oh my God! Are you kidding me? The only thing I knew was that Ashton had given him something to *sell* for him. I had a long talk with him about it and he promised-"

"He promised! Again with taking him at his word! You know better than that! You should have come right to me and your mother and told us this! Are you really that stupid to think that he wasn't using as well? How could you have been so ignorant to this? Do you have any idea how addictive these drugs are?"

"Jeff, stop blaming Becca for Jordan's mistakes," my mother chimed in.

"She should know better, Gail!" he shouted. "She *used* to have a brain. She used to be able to think for herself. She used to tell the truth. Now she's getting mixed in with this crowd and I don't even know my own daughter!"

"Mixed in with what crowd? I am NOT friends with Ashton Barrett!"

"Becca, what the hell has happened to you? Are you really that naïve? You are dating a very good friend of his. Do you think that he's not doing this stuff, too? I don't want you seeing him anymore."

My jaw dropped. How could he even lump Drew into this? I may not have been very familiar with drugs, but I wasn't stupid enough to not know when people were using, and I knew Drew *was not*. I shook my head and narrowed my eyes at him.

"Drew does not do drugs, Dad!"

"How do you know that, Becca? Huh? You've known him for a little over a month. You know nothing at all about this guy!"

"Yes I do!"

"What the hell do you know about him? Tell me!" he shouted.

The tears streamed down my face. Why couldn't he see how important Drew was to me and just accept it? "I know that he is the most giving and caring person I know. He allows me to be myself and not what everyone expects me to be. And I know that when I am with him, there is nowhere else that I want to be." My mother's eyes filled with tears as she looked away. "I am not going to stop seeing him. I won't allow you to punish me over something that Jordan did."

I grabbed my car keys and headed out the door, just feeling the need to get away. I couldn't believe that my father was going to use this as a tactic to get me to stop seeing Drew. I would never allow that to happen. I didn't care if it meant damaging my relationship with my dad. He was not going to take away my happiness like he always did when he didn't approve of something. I drove for some time before I found myself pulling into Krista's parents' driveway, not knowing what led me there, except for the fact that I needed my best friend now more than ever. I took a deep breath as I rang the doorbell.

"Becca! It's so nice to see you, Honey," Krista's mom greeted me with a huge hug.

"You too, Mrs. Hudson. I know I'm probably the last person Krista wants to see, but is she around?"

She gave me a sympathetic smile. "Yes, Honey, she's up in her room. We um- We've been having quite a time with her."

"What's going on?" I asked.

"Well, apparently she's been doing drugs for a few months. I didn't know... she was away at school and –" She began to break down in tears.

"Oh Mrs. Hudson, don't blame yourself. I'm her best friend and I was clueless."

"Her last semester, she was battling with bouts of depression. She tried to keep it from us but then one night she called me and she just sounded so desperate. My husband drove down to her school that night and got her. She never finished up the semester."

I shook my head and ran my hand through my hair. "She never told me."

"She didn't want anyone to know. We took her to the doctor

and got her on some antidepressants. Then you came home and she was going out and doing things like her old self again. A few nights ago she came home and she was a mess. I knew it was more than just alcohol and she finally admitted to me and my husband that she was using."

"Using what?" I asked.

Her mother closed her eyes and took a deep breath. "Pain Killers."

I was speechless. I knew Krista and Ashton were doing something that night in the bathroom and again I chose to ignore it the same way I had with my brother. A good friend would have told her parents right away. A good friend would have been there for her instead of shaming her into leaving. A good friend wouldn't have waited until well over two weeks to see if she was okay. Maybe I was selfish. Maybe I was so fixated with my own world that I stopped being concerned with what was going on with the ones I cared about most. My dad was right; I was ignorant, and unfortunately, that ignorance claimed two of the most important people in my life—Krista and my brother. I sat down on the step and shook my head at a total loss for words. "I am so sorry, Mrs. Hudson."

"This is not your fault, Becca. You had nothing to do with this. She's leaving for a recovery center out in California tomorrow. We were finally able to talk her into going." I nodded, still in shock, first my brother and now Krista. Maybe my dad was right; maybe I was naïve.

"Can I go up and see her?"

She smiled and nodded. My heart was racing as I walked up the stairs, finally reaching Krista's bedroom. I knocked lightly.

"Come in," she shouted. She looked up from her laptop in surprise. "Becca," she whispered. She didn't even look like my best friend. Dark circles encompassed her beautiful blue eyes. And her blonde hair that was always perfectly styled hung around her face like she hadn't washed it in days. I tried my best to stop my tears. I knew I had to stay strong for her.

"Hey chickie," I said, taking a seat next to her on her bed.

"I guess you heard. I'm a complete mess." She shook her head and gave a nervous smile.

"You're not a mess, Krista." She grabbed a tissue from her nightstand and wiped the tears that were flowing down her face. "I'm sorry that I wasn't there for you."

She shook her head. "It's not your fault, Becca. It's me. I'm so fucked up."

"Don't say that, Krista. You are not fucked up! You just need help. You're going to get it and everything is going to be fine. You are going to beat this! I know you will."

She looked at me and did her best to form a smile. "I wish I could be like you, Becca. You're able to handle any situation life throws at you. You have a killer course load at school and are able to maintain an awesome GPA, find time to volunteer, and you're an amazing friend. I couldn't even manage one of those things."

"You are a great friend, Krista!"

"Did you forget how we left things when we last saw each other?"

"Yeah, well, I don't want to think about that. Let's forget it ever happened and just concentrate on the future and all of the fun stuff we're going to do when you get back."

"I love you, Becca."

"I love you, too," I whispered, throwing my arms around her and hugging her tightly. I reached into my purse and dug around in the pocket, pulling out the chain with her half of the best friend charm. "I took this to the jeweler and had it fixed. I want you to wear this when you go because you'll always have the other half of my heart." She lifted her hair as I clasped it around her neck, letting out a loud sob before pulling me into a hug once again.

"I'm so sorry, Becca."

"It never happened, remember?"

She nodded and wiped her tears. "Becca, I don't want to upset you but please just be careful. I can't say for sure if Drew is involved in this whole drug thing, but I have seen him at a few parties hanging out with Troy Baker."

"Who's Troy Baker?" I asked.

"He's the biggest dealer around."

My stomach dropped. I had been clueless about my brother and Krista, who I knew better than anyone, so what made me so sure that Drew wasn't doing drugs? Maybe my dad was right. What did I really know about Drew? I didn't want to think about it now. My heart couldn't handle it. Instead, I just switched the topic, reminiscing about our younger years when life was uncomplicated, fun, free of drugs, and free of heartache.

After I left Krista's, I didn't want to go home. I had so much on my mind. I was worrying about my best friend, hoping she would be okay. She looked so weak and vulnerable today; so much different than the girl I had known my whole life. My mind began to shift to my brother. I didn't want him suffering the same fate as Krista, and I suddenly became angry at myself for not telling my parents about the incident with Ashton. If something were to happen to him, it would be all my fault. My father was right; I was stupid to believe Jordan. I only hoped that he wasn't right about his assumptions he was making about Drew. I couldn't even believe that I was doubting him. I was allowing my dad to unleash all of the insecurities that would flourish inside of me, once again. Whenever he didn't approve of something that I wanted to do, he would always tout the dangers or negatives to it, and normally, I would surrender and talk myself right out of it. But he wasn't going to talk me into thinking that Drew was a bad person. I *knew* Drew even if it hadn't been for that long. I knew there was something about him that was special. I started to second guess myself as I walked up to his door. I should have called him first, but my mind was going at warp speed, especially after what Krista had told me. I needed to hear it from him that both she and my dad were wrong.

An uneasy smile slowly stretched across his face as he opened the door. "Becca. Hey."

"I'm sorry I didn't call you first. I was just driving around thinking and I needed to talk to you about something."

He opened the door wider and kissed me on the cheek. He hurriedly grabbed the papers that were on his coffee table and shoved them in a folder; clearly he didn't want me to see what he was working on. "Sorry for the mess. I was just trying to get a jump start on some of the paperwork I need for next semester." I could tell he was nervous about something but I didn't know why. He took my hand and led me over to the couch. "This was a nice surprise." He smiled, sounding a little more like himself.

I smiled back, hoping that I wasn't going to jeopardize anything by confronting him. "Drew. Who's Troy Baker?"

His eyes widened. "He's a friend of Ashton's. Why?"

"Well, I went to see Krista today. She's really bad. She's leaving for a drug recovery center in California."

"Wow. I'm really sorry, Becca."

I nodded and sighed heavily. "Anyway, she told me that she saw you hanging out with this Troy guy and that he was bad news. Look Drew, I can't tell you who you can and can't hang out with but if you are involved in drugs in any way, I need you to come clean and tell me, because that's just something I can't deal with."

"What?" He laughed. "Where is this coming from, Becca? Just because I was talking to this guy? Just like you *assumed* I was like Ashton because I'm friends with him?" I could hear the frustration in his voice, making me sorry that I had even confronted him.

"I'm sorry, Drew. It's just been a bad day and I just –" I couldn't hold back my tears. "I'm sorry they made me doubt you."

"Hey come here." He stretched out his arms and I moved closer to him, resting my head on his chest. "What's going on, Becca?" I opened up and told him everything that was going on with my brother and my dad, including my dad's request to stop seeing him.

"I'm sorry that this happened. I don't like seeing you this upset."

"No, Drew, I'm sorry for even thinking that about you."

He rested his lips on the top of my head. "Just let this whole thing blow over with your dad and everything will be fine."

I lifted my head and looked up at him. "I really don't care if it doesn't blow over. I don't care if he never speaks to me again. I'm not going to stop seeing you." He pushed my hair from my face and that same look of apprehension washed across his face. The same look that he displayed when he opened the door. The same look as when I gave him the painting last night. "Drew, don't be nervous. I'm not expecting a marriage proposal or anything. I just have a great time when I'm with you. You make me happy and I'm not going to let him take that happiness away."

"You make me happy, too, Becca," he whispered in my ear.

"My father makes me feel like a little girl that can't think for herself and I hate it!"

"He just worries about you, Becca."

"Well, I wish he wouldn't. I know we haven't known each other very long, but I feel as if I know you almost better than anyone in my life."

He sighed heavily and kissed me on the top of my head. I looked up at him and was unable to resist kissing his perfectly full lips, instantly yearning to feel them all over my body. Maybe I was naïve to think that Drew would never do anything to hurt me, but I was willing to take that chance. He was definitely turning me on to an addiction, but it had nothing to do with drugs..... I was becoming totally and overwhelmingly addicted to him.

Chapter 23

My brother was on his best behavior as the weeks passed. My parents were watching him like a hawk, making him attend sessions with a drug counselor. I was hoping that Krista's situation would hit home with him and make him stop and realize what could happen. Still, I had learned to not assume anything when it came to my brother. My father and I were speaking only when necessary with my mother as the go between and even though it hurt like hell, I didn't back down. I continued to see Drew and didn't feel guilty about it.

"Come in!" I shouted when I heard a light knock on my door. I lifted my head from the text message I had just sent to Drew, smiling upon seeing my mother.

"Hey there," she said, taking a seat on my bed.

"Hey."

"What's going on? I feel like I never see you anymore." She was right; I had been dividing every free moment that I had between Drew and Mrs. Barrett's charity.

"Yeah, sorry. Just been busy," I said as I put down my phone.

"Have you heard from Krista?"

I shook my head. "Her mother said that she doesn't get phone privileges until she's been there for a month. I really miss her."

She gave me a sympathetic smile. "So Friday is your birthday! What did you want to do?"

I wanted to spend it with Drew. I only had a week and a half until I was back in school and I wanted to make the most of what little time we did have together. I shrugged my shoulders. "I don't know. I haven't really thought about it. It's just another day."

She took my hand in hers. "I know you want to spend it with him, Sweetie, and that's fine, but I would like to do something special for you. It is a very special day.....to me. So, why don't we have a little party here and you can invite Drew?"

Was she kidding me? My father and I had spoken approximately five words in the past two weeks and she actually wanted me to invite the source of that animosity over to a party.

"Mom, I don't think that's such a great idea."

"Becca, it seems like the two of you are becoming pretty serious and your father needs to come to terms with that. If Drew is going to be in your life, then he needs to get over it and move on."

I loved my mom for her logical way of thinking. Unfortunately, my father never listened to logic; it was either his way or no way. "Mom, I just don't think it's a good idea."

"I promise you it will be okay."

I took a deep breath. I wasn't even sure if Drew would even want to come over given the circumstances, and I couldn't say that I blamed him. "I guess I'll ask him and see if he wants to come," I relented with a very uneasy feeling in my stomach.

"Good!" She smiled, giving me a quick kiss on the cheek.

I had procrastinated all week with telling Drew about the party tomorrow night. Even though I wanted him there more than anything, I didn't want him to feel obligated. As I stood on his front porch, I was working up the courage to ask him.

"Hey there!" I smiled as he opened the door.

The wary look that was on his face scared me, and the little bit of bravery that I had mustered waiting for him to answer was quickly fading. His lips were on mine in an instant as he closed the door behind me, taking me totally off guard. He wasted no time lifting my shirt over my head and removing my bra. He didn't say a word as he took my already hardened nipple in his mouth. My body immediately responded in a positive way to his intensity as I removed his shirt and ran my hands up and down his bare back. We slid down to the floor and he swiftly removed my shorts and underwear, before removing his own pants and boxers. Immediately, I felt the fullness of him inside of me. It wasn't the normal relaxed and gentle lovemaking that I was used to with him. It seemed much more intense. He seemed to be filled with desire and I was more than willing to fulfill whatever needs he had. He moved in and out of me, breathing heavily. Each thrust turning me on more than the last. Our tongues collided and I felt myself coming undone around him.

"Oh my God, Drew," I screamed, never feeling anything that intense.

He continued with the same velocity and I could feel the momentum building up once again. *This couldn't be happening again, but it was.* I gently dug my fingernails into his back as he brought me to a second orgasm within minutes of the first. I closed my eyes and let out a gentle cry. He finally slowed down his pace and was staring down at me when I opened my eyes. Taking my face in his warm soft hands, he kissed me hard before picking up his stride once again. He buried his face in my hair and let out a loud groan as I felt the warmth of him filling me up. He was still silent, rolling over on his side and pulling me closer. My body was trembling while still feeling like it was having aftershocks from the pleasurable state that he had put it in. We both laid in silence on the cool hardwood floor. I was feeling so relaxed as he played with my hair and the warm summer breeze flowed through the open window above us.

"Can we just stay like this forever?" I whispered, finally breaking the long silence. He didn't respond, he just pulled me closer and rested his lips on the top of my head.

"Becca?" he finally whispered, his voice wavering.

"Yeah?" I lifted my head.

He stared up at the ceiling before finally looking at me with sadness in his eyes. "Promise me you will remember this forever."

I propped myself up on my elbow. "Of course I will. And I will remember all the times like this that are yet to come." He bit his bottom lip and stared back up at the ceiling. My heart immediately sank to my knees, he wasn't himself today and it was starting to worry me. "Drew, is everything okay?" I asked.

"Yeah, I'm just tired I guess," he whispered.

I lay back down and nuzzled closer to him.

"Then let's take a little nap." His heartbeat sounded like a beautiful melody. I had never felt so relaxed in my life as he gently caressed my back. After a while, his breathing began to change and I no longer felt his soft gentle fingers gliding up and down my back. I looked up at him and found him fast asleep. As I placed tiny kisses on his chest, I tried to keep my thoughts inside, but as hard as I tried, they finally escaped through my mouth. "I love you," I whispered.

Chapter 24

"Happy birthday, Becca. Blow out the candles!" my mother exclaimed.

I gripped Drew's hand as I blew on them, making sure that I got each one out. I was so happy that he had agreed to come, once I had finally got the courage up to ask him. He was still on edge; exactly how he was when I saw him yesterday. And each time that I asked him if he was okay, he would just dismiss it as nothing. My father was keeping his distance. But every now and then, I would catch him glaring at us out of the corner of my eye. I made sure that I didn't leave Drew's side. I didn't want him feeling awkward being left alone.

"Where are you going?" I asked. I could hear the panic in my voice when he let go of my hand.

"To the bathroom." He looked at me strangely.

"Oh, okay." I gave him a quick kiss and watched him walk away as I stared down at my wrist and the beautiful moon and stars charm bracelet that he had given me for my birthday.

"See, everything is fine!" my mother said, sneaking up behind me and causing me to jump.

"Yeah, so far so good." I smiled.

"Told you!" She placed her hand on my shoulder and gave me a warm smile before walking away. My stomach dropped when I saw Drew talking to my dad and the two of them entering the house together.

I nearly tripped over my own feet to get inside and see what was going on. "Becca! Sweetie!" Mrs. Hudson, Krista's mother exclaimed, stopping me dead in my tracks.

"Oh hi, Mrs. Hudson," I replied, placing a kiss on her cheek.

"Happy Birthday," she said while handing me a gift wrapped box.

"Thank you so much. You didn't have to do this." I smiled.

"Well, you know that Krista has never missed your birthday parties ever since you were little girls so I had to come and represent her this year."

I felt myself getting emotional just thinking about Krista. "Well, thank you."

"I talked to one of the counselors the other day. They said she's doing great. She......."

She went on and on, and at any other time I would love to hear about Krista and her recovery but right now, I was too on edge as to what Drew was being subjected to with my father. I paid attention as best as I could, keeping an eye on the back door for Drew. Relief swept over me as my mother came over and lured Mrs. Hudson into another conversation that didn't concern me at the same time that I saw Drew walking through the back door about ten minutes after he had entered with my dad.

"Hey, my father didn't give you a lecture in there, did he?" I asked once he finally reached me.

"Nah, it's all good." He gave me a nervous smile.

"Well, what did he say to you?"

"Um, nothing really. Just talking about school." I crinkled my forehead, wanting to believe that was true. But something about the sound of his voice and the look in his eyes told me differently. I decided to drop it and not press the issue. "I've got a really bad headache. I'm gonna head home and try and get some sleep."

"Oh, okay." I was trying desperately to hide my disappointment, hoping that this *headache* wasn't brought on by my father.

Taking his hand in mine, I walked him out to his car. I stood on my tiptoes and placed a gentle kiss on his lips, swiping the side of his face with my hand. "Go home and get some sleep and I'll see you tomorrow."

He took a deep breath and looked away before nodding. "Happy Birthday, Becca," he whispered, resting his lips on my forehead before looking into my eyes and getting in his car. I stood in the driveway long after he drove off, trying desperately to shake the uneasy feeling in my stomach and the worry that was creeping into my heart. Something was off with him these past few days and I couldn't quite put my finger on it. I walked back into the party, putting on my best happy face.

"Is everything okay?" my dad asked, sneaking up behind me and causing me to drop my piece of cake that I had just picked up from the table. "Oh, I'm sorry," he said, bending down at the same time as me to pick it up.

"Yeah, everything is fine. Why wouldn't it be?" I asked, immediately being put on the defense.

"I don't know. I just noticed that Drew left. Did the two of you have a fight or something?"

I stared at him blankly. "No, Dad, we didn't! He just wasn't feeling good and went home to go to sleep."

He closed his eyes briefly and nodded. "So now that you're heading back to school, you'll be done with your work on this charity, right?"

"Well, I told Mrs. Barrett if she needs me to help out when I come home on the weekends or during my breaks that I would."

"Becca, I don't think that's wise with the amount of courses you've taken on next semester."

"I can handle it, Dad."

"Becca, if I'm going to be paying for your education, then I insist that you stop this work with this charity. You need to concentrate one hundred percent on your studies."

"Geez, Dad, what is it with you? Why do you feel like you always need to control me?"

"Becca, that's not what I'm trying to do. You're just biting off more than you can chew and your studies should come first and foremost."

"I won't ignore my classes, Dad, but as far as coming first and foremost Drew now holds that title."

I held my breath in angst, waiting for him to blow up on me but instead he remained quiet, looking a little wounded. "Becca, you really need to get your priorities straight."

"I do have my priorities straight, Dad!" I shouted, getting the attention of some of the guests. "I'm not a baby and I'm sorry if you want to still treat me that way. I care about Drew a lot and I'm sorry if you don't approve of that but my feelings for him will never change....not ever!"

"I just don't want you throwing your whole life away over something that's not going to last."

I shook my head in anger at him and stormed into the house, knowing now more than ever that he must have said something to Drew tonight to cause him to leave. I dialed Drew's number, wanting to apologize to him for whatever it was that my father said or did. When it went straight to his voicemail, I decided to go see him face to face. I was feeling horrible; he didn't deserve to be subjected to my father like this.

I arrived at Drew's and knocked gently on his door. I couldn't wait to throw my arms around him and let him know that no matter what my dad may have said to him tonight, I didn't care. All I wanted was to be with him.

He slowly opened the door and looked surprised to see me standing there. "I know you're tired and have a headache, but I just wanted to see you to make sure that everything was okay. You seemed kind of off tonight."

"Yeah, everything's fine," he replied, still looking like he was on edge.

"I'm really sorry if my dad said something wrong to you tonight." I wrapped my arms around his neck and he pushed me away, taking me totally off guard. "Drew, what's the – ". I stopped myself mid-sentence when I saw the suitcase sitting in the middle of the living room floor. He ran his hand through his hair and let out a deep breath. "Are you going somewhere?" I asked.

He looked away. "Yeah, I'm going back to California."

"To visit?" I could hear the panic in my voice. He shook his head, still unable to look at me. "Drew, what the hell's going on? You're moving back to California?"

"Yes," he replied with his eyes finally meeting mine.

"Why?" my voice cracked with emotion and the first teardrop rolled down my face. I could feel my entire body begin to tremble. "You weren't even going to tell me?"

"I'm sorry, but trust me you're better off." I shook my head in disbelief. This couldn't be happening. "It just has to be this way, Becca."

"What the hell are you talking about, Drew? What way? What did I do to make you want to leave?" I shook my head, finding each breath a little harder to make. "Please don't leave me! Whatever I did wrong, please just tell me!" I grasped tightly to his arm.

"You didn't do anything. It's me. It's all me."

"Drew...no." I moved closer and pulled him into a hug. "I'll do whatever it takes for you to stay. I'm sorry if I've become too needy with you. We can slow things down. Just please say that you'll stay."

"Becca, don't; please, just don't. I care about you a lot. Please don't think that you did something wrong."

"Then why are you -" I couldn't even speak through my sobs.

"Because I have to."

I shook my head. "Why?! Damn it, Drew, tell me why!"

"Becca, just go." He looked away and turned his back to me.

My heart dropped to my knees. "You let my father get to you, didn't you?"

"No." He ran his hand over his face and turned back around to face me.

"You're a liar! Everything I thought we had was a lie. You let him buy you! I hate you! God, I hate you so much!" His eyes were building with emotion before he looked down at the ground.

"Becca—" I yanked my arm from him as he went to grab it and I pulled off my bracelet, throwing it at him just before I ran out the door. I couldn't get out to my car quick enough. My hands were trembling as I tried to get the key into the ignition.

Pure anger overtook me once I was finally pulling in my driveway from my tear filled drive home. I walked in the house, looking for my dad. I slammed the door and headed out to the patio where my mother and father were still entertaining guests.

"Becca, what's the matter, Sweetie?" my mother asked. I looked right past her, focusing my attention completely on my father.

"You just couldn't stand to see me happy, could you?"

"What are you talking about, Becca?"

"YOU made him leave! Tell me, Dad, did I at least cost you a lot of money?"

"Becca, this is not the time or place for this."

"What's going on?" my mother asked.

I totally ignored her as I glared into my father's eyes. "Well, congratulations! You succeeded. Not only do I hate him, but I hate you, too!"

"Becca, that is enough!" my mother shouted as all of their guests looked on in shock.

My legs were trembling as I ran out of the back yard. My brother grabbed onto my arm as I whisked past him. "Becca, just calm down!"

"Just let go of me!" I screamed before breaking free. "You were right, Jordan, maybe I should start living a little!" I shouted. "Maybe I should start acting like you and just not give a shit. Then maybe *he* would stop treating me like a mindless fool!" I ran out of the backyard and jumped in my car, not knowing where I was headed. My mother came running out into the driveway to try and stop me, but it was too late; I was already barreling out of the driveway. If my father wanted to feel as if he couldn't trust me with the decisions that I made, then I was going to give him what he wanted.

Chapter 25

It seemed like I had been driving forever, without any destination in mind. I had gone to all of the familiar places that Drew and I had frequented over the summer, feeling like a piece of my heart was being ripped from my chest. Just twenty four hours ago I was in his arms and now it was over, without any explanation as to why. I thought back to Krista's warning about him. How much did I really know about Drew? Could he have been involved with drugs and stupid little me was just too naïve to see it? Maybe I was blaming my dad for something that he really didn't do. I wasn't sure which scenario made me angrier….him having a whole other secret life or him choosing my father's money over me. Either way, I knew that it was ultimately Drew that I should be angry with. He played me. He made me fall in love with him. He made me believe that he felt the same way and then he left me. Everything that I thought we had was a big sham.

The thick fog seemed to be the only thing on my side tonight. It was blocking out the moon and stars which was another painful reminder of the one person I was trying to forget. I sat in the park alone in the darkness, resting my face against the chain of the swing. A million thoughts were coursing through my mind. I thought of Drew's reaction when I gave him that painting and his odd behavior yesterday after we had made love. I couldn't believe how stupid I was to think he was special. He was the same as every other guy out there. All along I kept convincing myself that he wasn't like Ashton—turns out he was worse. At least Ashton put it out in the open that he was a sleaze. He didn't turn on the charm and make you fall in love with him first. I needed something to dull my pain. Maybe I could stop off at the liquor store and bury my heartache in a bottle of alcohol or maybe I could ask my brother to give me something from his supply. I needed to get the taste of Drew off my lips, the feel of him inside of me out of my body, and most of all, the memory of him from my heart. I closed my eyes and took a deep breath. If this was what falling in love and having your heart ripped to shreds felt like, I vowed to never do it again. I got up from the swing and headed back to my car with only one thought in my head. A thought that was more dangerous than alcohol or any drug out there. A thought that I never imagined would cross my mind, but for now it seemed like the only thing that would dull the pain, wash away Drew's memory, and at the same time, prove that I was no longer the same sweet Becca that everyone made me out to be.

"Well, well, well. To what do I owe this honor?" I stared at Ashton blankly as he opened the front door. "My mom's not here if that's who you're looking for. Her and my dad-" I pushed my way in, taking him totally off guard.

"I didn't come to see your mother." He raised his eyebrow and his signature devious grin stretched across his face. "I need you to fuck the memory of him away. I want both him and my father to know that I am no longer their sweet little Becca." He stood there silently, and if I had to guess, I would say that he was just as shocked as I was over my uncharacteristic behavior. The last thing that I ever thought I would be doing was asking Ashton Barrett to have sex with me. But I needed to feel depraved. I needed to feel as low as I possibly could. I wanted to erase the memory of Drew and at the same time live up to my father's *stupid girl who couldn't think for herself* perception that he had of me.

He pushed me up against the wall and ran his hands up and down my body. "I want you to say it, Becca," he whispered in my ear.

"Say what?"

"That you want me."

I turned my head and looked away. He grabbed my face in his hand, forcing me to look at him. "Say it!"

"I want you, Ashton."

I felt like a robot, knowing that there were no true feelings in those words. He was just a means to an end. He led me up to his bedroom and his tongue was down my throat in an instant as he lifted my sundress over my head. He laid me down on his bed and removed his shorts and boxers. I closed my eyes when I felt him climb on top of me, running his tongue down my neck and to my breasts. I needed to do this to feel lower than I already was feeling. I needed to do this so I could remove the distinct title that I had given Drew of being my one and only. And most of all, I needed to do this so my Dad could see that he couldn't control me by taking away everything that I cared for so much. He grabbed a condom from his nightstand and placed it on him. Standing on the side of the bed, he gripped my thighs and roughly pulled me to the edge as he hastily entered me, taking me a little off guard. I closed my eyes, trying to block out what I was doing and who I was doing it with while he relentlessly slammed into me, over and over, letting out a groan every now and then. He was completely into it, clearly only thinking of his own needs, not that I was expecting any gratification out of it other than getting back at my father and Drew. He finally let out one last grunt and hastily removed himself from inside of me. I laid there for a minute staring up at the ceiling, finally coming back to my senses and instantly regretting what I had just done.

"Anytime you need me to help you forget, I'm ready, willing, and able." He pulled on his shorts and I felt the bile rising up to my throat. I sat up and stared into his piercing blue eyes for what seemed like eternity while he glared back at me.

I jumped upon hearing the knock on his door, quickly grabbing my dress from the floor. "Ashton, what's Becca's car –" Mrs. Barrett covered her mouth in shock while I frantically tried pulling my dress over my head. I jumped up from his bed, running down the steps and out the door.

Had I known that Ashton's eyes would be the last set of eyes that I would ever look into, I would have looked away. If I had known that I would never see a sunset again, I would have taken in every last detail of the beautiful one that I had taken for granted earlier that night. And had I known that one reckless act would change my life forever and take away my power to see, I would have thought twice before I pushed my car to the limit, losing control and crashing into a concrete median. But I needed the adrenaline rush to help me forget what my father had done, that I had just had sex with Ashton, and that Drew was really gone and everything I thought we had was a lie. Maybe I did it to get back at all of them. Maybe I did it to prove that I couldn't always be in control of myself, or maybe I did it because I couldn't fathom a life without Drew in it.

Part Two

Mason

Chapter 26

Mason

Six years later........

After an eight hour flight, three layovers, and two delays I was finally home. Well, what I temporarily considered home. I couldn't wait until the day I could go back to my real home; River Ridge Louisiana, a suburb just outside of New Orleans. But for now New York City would have to do.

"Hey gorgeous girl, did you miss me?"

Liz lifted her head from her desk, greeting me with a huge smile when I walked into the office. Agent Liz Diaz was a co-worker and a very good friend of mine. We had known each other since I had gotten transferred to the New York office, well over three years ago. I knew she always had my back and I trusted her with my life. She was tough as nails and didn't take shit from anyone. She told you like it was and if you didn't like her for it, she could care less.

"Well, well, Mason Boudreaux in the flesh. How does it feel to be back to civilization?"

"I'll tell you once I get a decent cup of coffee and a hot shower."

"You didn't have fun charming those ladies down in South America?"

"Oh yeah, loads." I rolled my eyes in sarcasm. "Oh, congratulations by the way; I heard you and Natalie are officially engaged."

"Yup, haven't set a date yet, but soon we will be wife and wife." She laughed. "And you better be there."

"Wouldn't miss it for the world," I replied, taking a seat opposite her desk.

"And condolences to you; I heard you and Gina are officially over. You know I never liked her, right?"

"Yeah, I do recall you telling me that *several times*." Gina and I had been seeing each other for the past two years. She wanted more and I didn't, so she decided to find more with someone else. "It was for the best," I said.

"It's hard trying to maintain a relationship when you have to spend months at a time being someone else. Oh well, I'm sure it won't be long before you're smooth talking some other little chick with your sexy southern charm."

"Boudreaux, welcome back, my man!" Matt, another agent, said as he walked into Liz's office, shaking my hand.

"Yeah, hopefully I will be back for a while."

"Heard about you and Gina—sorry, Man."

"Geez, what, has my love life been the topic of conversation around here for the past six months?"

"Pretty much." Matt chuckled. "Did you miss us so much that you had to stop in and see us as soon as you got back?"

"Don't flatter yourself. I have to be at the prosecutor's office at ten. Apparently the Mueller case is *finally* going to the Grand Jury, after five long months of working undercover."

"Well, let's just hope that he gets put away for a very long time after all your hard work," Liz said.

I leaned my head back in the chair and stared up at the ceiling, wondering how long I would be able to continue being myself before I was sent off on my next case and forced into a whole new way of life. I loved the excitement that this job brought, but sometimes it was nice just to be me and bask in the calmness of my own life and not have to worry about compromising a case by slipping up and saying one wrong thing.

"So Harrison said you're up for a promotion?" Matt said, breaking me from my daydreaming.

I nodded.

"That would take you out of the field and put you behind a desk. Are you cut out for that?" Liz asked.

I shrugged my shoulders. "Don't know, some days I think yes and others, no."

"Well, you are one of the best damn undercover agents out there, but I get how it could burn you out after doing it for so long," she said.

"Yeah, it can." I stared out the window deep in thought before finally looking up at the clock and noticing the time. "Oh shit, I gotta get!"

"Drinks tonight?" Liz asked.

"Yup, text me the time and the place."

"Sounds good." She smiled as I got up from the chair and walked out of her office.

I waited for the receptionist to finish up with her phone call.

"Can I help you?" she asked with a slight roll of her eyes, seeming bothered by my interruption.

"I'm Agent Boudreaux. I have a ten o'clock appointment with Frank Davis."

Her mood suddenly shifted. "Oh yes! Mr. Davis is expecting you." She picked up the phone to let him know I was here.

"Mason Boudreaux," Frank said, coming out of his office in an instant. "How are you?" he asked, patting me on the back.

"I'm doing good." Frank and I had worked on cases previously. He was one of the best damn prosecutors around, in my opinion. His deep voice was just as intimidating as his six foot five stature, but once you got to know him, he was really a giant teddy bear.

"It's been a while since you and I have worked together," he said.

"Yes, it has."

"Well, I'm glad to see that this one is finally going to the Grand Jury. Let's just hope we have enough for the indictments."

I nodded. "No doubt in my mind that we do."

"I'm actually going to have one of my newer prosecutors sitting in on this one. I'm going to be letting her handle most of this case, so you will be working closely with her." He led me through a maze of cubicles before stopping and knocking lightly on one of the office doors. "Becca, you have a minute?"

"Yeah, sure."

I was speechless as I stood in the doorway staring into those beautiful blue eyes that I tried so desperately to forget for the past six years. My heart descended to my knees as I tried my hardest to think of what I was going to say to her.

"Becca, I have Agent Mason Boudreaux with me here. He was the undercover on the Mueller case." She looked past me and smiled. There was no way in hell that she didn't recognize me. She stood up and extended her hand, waiting for me to take it, still staring in the same spot.

"Hi, I'm Becca Keeton. It's very nice to meet you." I creased my forehead in confusion as I took her warm soft hand in mine. "Just in case Frank didn't tell you, I'm blind."

Blind? What the hell happened to her? I finally pulled it together and cleared my throat. "It's … it's nice to meet you, Miss Keeton."

"Please, call me Becca. You're accent? Where are you from?"

I swallowed hard, remembering that when Becca had known me or at least who she thought I was, I had to talk without my accent to keep up my cover. "New Orleans," I responded.

"I like it."

Frank excused himself to take a call, leaving me alone with Becca. I couldn't stop staring at her as she began to speak. She was just as beautiful as the last time that I had seen her. So many questions were going through my mind. But the main one was *how*? What had caused her to lose her sight?

"So Mueller was basically funneling the money through three different accounts?"

"I'm sorry, what?" I asked, realizing that I hadn't heard a word that she had been saying for the past five minutes of our conversation.

"Okay, Agent Boudreaux, let's get the elephant out of the room. Does it bother you working with me because I'm blind?"

"What? No....not at all. I just didn't get much sleep last night, I'm tired."

"Well, sorry. I'll try and keep this short. You don't mind if I record this, do you? It just makes it easier on me when I have to go back and research since I can't....well you know....see." She forced a smile.

"What happened to you?" The words were out before I could even stop them.

"What?"

"I mean, when did you lose your eyesight?"

Pain shot through her eyes and right down to her face. She swallowed hard. "Six years ago. I was in an accident."

"What kind of accident?" I blurted out. I needed to know.

"Boy, you ask a lot of questions! Are you sure you're not a lawyer, too?" she said with a nervous laugh.

"I'm sorry."

"No, it's okay. Most people don't like to talk to me about it. You know, they act like it's some kind of disease that they're going to catch if they do." Her eyes shifted and looked like they were staring right into mine. "I was in a car accident. I was.....I was at a really bad point in my life." I briefly closed my eyes, hoping that bad point she was referring to had nothing to do with me. "But, that's in the past. Guess we all gotta live with our mistakes. Some of us just make bigger ones than others."

I stared at her perfectly red lips and was instantly brought back to how it felt to have them pressed up against mine and all over my body. This couldn't be happening. Becca Keeton, the one and only girl that I ever loved. The girl who plagued my thoughts more times than I cared to remember. The girl that I thought I would never see again couldn't be sitting right here in front of me.... but she was. I often wondered what would happen if we had ever met up again. Would she hate me for what I had done to her? Would she be able to look past it and understand that my leaving had nothing at all to do with her? Would she be able to fall in love with the real me instead? Never in a million years did I imagine that she would be staring into my eyes, feeling absolutely nothing at all.

Chapter 27

Six Years ago

It had been two months, twelve days, and six hours since I had been assigned to this case. I knew it could have been a lot worse. I could have been in some third world country working with ruthless drug cartels instead of over privileged college kids, trying my best to be one of them. So, instead of being Mason Boudreaux, a twenty five year old, DEA agent, who came from a modest family which included my mother, father and sister, I was now Drew Bryant, twenty two year old college student from California who had inherited his family's fortune after they passed away tragically. The investigation was focusing on Ashton Barrett, who had been on the radar for some time. When the agency had gotten some information that he was starting to branch out to distributing to bigger targets, it piqued their interest and that was where I came in. So here I was at Ashton Barrett's party, hoping to get some leads while listening to him go on about the girl that he fucked the night before, trying to seem genuinely interested. When the truth of the matter was, I could care less who this obnoxious prick was getting it on with. My attention was broken from Ashton when I saw the two girls that had just walked in, paying particular attention to the taller one. God, she was beautiful. I looked her over, trying to guess her story, something that I always did when new people piqued my interest. I could tell right away from her stance that she didn't realize just how beautiful she was. She seemed timid and out of place, standing in the same spot as her long chestnut brown, wavy hair was blowing from the ceiling fan overhead. I looked away, not wanting her to see me checking her out.

Ashton looked over in her direction and I immediately wanted to knock the arrogant grin right off his face. "I have been after that piece of ass since the fifth grade and I will bet any of you dick wads that I will get it by the end of the summer." He took another sip of his beer and licked his lips, still staring at the girl.

"Dream on!" Ashton's friend, Jack said. "Becca Keeton doesn't give any guy the time of day....especially not you."

"Oh, I have my ways.....trust me." Ashton smirked. God, I wanted to knock this jerk off on his ass so bad. "Watch and learn, Jack," Ashton said as he approached her.

"Well, well, well, the beautiful ladies finally showed up, now all the rest of these bitches can go home!" he said. He moved closer to her and whispered in her ear. I couldn't keep from laughing at the repulsed look on her face just before she pushed him away. This girl may have been reserved but she certainly wasn't stupid. Not like all of those other foolish girls that Ashton had eating out of the palm of his hand. He held his hands up in defense. "Well, you can't blame a guy for trying?" he said, walking away with his tail between his legs.

My attention was suddenly focused on the guy who just walked in the door, Troy Baker; one of the main guys that Ashton was dealing with. He had a rap sheet a mile long, but nothing was sticking out just yet. He wasn't the source of Ashton's supply, there was someone else involved and I was having the hardest time trying to figure out who it was.

"Yo, Troy!" Ashton shouted, handing him a beer.

"What's up, my man?" Troy responded, totally amped up on

something. "You got my stuff?" he asked.

"Of course. You got my money?" Troy pulled out a wad of hundreds from his pocket. "Then follow me, my man," Ashton said, leading him up the stairs.

"Fuckin' Ashton, man. His parents have more money than God and he's got his hand in shit like that," Jack said, taking a swig of his beer.

"Where's he get his stuff from?" I asked Jack, knowing that he was buzzed just enough to tell me if he knew anything.

"Well, the rumor I heard was from his old man."

"His father?" I asked in total shock.

"Well, his dad certainly has access to all the stuff he wants; he's an orthopedic surgeon. Don't know how true that is, but that's what I heard."

Holy shit! I never in a million years would have made that connection. But it would make perfect sense. His parents were supposedly pillars of the community so no one would be suspecting them to be using their son to be pedaling their wares. Now I had my work cut out for me. I had to get an in with his parents. *How the hell was I going to do this?* Ashton never hung around his house, so it wasn't like I could use my *friendship* with him as a connection. I was deep in thought when Ashton's big mouth broke my concentration. He was standing on the landing of the steps swaying back and forth. "I have something to say! I just want to thank everyone for coming to what will be my first epic party of the summer." His eyes surfed the crowd of people until they finally locked eyes with the pretty brunette that he was trying to get with earlier. "Tonight we are privileged by a very special guest. The ice princess, dick tease, Becca Keeton has honored us by lowering herself to be here tonight. Some of you may remember her from high school. Well, college hasn't changed her much, she still has that same stick up her ass!"

I looked over at the girl as the rest of the crowd started to laugh. I could see even from across the room that she was mortified. *He was such a fuckin' asshole.* He continued rambling on as the girl ran out of the house.

As I took a walk out to my car to text over the information that I had learned tonight to my boss, I noticed the pretty girl that Ashton had just humiliated, standing up against a car. Her moonlit silhouette was just as beautiful as the starlit sky she was staring up into. I knew I should just keep walking and pretend like I didn't see her standing there, but I just couldn't. I could tell she was upset and I wanted to make sure that she was alright.

"Hey, are you okay?"

She jumped and quickly wiped her eyes before turning around to look at me. "Oh yeah, I'm good." She mustered her best smile.

"So do you like looking up at the stars?"

"Yes, as a matter of fact I do!" she snapped.

"No need to take offense. I just thought I was the only one that liked stargazing."

She sighed and gave a small smile. "In case you didn't hear Ashton's little speech, I'm Becca Keeton. The ice princess or dick tease, take your pick," she said, extending her hand out to me.

"I'm Drew Bryant." I took her hand in mine.

"So, are you a friend of Ashton's?"

"Yeah, college buddies." She nodded as her eyes fixated on mine. "Why don't you come back inside?" I asked.

"Umm….no. I think I'll just wait out here for my friend."

I leaned up against the car and stood next to her. "So, Becca, tell me about yourself." *What the hell was I doing? I had no business getting to know this girl. She had nothing to do with this case.* But I just couldn't help myself.

"Well, you already know that I'm a stuck up bitch."

I shook my head and smiled. "I don't believe one word of it."

"Well, that's very kind of you. But you're going to take my word over your buddy's?"

"I got a mind of my own. Plus I'm really good at reading

154

people and I can tell you're not," I replied in all honesty. Little did she know but I thought Ashton Barrett was a complete asshole as well.

"Well, thank you." She nervously raked her hand through her hair. "So what's your story?"

"What do you mean?"

"I mean, you obviously go to Fairfield, but where are you originally from?"

"California." I still couldn't get used to saying that. "What about you?" I asked.

"Born and raised in this uppity town my whole life. Finally got away from it three years ago when I went off to college. Columbia. Pre-law."

I raised my eyebrows; apparently this girl *was* a lot smarter, just like I had thought. "So, how long have you known Ashton?"

She rolled her eyes. "Too long. His parents and mine are really good friends. His dad and mine are both in the same medical practice. His parents are such nice people; I just can't believe they have a son like that."

And there's my connection.

She placed her hand over her mouth. "Oops sorry, don't mean to be talking about your buddy like that."

I shook my head and chuckled. "Nah, it's all good. So –"

"There you are!" The other girl that she had come to the party with shouted just as I was about to ask Becca if she wanted to go out sometime.

"Oh hey!" Becca smiled.

The girl looked at Becca and then at me. "Well, I was going to see if you were ready to leave, but if –"

"Nope, I'm ready!" Becca said all too willingly. "It was great talking to you, Drew," she said while jumping into the passenger's seat.

"Yeah, you too." I watched as they drove away. Who would have thought that a beautiful woman just may be the "in" that I needed? For the first time since I started on this case, things were starting to look up.

Chapter 28

"Over here!" Liz shouted from the bar area of the restaurant. I sat down next to her and ordered a beer. "Please tell me you're hungry because I put our name on the wait list for a table....I'm starving."

"Yeah, that's fine." I was still feeling a little out of it after running into Becca.

"So, how did everything go at the DA's office today?"

"Okay, I guess." I took a swig of my beer and ran my hand through my hair.

"Mason, what's the matter? You are so not yourself tonight. Have you forgotten that you're not working undercover anymore?" she joked.

I stared off into space before turning my attention back to Liz. "That female prosecutor....the blind one."

A smile stretched across Liz's face as she lifted her wine glass to her lips. "Oh yeah, Becca. She just started about six months ago. Love that girl! She is a sweetheart." I sighed deeply. "What about her?"

"I slept with her."

She choked on the sip of wine that she had just taken. "What?! When?"

"Six years ago, when I was working on this case. She had close ties with the source of the investigation and…" I took a deep breath and looked away.

"Wait, wait, wait, let me get this straight. You slept with Becca Keeton when you were undercover so she thought you were someone else?" I nodded. "Mason, what the hell is wrong with you?"

"I know. I needed to make a connection and she was my in. She was just so beautiful, Liz. I couldn't help it.

"You fell in love with her, didn't you?"

I nodded. "I thought about coming clean with her and giving up everything for her, but I knew she would never forgive me. She would always think that I had ulterior motives. At first I did, but it didn't take long for all of that to change."

"So, she has no clue who you are?"

"Nope. When she knew me, I was Drew Bryant from California."

"How did it end?"

"Not good. I got pulled off the case when they got all of the information that they needed for the arrests. I told her I was going back to California. I never gave her a reason why. The last memory I have of her was me breaking her heart. When I asked her how she went blind, she said it was a stupid mistake and she was at a really bad point in her life. God, I hope I had nothing to do with that."

"Wow!" Liz said shaking her head.

"Do you know how many times over the years that I wanted to just look her up to see what she was up to, if she ever graduated law school, or if she was married? But I just couldn't do it. The mere thought of her and what I did to her tore me up inside. So I figured if I pretended that she never existed then maybe that would help me forget about her."

"Did it work?"

I shook my head. "When I saw her today, it just brought back all of the memories of her. She's even more beautiful than I remembered. I just can't believe she's blind."

"Mason, stay away from her! You work with her on this case and give her whatever information she needs, but DO NOT try and rehash whatever unfinished business you have with her."

I looked down at the bar and began peeling off the label from my beer bottle. "Liz, you don't know what I had with this girl."

"YOU, didn't have anything with her. Drew Bryant, a man that doesn't exist, did and I'm telling you now, it's going to end ten times worse than it did last time, if you try to start something up with her again."

"Ah, Liz, what the hell do you know about women?" I joked.

"A hell of a lot more than you'll ever know, smart ass. Come on, let's go see if our table is ready," she said, getting up from the bar and smacking me on the back of the head.

"What the hell was that for?"

"For breaking my favorite prosecutor's heart." After seeing Becca today and looking into those beautiful empty eyes, I knew that I deserved more than a smack on the head.

I grabbed my ringing cell phone as I jumped into the taxi to head into the office. "Hey Mason, it's Frank Davis. Do you have some time to stop in this morning and meet with Becca to go over a few things?"

Becca. Just hearing her name ripped me apart. "Yeah, sure." I looked at my watch. "Is now good?"

"Now would be perfect. I'll let Becca know that you're on

your way."

"Okay, thanks." I stopped off for coffee along the way. I still remembered exactly how she drank hers: Hazelnut, vanilla creamer, and one *sweet 'n' low*.

"Becca, Agent Boudreaux is here," the receptionist said as she led me back to her office. She took the earplugs out of her ears and looked up.

"Thank you." She smiled. "Good morning, Agent Boudreaux," she said, looking right past me and through the door.

"Morning," I replied while trying to stop myself from staring at her. I placed the coffee cup down on her desk and watched as her mouth began to form a slight smile.

"Is that hazelnut coffee I smell?"

I nodded and then quickly responded, "It is."

"For me?" Her smile became bigger.

I nodded again. *Damn it, I have to remember to stop doing that!* "Yup!"

"Well, thank you. Hazelnut is my favorite."

She picked up the cup and took a sip. "Agent Boudreaux, how did you know exactly how I take my coffee?" She giggled.

"Lucky guess.....I guess." *Damn it, Becca, it's me!* I moved in closer, breathing in the faint scent of her perfume. How I had wished so badly that she knew who I really was. I took a seat in the chair across from her desk and tried my best just to focus on the questions she had for me.

"So, I was listening to some of the recordings from the wire that you wore. That was really risky. Mueller is pretty ruthless. He would have had no problem taking you out if he had found out."

"It's all in a day's work. I've been in tighter spots than that."

She shrugged her shoulders. "I guess it takes a special kind of person to work undercover." She lifted her coffee to take another sip. I gazed at her perfectly full lips touching the lid of the cup.

How I wished I could get the image of her lips on mine out of my mind. "Guess your time in the Marines helped out a lot, too." *How the hell did she know that?* "Frank let me in on that little bit of info," she said as if she was reading my mind. "I know I'd be scared to death. I'm not that brave."

"I guess we all fear different things. You're braver than me when it comes to living and I'm braver than you when it comes to dying."

"What do you mean?" She furrowed her brows.

"You're a lawyer and you're –"

"Blind," she whispered.

"How did you do it?"

"Do what?" she asked while taking another sip of her coffee.

"Get through law school without being able to see. That couldn't have been easy."

"Well, after my accident I went into a horrible depression for three long months. I didn't want to talk to anyone. Didn't want to eat. Didn't want to leave my bedroom. Then one day I finally woke up and realized this was the hand that I was dealt for the rest of my life so I may as well make the most of it. I knew I would never be able to do what I really wanted to do without my sight so I figured I may as well finish what I had started. I learned braille in record time. Finished up my last year of school at a college for the blind and was accepted into a really good law school. Passed the bar exam and here I am."

"What is it that you really wanted to do?" I asked, already knowing the answer.

"Paint." She smiled. "Now the only pictures I can create are the ones inside my mind."

I felt like I had been kicked in the balls. She had so much talent and it was all taken away in the blink of an eye. Why didn't I tell her the truth back then? Why didn't I tell her that I was really in love with her? Why didn't I just give up everything to be with her? I cleared my throat, trying to pull it together.

"You can still paint," I whispered.

"Umm....I don't think anyone would be interested in any paintings that I would be creating unless they were into that crazy art stuff." She laughed it off.

"You went through law school, passed the bar exam, and have a great job without your sight. Are you telling me that you can't make a stinkin' little painting?"

She raked her hands through her hair. "No, that's just a dream that will never happen again." I could see her eyes filling with tears. She took a deep breath. "So where were we?" She clicked on her tape recorder and forced a smile.

I sat there listening to her talking, feeling like I was working undercover but in my own life. And for the first time, I wanted to go back and be one of my aliases. I wanted to be Drew Bryant again. I wanted to be that couple that Becca thought we were back then. I wanted to feel her in my arms once again. Taste her lips and her warm soft skin. I wanted to be inside of her and know that I was the only man that had ever been there. I wanted to tell her how I felt for her back then. That all I cared about was her. That I had no choice but to leave her and that keeping her safe became my one and only priority. And most of all, I wanted her to know those three words I never said but felt inside of me every time I was with her.....I love you.

162

Chapter 29

Six Years ago

Becca was definitely the key that I needed into the intricate drug ring that expanded so much further than I had ever imagined. Dr. Barrett and his wife were using their charities as a front for their expansive drug business they had going on and also using Becca as a runner for all the deals. She was clueless as to what they had her doing and the danger that they were putting her in. I made sure that I went along with her to each one of the deliveries they had her going on to keep her company or so she thought. I was able to get a good amount of names of the individuals involved from the spreadsheet that Becca had been working on. Allowing me to piece together just how far this whole operation ran.

The name that stuck out more than any was Carlos Simms, a big time dealer who had his hand in more than just the drug business. The FBI had been watching him for months because of his ties with human trafficking. The thought of Becca going to his house to make deliveries scared me half to death. I knew that once he laid eyes on her, he would have more than drugs in mind. We had gone to his home last week and he wasn't home, for which I was grateful. I was hoping that was the only time that Becca would have to go there, but this morning when she had told me that she was going again, I jumped right in to let her know that I *would* be going with her. I knew that she thought it was a little strange that I wanted to go, but I didn't care; there was no way in hell she was going there by herself. After getting a little pat down by one of his men, I was glad that I had listened to the little voice in my head, telling me not to wear a wire or carry. If he had found either one on me that would've been it; my whole cover would have been blown and then who knows what would have happened to Becca. I was trained to remain calm in tense situations so I knew that this would be no different than any other I had been in. I was just a little nervous because I knew Becca was involved in it. I was finding that keeping her safe was more important than anything else about this case. It was quickly becoming my main priority as I was uncovering more information and realizing just how dangerous some of the people they had her delivering to were.

Almost two hours after our visit with Simms, Becca's nerves were finally settling down. We stopped off at an old stable that she wanted to show me and sat by the water. I couldn't stop staring at her. She looked like an angel as the sunlight shone through her hair, creating a beautiful silhouette all around her. My head had been consumed with thoughts of her lately and each time I was with her those thoughts were becoming permanently etched in my mind. I knew that I shouldn't have crossed that line and slept with her, but I just couldn't help it. She was the most beautiful woman that I ever laid eyes on. She was so sweet and innocent and the thought of that ruthless, heartless monster from earlier today getting his hands on her drove me insane. The look in his eyes when we walked out that door confirmed everything I already knew. He was eyeing up Becca like she was his next meal and I had to let him know that would *never* happen. I hated putting on an act with the Barretts' when I was with Ashton, pretending that I didn't know what was going on. I wanted to kill both of them for putting Becca in these dangerous situations without even blinking an eye, all for their own personal gain.

I listened to Becca reminisce about her horse, Chestnut, and the time they would spend together in this very spot. Sadness filled her eyes when she began to tell me about her father taking him away and I wanted to take away her pain, if only for a second. I moved my head closer to her and placed my lips on hers. She jumped when her phone began beeping.

"Your phone has the worst possible timing ever."

She laughed that cute little laugh that I loved so much as she pulled her phone from her pocket and read over the text message that had just so rudely interrupted us. "Hey, do you feel like meeting my friend Krista and whoever Brad is for dinner?"

There was something about her friend Krista that I didn't like from the first time I had met her. That was confirmed after we were done kayaking yesterday, and she showed up at Ashton's beach party. It was so apparent that she had some deep seeded jealousy issues with Becca. "Yeah, that's fine, I guess." I tried putting on my best game face as always.

"Ready?" she asked after she texted Krista back.

"Yup." I got up and grabbed her hand.

She stood up and silently looked out at the water before turning her attention back to me. "Can I tell you a little secret?"

"What's that?"

"I liked being here with you just as much as Chestnut, and I got lots of pictures in my mind to put on paper."

This girl was completely owning me and I knew that wasn't good, but there was nothing I could do to stop how I was feeling about her. "Oh yeah?" I smiled. She looked up at me and my whole body felt like it was in overdrive just staring into her beautiful eyes. "Is one of those pictures this?" I grabbed her face and let my tongue express to her just how I was feeling. She let out at little sigh once the kiss ended and my lips were gently touching hers.

"I don't need to paint a picture to remember that, Drew. Some things don't need to be displayed to see them clearly. Some things are best seen if we just close our eyes and look inside our hearts...."

and that kiss will remain in mine for the rest of my life."

And the memory of you will be in my heart forever, too, Becca.

Chapter 30

"I'm starving....dinner?" I asked Liz as I poked my head in her office after a long day of sitting behind a desk, catching up on paperwork and reports from the case that I had just come off.

"I would love to, but Natalie's parents are in town so I have a dinner date with them."

"Ah, I see how I rate," I teased, pulling my ringing phone from my pocket. "Boudreaux," I answered.

"Hi Agent Boudreaux, it's Becca Keeton." She didn't need to tell me who she was. I knew that voice anywhere. "I know it's kind of late, but I was wondering if you had time to stop by my office just to go over a few questions I have from the tapes that I listened to today."

"Yeah, no problem," I replied, hoping that I didn't sound too eager. "On one condition."

"What's that?"

"Well, I'm starving and no one wants to go out to dinner with me." I looked over at Liz, who was shaking her head at me. "So, if you agree to dinner, then I agree to answer your questions."

She laughed. "Umm....okay, that sounds fair. But only because I'm pretty hungry myself."

"I'll meet you at your office in ten," I said before hanging up the phone.

Liz was staring at me as I placed my phone in my pocket. "What unsuspecting female did you just con into going to dinner with you?"

"Don't you worry about it, Lizzy." I looked away.

"Mason! No! Don't even tell me it's Becca."

"Liz, just calm down. It's work related."

"Mason, I know you better than anyone and I know that you have more than work on your mind when it comes to her. I'm telling you.....don't!"

"I'm a big boy, Liz. I know what I'm doing."

"I know you are, but have you ever stopped to think how it's going to affect her if you two start something up again?"

I didn't want to think about that at the moment. All I wanted to think about was being with Becca and spending time with her again. I wanted her to be able to see the real me. I wanted her to realize who I was without telling her. "Have fun with your in-laws." I gave her a quick grin and hurriedly exited her office, sparing myself from another lecture.

I arrived at Becca's office and was greeted by a security guard sitting at the front desk. It was after hours and the rest of the office staff had gone for the day. I flashed him my badge and told him my reason for my visit before he buzzed me in and I made my way back to Becca's office. Becca skimmed her fingers along a piece of paper as I stood in her office doorway, silently watching her. I knocked lightly and jumped when I was greeted by a barking dog.

"Oh shit," I whispered.

Becca began to giggle. "Did she scare you?" she asked as a Golden Retriever stuck her head out from underneath her desk.

"Just a little."

"This is Lilly....She's my eyes."

"Well, it's nice to meet you, Lilly," I said.

"Go ahead girl, you can go and say hello."

The dog got up to greet me and I bent down to pet her. "She's a sweetheart."

"Yes, she is. She's my baby. Aren't you, girl?" She perked up at the sound of Becca's voice and went running over to her with her tail wagging back and forth. "Since it was such a nice day, I decided to walk to work, so Lilly had to come with me to help me get here." I bit my lip, still having such a hard time grasping the fact that she was blind. "So would you mind stopping off at my place to drop her off before we grab a bite to eat?"

"No problem."

She reached down on the floor and moved her hand around until she located her briefcase, grabbing all the papers that were written in braille from her desk. I was amazed by how well she had adapted to everything without her sight. She grabbed Lilly's leash, feeling around for the latch on her collar. "Ready?" she asked, grabbing onto her briefcase with one hand and Lilly's leash with the other.

Her apartment was right up the street from her office. I watched as she unzipped her purse and grabbed the key ring. I was readying myself to help her insert the key into the lock, but stopped myself when I saw her do it with ease. "I just want to feed her dinner and get her some water before we go."

"No problem." I stood in the middle of her living room as she maneuvered her way through the tiny kitchen like she had twenty-twenty vision.

"Do you mind if I change really quick?" she asked after she took care of Lilly.

"No, go right ahead."

"Have a seat, if you aren't already." She smiled.

"I'm good."

She walked off to her bedroom as I began taking everything in her apartment in. It was decorated to perfection and part of me wondered why she needed all of the elaborate paintings and portraits that were hanging on her wall if she couldn't see them. My eyes skimmed over them and my heart sank when I saw the one hanging over her sofa. The same one that I had hanging in my apartment. The one that Becca had made for me all those years ago. I moved closer, examining the details of that star filled sky that had been so beautifully captured on canvas. It was filled with so much intricate detail and was almost identical to mine with the exception of the moon. She had put her whole heart and soul into those paintings. I closed my eyes, remembering the night that she had given it to me. I was speechless, especially when she explained the symbolism of the moon, making me feel like total shit for lying to her and leading her to believe that I was someone that I wasn't. The only thing I wasn't lying about back then were my feelings for her. Every emotion. Every kiss. Every touch was real. Becca Keeton made me feel things that no other woman ever had been able to make me feel before or after I had met her.

"I'm ready," she said, walking out of her room. "Do you mind if I use you to help me out a little? I'm perfectly fine in here but once I get outside, I get a little lost."

"Oh, not at all," I said, walking over to her and looping my arm in hers. It felt so good being this close to her again. We walked out of her apartment building and I flagged down a taxi. "Do you like Italian?" I asked, already knowing the answer.

"Love it," she replied as I helped her in the cab.

I gave the driver the name of one of my favorite restaurants and we headed on our way. "Sorry for making you wait so long. You must be really hungry by now."

"Nah, it's all good," I said. I was finding that trying to make small talk with someone that you pretty much knew everything about was pretty hard. I was relieved when we finally arrived at the restaurant. I helped her out of the taxi and we headed inside. She opted to sit in the outside seating area and since it was such a nice night, I didn't object.

"Umm....I hate to be a pain but would you be able to tell me what is on this menu?" She smiled.

I looked over the menu, finally locating her favorite. "Pasta primavera -"

"Say no more.....I'll take it!" she said, taking a sip of her wine. I smiled at her as I gazed into her eyes. She was still the same girl from all those years ago. I just wished that I was the same guy. "So, Agent—"

"Mason," I Interrupted.

She furrowed her brows. "I'm sorry-what?"

"Call me Mason. That's my name."

She nodded. "Oh. Okay."

"So Becca, do you have a boyfriend?" I blurted out.

"Oh….um, no." She shook her head, seeming a little embarrassed by the question. "No guy in their right mind would want to be burdened by me."

My heart sank to my knees. "What do you mean?"

"Well, for instance, look what just happened now. I can't even read my own menu. It's like going out with a three year old. Sometimes I just feel so helpless and I would never place that load on anyone else."

"Are you crazy? You are a beautiful, intelligent girl with a great personality."

I was happy to see the remnants of a smile adorn her face. "Well thank you very much, Agent…I mean, Mason. But unfortunately, my perception of how others see me will always be tainted."

"I don't see you that way, Becca, and I would love to take you out on a non-business date some time."

She began to fold her napkin and I could see she was feeling uneasy over the whole situation. "That's so sweet of you. But trust me; my inability to see isn't my only defect." She shook her head and sucked in her bottom lip as she silently stared into space. She looked down at the table and began to speak again, totally changing the subject. "I've gotten through half of the tapes so far and I'm just a little confused. How did you know that Mueller was involved with the Trent Roberts deal?"

I couldn't stand the pain in her eyes. How could she feel that way about herself? To me she was still that same beautiful Becca from all those years ago. I took a deep breath, trying to shake off the sadness in her eyes and answer her questions. "Easy. Trent Roberts was one of Mueller's main *customers* in both the drug business and his prostitution ring that he ran. Mueller was using his women to transport the money and drugs. Roberts, who was the *All American Guy* in everyone's eyes—perfect husband, perfect father, CEO of a very reputable company—was living this whole other life. And in return for drugs and free women, he allowed Mueller to funnel the money through his charities that he was running and a few of his company owned bank accounts. It's a very common thing. I've worked on a lot of cases like this one."

"The night of the bust….the amount of drugs that were seized, that is unheard of."

"Yeah, they were rolling in drugs and money until it all came crashing down."

"So, you were Alec Williams, the bartender in Mueller's once booming restaurant?"

I nodded, as she sat there staring at me blankly. "That is correct," I finally answered. I rubbed my hand over the scruff of my face. "Ninety percent of the deals went down there. So it was the perfect *job* for me. Plus, I learned how to make a pretty mean martini."

She raised her eyebrow and let out a giggle. "I can't even imagine pretending to be someone else. How do you do it?"

I looked away. "Some cases are easier than others."

We continued going over the case until the waiter brought us our food. She felt around on the table for her fork and tasted a piece of her pasta. "I feel like such a pain, but is there salt?" I picked up the shaker and placed it in her hand. "Thank you," she whispered.

"So, is it hard going into a courtroom and not being able to see?"

"Well, at first it was a little scary. I don't get to actually lead the case. I'm just what they call a second chair. I assist the main prosecutor. You'd be amazed by how in tune your other senses become when you lose one of them. I hear and smell things that others can't. I could just sense certain things almost as if my other senses are picking up the slack for my lack of vision. Plus, we have a few part time college students that read for me."

"What do you mean?" I asked.

"Well, they read police reports and rap sheets and stuff like that to me and I just make my notes in braille."

"Wow, that's pretty amazing."

She shrugged her shoulders. "Well, it's not exactly how I had hoped to be practicing law. I wish that I could be walking around the courtroom, making eye contact with people and gauging their reactions, but I guess it's better than nothing, right?" She had a look of defeat on her face as she took another bite of her pasta.

"You should be very proud of yourself. Most people don't achieve half of your accomplishments even with their sight."

Her eyes filled with tears as she stared into mine. "Well, someone once told me to not ever let anything prevent me from what I wanted to do. If I wanted it bad enough, it's always obtainable no matter what obstacles are in the way." She quickly wiped her eye with the back of her hand and I felt my heart ripping from my chest as I remembered saying those words to her like it was just yesterday. She shook her head, trying to shake it off. "Even though I want to forget the person that said it, those words stuck with me and kind of kept me going....weird, right?"

I shook my head, before clearing my throat and pulling it together. "No, it's not weird at all," I whispered. I ran my hand through my hair, answering her questions about the case even though my mind was a million miles away. How could I have been so stupid to think that she actually *wouldn't* hate Drew Bryant for what he did to her? The look in her eyes the night I told her I was leaving, haunted me for the past six years of my life. I knew I was saying goodbye to the best thing that had ever happened to me.

Chapter 31

Six years ago

It was Becca's twenty second birthday, and I had gotten the call yesterday, telling me that the arrests were going to go down and I was being pulled off the case. It was the day that I couldn't wait for when I had started this case and the day I had most dreaded after I had met Becca. I knew that the FBI was still trying to get Simms on the human trafficking charge and I was praying that they weren't going to try and use Becca as bait. When I asked, I was told that it was privileged information that I didn't need to know and my part of the case was over. I was going completely crazy not knowing what to do. I wanted to warn her, but I knew if I did it would jeopardize the whole case and put my job on the line. I was spent from over thinking it all and I knew that Becca was picking up on it. She was so on edge at this party and I knew why. She was afraid that her father was going to say something to offend me. Little did she know, her dad was the least of my worries right now and, ironically, the one person that I felt I could divulge this information to. I knew that Becca's safety was his first priority.

"Where are you going?" Becca asked when I let go of her hand for the first time all night.

I hated that she was such a nervous wreck. "To the bathroom."

"Oh, okay." She stretched her neck and gave me a quick kiss.

I awkwardly stood around waiting for her father to wrap up his conversation that he was in. "Dr. Keeton. Can I talk to you for a minute?" He looked surprised when he turned around to face me.

"Sure. What is it, Drew?" I could hear his dissatisfaction for me in his voice.

"In private."

He nodded, leading me into the house and into his study.

"If you're here to tell me that you have nothing but good intentions with her, save your breath. I'm not buying —"

I shook my head and put my hand up to stop him from talking. "Dr. Keeton, I need to tell you something and I need to know that this is going to stay in this room." He gave me an uneasy look and nodded. "My name isn't Drew Bryant, it's Mason Boudreaux. I'm not a college student, I'm a DEA agent that was sent here to bust up an illegal drug ring that was supposed to have revolved around Ashton Barrett, but I've found out it's so much bigger. Your medical practice is being investigated. Ashton's father is now the new target. They pulled me off the case because they've got all the information that they need for the busts and they're afraid that my cover may have been compromised. I have to report back by tomorrow morning." I looked out the window, trying to pull it together. "I can't say anything to Becca. I can't put her at risk. But please, I'm begging you, get her off this charity. They're using her as a drug runner to transport the drugs back and forth. That's why I had been going with her to all of them. I found out that they have another one set up this coming week to one of the biggest dealers in this area. He's in the drug business and other illegal businesses that involve young girls. They want to take him down before they close the case. I'm not sure if the Barretts' are going to try and get Becca to do the delivery or not. I'm not even supposed to be here and I may be blowing this case wide open and lose my job by telling you this, but Becca is my first priority right now. Just please do whatever you have to do to make sure that she doesn't go." He was speechless. "I may have lied about who I was and my intentions, but I never lied about my feelings for Becca."

He shook his head and took a seat behind his desk. "You took advantage of my daughter, made her fall in love with you, knowing the whole time that you were going to leave her. Was this all some sick game to you!?"

I looked down at the ground and then back up at him. "No sir, it wasn't. I care about Becca more than you will ever know. I would give everything up right now and walk away from it all for her, but you and I both know that she would never forgive me for not telling her the truth." I was hoping for some type of indication from him that maybe Becca could get past this so we could have a future together, but there was none.

He had an uneasy look on his face. "Do you have any idea what this is going to do to her?"

I got a sick feeling in my stomach, thinking about how much it was going to hurt her. "I didn't mean to fall in love with her. I just wanted to protect her. But you know better than anyone what an amazing person she is."

He took a deep breath and briefly closed his eyes. "I'm sorry, but this is just a lot for me to take in right now."

"I felt that it was only fair to warn you for both professional and personal reasons. The Feds are going to be all over your medical practice; just give them whatever information they ask for. It's Barrett that they're after."

"I have nothing to hide," he whispered. "My main concern is Becca right now. She's going to be devastated."

I looked away and nodded. "I'd rather have her hate me for the rest of her life and know that she's safe. These people are dangerous. You may think you know them, but they are using your daughter for their own personal gain. She's exactly what they wanted. A young, innocent girl. I can't protect her anymore, so I'm leaving it up to you."

He ran his hand through his hair and nodded. "I'll make sure that she doesn't go and I promise you I will not breathe a word of this to anyone. Thank you for watching over my daughter."

"You're welcome." I hung my head low and began to walk out of his study.

"Agent Boudreaux," I turned around and stared into his eyes, "I'll take the blame for you leaving."

"I appreciate it, but that's not necessary, sir. Becca will never forgive me for this no matter what, so it doesn't matter how much she hates me. You're her dad. You will be in her life forever. I don't want her hating you, too. I just need you to know that I truly do love your daughter and I always will."

I packed up the rest of my clothes and double checked to make sure that I wasn't leaving anything behind, with a very heavy heart. This place was filled with memories of me and Becca. There wasn't a room in this entire house that we hadn't made love in. I shook my head, trying to shake off those memories. I felt like such a coward for not giving her an official goodbye, but I knew it was better this way; neither of our hearts could handle it. My stomach dropped when I heard a knock at my door and saw Becca's car in the driveway. I didn't know if I was going to have the strength to do it. I took a deep breath and opened the door. I couldn't even look at her, knowing that I would never be seeing those beautiful eyes again.

"I know you're tired and have a headache, but I just wanted to see you to make sure that everything was okay. You seem kind of off tonight."

"Yeah, everything's fine."

"I'm really sorry if my dad said something wrong to you tonight." She wrapped her arms around my neck and it took everything inside of me to push her away. I knew that if I hugged her back, I would never be able to let her go. I felt like I was being kicked in the balls over and over again when I saw the look on her face. "Drew what's the –". Her eyes focused on the suitcase that was sitting on the living room floor. I ran my hand through my hair and let out a deep breath. "Are you going somewhere?"

The pain in her eyes was killing me. "Yeah, I'm going back to California."

"To visit?" Her voice quivered. The best I could muster was a shake of my head. "Drew, what the hell's going on? You're moving back to California?"

"Yes." I could feel my eyes stinging as I finally found the courage to look at her.

"Why?" She began to cry. "You weren't even going to tell me?"

"I'm sorry, but trust me you're better off. It just has to be this way, Becca."

"What the hell are you talking about? What way? What did I do to make you want to leave?" She was trying her hardest to speak over her sobs. "Please don't leave me, Drew. Whatever I did wrong, please just tell me!" she yelled as she gripped my arm tightly.

"You didn't do anything. It's me. It's all me."

"Drew…no." She wrapped her arms around me and hugged me, and this time I just couldn't resist hugging her back. "I'll do whatever it takes for you to stay. I'm sorry if I've become too needy with you. We can slow things down. Just please say that you'll stay."

Everything inside of me was telling me to come clean with her. I knew it was now or never. But I also knew that *if* she were to forgive me, she deserved a much better life than I could ever give her. She didn't deserve to be with someone who was only going to be in her life on a part-time basis whenever he wasn't working on cases. As much as it was tearing me up inside, I knew that this was what would be best for her. She had a great future ahead of her and I knew after a little bit of time I would just be an old memory to her, but she would remain in my heart forever. "Becca, please don't. I care about you a lot. Please don't think that you did something wrong."

"Then why are you-"

"Because I have to."

"Why?! Damn it, Drew, tell me why?"

"Becca, just go." I couldn't stand looking at her hurting so badly and knowing that I was the cause of it.

"You let my father get to you, didn't you?"

"No." I turned back around to face her. I couldn't have her blaming her father for this for the rest of her life.

"You're a liar! Everything I thought we had was a lie. You let him buy you! I hate you! God, I hate you so much!"

"Becca," I whispered. I tried to grab her arm but she hastily pulled away in her rage, taking the bracelet that I had given her off of her wrist and throwing it at me, just before running out the door.

I picked up my keys, readying myself to go after her and tell her everything before stopping myself as I was halfway out the door. I knew this was for the best. Becca needed to get on with her life without Drew Bryant because after tonight he was no longer going to exist. I stood in the doorway looking up at the star filled sky and heard Becca's voice so clearly in my mind:

When we go back to school, we can each have our paintings and know that we're looking up at the same star filled sky. I can be the first quarter and you can be the third quarter, and together we can be the full moon.

"Becca, Baby, I will always think of you when I look up at those beautiful stars," I whispered as I ran my hand through my hair, fighting the burning in my eyes. I walked back inside and grabbed my suitcase, Becca's bracelet, and the painting that she made for me. I walked out the door and took a deep breath. As I locked the door behind me, I said goodbye to Drew Bryant and the beautiful girl he had fallen so in love with forever. The only traces of evidence that either one of them existed was the painting in my hand and the memories in my heart.

Chapter 32

I took Becca's arm as we walked out of the restaurant. It was the perfect early summer night. "Did you want to walk back to your place?" I asked.

"Yeah, sure, that would be great." Even though the weather *was* beautiful, I knew the real reason that I wanted to walk. I wasn't ready to call it a night just yet. I wanted more time with her. I wanted to feel her close to me.

"So, Mason, how old are you?" she asked as we began to walk.

"How old do you think?"

"Hmm….judging by the sound of your voice, I'd say…..thirty?"

"Close. Thirty one."

She stopped walking and smiled. "Do you mind if I just do something?"

I shook my head and then quickly responded, "No."

She lifted her hand and gently traced her fingers along my jaw line. Closing her eyes, she moved her hands up to my hair. I took a deep breath and breathed in the light scent of her perfume wafting through the warm summer breeze.

"What color is your hair?"

"Brown," I whispered as her hands rested on the side of my head. She opened her eyes and stared up at me as if she could see me clearly. Her fingers glided back to my face and she placed her thumbs under my eyes. "And your eyes?"

"Grayish, blue," I responded, with my heart beating at warp speed as I stood there, foolishly wondering if she would put together the pieces and figure out who I really was.

"Smile," she said as she began to outline my mouth. "You have a dimple in your left cheek."

I swallowed hard and nodded once again, knowing that her hands were still on my face and she would be able to feel my response. She bit her bottom lip and gave me a slight smile.

"I can see you clearly," she whispered.

How I wished that was true and that she knew exactly who I was and still be perfectly fine, standing here talking to me instead of hating me for what had happened in the past. I took a deep breath and pulled it together. "Do you like what you see, Becca?"

Her smile broadened. "Yeah, I think I do."

I sat behind my desk, finally finishing up with the last of my paperwork that was needed to wrap up the case that I had just come off of. It had been three days since I had spoken to Becca and I was trying to think of any excuse just to call her.

"Got a minute?" Agent Erickson, my supervisor in charge, asked.

"Yeah, sure." I got up from my desk and followed him into his office.

"Have a seat," he demanded as he took a seat behind his desk.

He leaned back in his chair and intertwined his fingers behind his head. "I don't need to tell you that you're one of my best damn under covers."

I nodded. "Thank you, sir."

"Johnson is retiring in three months and Knox wants to bring you in from the field and have you in the office full time. You would be in charge of your own team. There's no doubt in my mind that you can do it and it will be a nice promotion for you." He sat up straight in his chair and leaned forward. "But will you be happy sitting in an office all day?"

I looked out the window, not knowing how to answer that question. "You know, there are days that I would give up anything to just be able to be myself for the rest of my life, and then there are days that I just get off on being someone else."

"It's in your blood. That's why you're so damn good at it! Well, you think about it. Just say the word and I will have your letter of recommendation printed out and ready to go."

"Thank you, sir," I said as I started to get up.

"How's the Mueller case going?"

"Pretty good, as far as I know. It's going before the Grand Jury in a few weeks."

He nodded. "Well, I'm fairly certain that's going to be an easy win."

"Yeah. I agree."

"Well, I've got a few busts that are going down this week. I'm going to need you there to assist with the arrests."

"Not a problem, sir."

I walked out of his office with mixed emotions. It would be great to finally have an office job. More money. A regular schedule. Never having to lie to anyone about who I was. But I still wasn't sure if I was one hundred percent cut out for that just yet. For me, that was a whole lifestyle change. I had spent so many years pretending to be other people that I had to adjust to being myself. I wasn't afraid of being put in rough situations where my life was on the line. I actually thrived on that. But as I stood looking out the window with my phone in my hand, contemplating calling Becca to ask her out on an actual date, I was scared to death. I finally got the courage to dial her number, feeling much like a teenage boy getting ready to ask his first crush to the school dance.

My heart raced from just hearing her voice. "Becca Keeton."

"Hey, Becca. It's Mason."

"Agent – I mean, Mason. How are you? Is everything okay?"

"Oh, yeah. Everything is good. I – umm. I wanted to see if you would like to get together. This time, non-business related."

There was a short pause that seemed like eternity to me as I waited in angst for her reply. "Oh, well when were you thinking?"

"Whenever is good for you," I said.

"Well, I have a dinner that I have to go to tomorrow night but I'm pretty much free the rest of the week."

"Okay, how about Wednesday night? I'll pick you up at seven?"

"Uh… yeah, sure. That'll be great." I could hear the slightest bit of hesitation in her voice that I had wished I could make disappear. "Wait, you're not doing this because you pity me for what I said the other night about me dating?"

"Not at all, Becca, and to prove that I'm not, I'm going to have you order for both of us without even reading you the menu."

"Oh boy, that could be scary," she giggled.

"I'll see you Wednesday, Becca."

We said our goodbyes and hung up. I continued to stare out the window, suddenly questioning everything in my life. *What was I going to do about this promotion? What was I doing with Becca?* I knew that it was wrong to try and start something back up with her just like I knew it was wrong back then, but in both cases, I couldn't stop myself even if I had tried. I had spent my entire career trying to convince others that I was someone else. Now, here I was trying desperately to get Becca to see who I really was and fall in love with me all over again. I knew that it wasn't going to be easy. But the more difficult the challenge, the more rewarding the results.....and Becca was worth the fight.

Chapter 33

Wednesday was finally here. After a long day of some pretty big busts, I stopped home and took a quick shower before heading to Becca's to pick her up. I was shocked when I opened the door to leave and saw Gina standing on the other side.

"Welcome back, Mason." She smiled as she took a step inside. "Thanks." I looked away.

"I found this when I was going through some old things. You must have left them at my place." She handed me a box containing all of my vintage CDs.

I did my best to manage a smile. "I was wondering what happened to those."

"You look…..you look really good." I could see her eyes beginning to fill with tears. I nodded, not knowing how else to respond. *Do I tell her that she looks really good, too?* Gina was gorgeous, she knew it and everyone that came in contact with her knew it, too, but she was nowhere near as beautiful as Becca. "Are you headed out somewhere?" she asked.

"Yeah, I am," I responded, running my hand through my hair.

"Mason, I didn't mean to hurt you. It's just that Nathan, he's always around when I need him. It's like even when you weren't working undercover you were never really fully here. Your mind was always off somewhere else and I just needed more."

"That's perfectly fine, Gina."

"I'm not quite sure if that comes with the territory of your job or if it's because you're still pining for someone in your past. Maybe if I could have just understood which one it was a little better, then maybe –"

"It doesn't matter anymore, Gina. What you and I had is in the past and I really do wish you nothing but the best with him."

She bit her bottom lip and nodded. "Yeah well, I wish you nothing but the best, too, and maybe one day you'll find that girl you're after. The one that made you that painting that you so carefully display. The one whose photo you still keep in your nightstand drawer. She really is a lucky girl to have someone like you carrying a torch for her because I know from firsthand experience, that's no easy feat." She stared at me one last time before sweeping a kiss across my cheek. "Be safe," she whispered.

"Always am." I raised my eyebrows at her and gave her a quick smile. She wiped the tear that was rolling down her face and walked out the door.

I stood there staring into space long after she disappeared out of site, wishing that I could be feeling some type of emotion, whether it was hurt over the end of our relationship or anger over the fact that she cheated on me. But the only feeling I could conjure up was relief. I was never in love with Gina, far from it, and I hated knowing that she had fallen in love with me. I felt guilty for not being able to reciprocate those feelings. She was right; the girl who made me that painting and whose picture I kept tucked away was the reason why. Becca was the one and only girl that would ever own my heart and it was an unfair advantage for any other woman that even dared to try and find their way in.

"Okay, make me feel like a total idiot!" I said as I watched Becca pick up her rice with her chopsticks like she was eating off a fork.

"Why is that?" She laughed.

"Because you're showing off with your chopstick skills and I can't even hold the damn things!"

She began to laugh even harder. "Oh Drew – it's not that hard!" The smile instantly disappeared from her face as well as mine. "Oh my God. I am so sorry. This just brought back a memory of something for me." I closed my eyes for a brief second, knowing exactly which memory she was thinking of—the night she had given me the painting. She was silent, lifting up her glass and taking a sip of water.

I decided to break up the awkwardness of the moment. "So, Becca, have you ever tried Cajun food?"

"No, can't say that I have." I was happy to see a smile coming back to her face.

"Well, I make the meanest jambalaya around."

"Is that so?"

"Yup, it is. You'll just have to come over one night and try it."

"Well, on one condition."

"What's that?"

"You have to promise to eat it with chopsticks."

I couldn't hold back my amusement as I reached over the table and grabbed her hand to shake on it. "Deal," I said.

"Okay, in that case I would love to try some of your jambalaya."

Her eyes moved and finally locked with mine. "Well then, how about Saturday night?"

"Can't....going to the movies."

"Oh well then....."

She started to giggle. "I'm kidding! Kind of pointless for me to go see a movie, don't ya think?"

"I don't know. I thought maybe you just listened to it or something."

"Nah, I was never a big movie person even when I could see."

I looked at my watch as the waiter brought the check. Just enough time to get to Battery Park and see the sunset, which used to be one of Becca's favorite things to do. Becca cracked open her fortune cookie and handed me the paper inside. "Read it to me, please."

I took it from her hand and read it aloud. "Don't be afraid to smile, you never know who's falling in love with it."

Her grin became wider. "Hmm....wonder who that could be? The waiter maybe?" She joked. "What does yours say?"

I opened my cookie and read the fortune inside to myself. "There's not one in there," I lied.

"What do you mean there's not one in there?" she asked. "Mason, do you not want to tell me your fortune?"

My laughter gave it away.

"Can I take the check, sir?" the waiter asked as he walked over to the table.

I nodded.

"Excuse me, Mr. Waiter, can you please read to me the fortune that this man sitting across from me either has in his hand or sitting in front of him on the table?"

I let out a loud laugh, finally surrendering my fortune over to the waiter as he picked it up and read it to Becca.

"He likes to flirt, but toward you his intentions are honorable."

Her smile deepened and so did mine.

"Now what was so bad about that? I actually think that was sweet!"

I stood up and took her hand, leading her out of the restaurant. The profanities were spewing from my mouth as I tried without success to flag down a cab. "What's the hurry?" she joked.

"You'll see," I said, feeling relieved when an empty taxi finally pulled up. "Battery Park," I said to the driver.

Becca looked at me strangely. "Why the big rush to get to Battery Park?" she asked as we got in.

"Because we're going to watch the sunset."

"Oh, well….I think you have forgotten one thing."

"What's that?"

"I can't see it." I knew she was trying to make a joke, but I could see the pain in her eyes.

"You will, Becca….I'll make sure you do, and it will be the most beautiful one you've ever seen."

The sadness that was all over her face was beginning to wash away. "Okay, I'm going to hold you to that."

"You got it!"

Chapter 34

We took a seat on an empty bench just as the sun was setting. "Did we make it in time?" Becca asked.

"With about a minute to spare. Close your eyes, Becca," I said as I stared out into the river. "Tell me what you see?"

She sighed deeply and appeared to be deep in thought. "The sky is lit up in shades of pink and peach. Oh, and now I see some lavender. So many different colors. Colors that I never even knew existed." The smile came back to her face and I couldn't hold back mine from just seeing the enjoyment she was getting from this. "The sun is so bright. It looks like a giant yellow ball with a beautiful pink halo. Its rays are reflecting off the water like angel wings. It's so big but it's becoming smaller with each passing second as it sinks into the skyline, leaving just the remnants of the day and hope for a new one." She took a deep breath and her eyes remained closed. "It's so beautiful," she whispered as a tear rolled down her face. I looked down at her hand that was now on top of mine, wanting to grasp it tighter.

"Keep that picture in your heart forever, Becca, and you'll always be able to see the sunset whenever you want."

I moved my head closer to her and grazed her lips. I hoped that it wasn't too soon for her, but I just couldn't resist. A slight smile stretched across her face, putting my mind at ease. I stood up and grabbed her hand. As we strolled along the pier for some time with our arms looped together, I could feel her moving closer to me. I didn't want this moment to end. I wanted to be here with her forever. There was a comfortable silence between the two of us; the kind that you only experience with someone who knows you just as well as you know yourself.

"Is the moon out yet?" she asked once we finally came to a stop.

"Yes."

"Tell me what it looks like, Mason."

I looked up at the star filled sky that looked so much like her painting, wishing so badly that she could see just how beautiful it looked tonight. "It's a half moon," I whispered.

"Which half is out?"

"The right."

She closed her eyes and bit her lip. "It's waiting for its other half to make it complete."

"Do you think it will find it's other half and become a full moon?" I asked.

"It's not proper to ask the moon of its intentions. It's best to just wait and see how the phases play out and if it's meant to be then that full moon will shine brightly."

My hand swept down her face and my lips were gently pressing into hers. I waited for her reaction before I continued. She opened her mouth, allowing my tongue access and bringing me right back to the night of our very first kiss. I pushed her hair behind her ear and stared down at her once our lips disengaged. We were both silent for a moment as I tried to get over the excitement of feeling her lips on mine once again. I closed my eyes as her soft gentle fingers swept across my face while her other hand reached for mine.

"Thank you for allowing me to see the sun and the moon again," she whispered.

"Anytime, Becca." I looked up at the moon once again, hoping that it would find it's other half. Hoping that Becca would see that she and I were meant to be.

"Hello? Earth to Mason," Liz said, waving her hand in front of my face.

"What's up?" I asked, lifting my head from my computer.

"When is the Grand Jury hearing for the Mueller case?"

"Two weeks."

"Are you all prepared with your testimony?"

"Yup. Good to go."

I knew where this was going. This was her way of indirectly trying to find out what was going on with me and Becca and I wasn't biting. I didn't feel like hearing another lecture. Liz would never completely understand how I felt about Becca and that I couldn't control how I was feeling in my heart.

She took a seat opposite me as I tried my best to look busy, hoping she would just leave. "So, Natalie and I are meeting up with a few of her coworkers for drinks tomorrow. There's going to be some cute single girls there. Would you like to join us?"

Okay, she was using another tactic. I laughed to myself at how well I could read her. "Nah, already got plans."

"Oh? Do tell?" she said with a raise of her eyebrow.

"A gentleman doesn't kiss and tell, Liz. Even you should know that." I smirked.

"These plans wouldn't happen to be with a certain prosecutor, would they?" I pretended to be interested in something on my computer, completely ignoring her question. "Mason!"

"What?" I raised my voice in annoyance.

"You're smarter than this."

"Liz, just stop, okay? I appreciate your concern, but I got this all under control."

She was so damn stubborn. I knew she wasn't going to just let it go. She shook her head and gave me her trademark look of disapproval that I had grown so accustomed to over the years. "Okay, so what's going to happen when she wants to introduce you to her family and her friends….hmmm?"

"I'll deal with that when and *if* that time comes."

"Look, Mason, I get it. You were in love with this girl, but don't you think she's been through enough heartache? Don't lead her on again just to believe another lie. If you're going to make a go of it with her, then you need to come clean and tell her everything."

I knew she was right, but I knew if Becca knew the truth then it would be over before it even began. "I will when the time is right." She sighed heavily, stood up, and started to walk away. "Hey Liz." She turned around and stared at me, waiting for me to speak. "Does your friend, Derrek still have that art studio?"

She looked at me strangely. "Yeah, why?"

"Can you do me a favor and ask him if I can use it for a couple of hours tomorrow afternoon?"

She let out a loud laugh. "Mason Boudreaux, you don't have a creative bone in your body!"

"I know I don't."

The smile quickly vanished from her face. "O-h-h!" She shook her head as I gave her a pitiful pleading look. "I cannot believe that I'm going to be an accomplice to this!"

"Love you, Liz!" I grinned.

"I'll see what I can do. Just promise me that you'll think about what I said?" I nodded. "Preferably, before she falls back in love with you."

Chapter 35

Even though Liz talked a good game, she had arranged with her friend to allow us to use his studio for a few hours. She had texted me the address, the combination to get in, as well as letting me know that he had set everything up for Becca to be able to paint. Of course she had to type out: *I CAN'T BELIEVE I'M BEING A PART OF THIS! TELL HER!* at the end of her message. I arrived at Becca's to pick her up, waiting for her to say her goodbyes to Lilly like she was never going to see her again. "Is she okay, being left alone for long periods?" I asked.

"Of course! My Lilly is an angel. Actually my neighbor, Linda, that lives across the hall is a big help with her. She takes her out for me all the time when I'm going to be gone for long periods of time." We walked out of her apartment and into the bright sunlight. "Wow, it's pretty warm out," Becca said while grabbing the hair clip off her purse and twisting her hair up into a sexy messy bun with ease. "So what is your big surprise?" she asked.

"You'll see." I flagged down a cab and opened the door, helping her in. I gave the driver the address and I could see Becca's mind instantly working, trying to figure out where we were going. "Give it up. You're not going to figure it out!" I laughed.

"Well, it was worth a try!" She giggled.

Her phone began to beep loudly as a pre-recorded woman's voice came through the speaker. "Call from Jordan." She dug through her purse until she had her phone in her hand.

"I'll just be one second," she said.

"No problem."

"Hey you, what's going on?"

I looked out the window as Becca listened to her brother on the other end before speaking again. "Well, I would love for you to come and visit me! Just let me know the dates so I can schedule a few days off......Okay, love you, too!" she said before hanging up the phone.

"Sorry, that was just my brother."

I nodded. "You just have one brother." I posed it more as a statement. I hated pretending like I didn't know.

"Yeah, Jordan. He's four years younger than me. If one good thing came out of my accident, it was that it straightened him out."

"What do you mean?" I asked.

"Well, he was getting into his fair share of trouble with stuff that he had no business being involved in, and after my accident it totally made him grow up. He stopped all the nonsense and was there for me more than anyone." I closed my eyes and swallowed hard. "He went to college out in Colorado and decided to stay after graduation. He says it's because of the great teaching job he found out there. I say it was to get far away from my parents."

"Doesn't he get along with them?" I asked.

She shrugged her shoulders. "I guess just about as well as I do, anymore." I knew that Becca and her dad had their problems in the past, but I thought that maybe they had resolved them. "My dad....he always treated me like I was two years old. Never let me make my own decisions and when I did, he would make sure that he would fix it so it was always his way." She sighed deeply and closed her eyes. "You know, I think he was actually happy after I lost my sight because it made him feel like he could control me more; so that just made me more determined. I wasn't going to let him win. He took everything that I ever cared about away from me. I wasn't going to be his poor blind little girl that he had to take care of." The tone in her voice was now turning to anger. "When I got this job and told him I was moving to the City, he told me I was crazy and it was going to be too hard and too dangerous for someone like me." She laughed. "*Someone like me*....A blind, naïve girl. That's how he views me, just a stupid blind girl. That's always how he viewed me, only before I was just a stupid girl who could see. No matter how hard I tried, it was never good enough." She wiped the tear that was rolling down her face. "Oh God, I am so sorry for unloading this all on you. I just get so angry sometimes when I think about him."

"It's okay, Becca." I stared out the window, feeling somewhat responsible for her resentment that she was harboring against her father. I knew that our relationship back then was the source of the animosity between them. Not to mention that Becca thought that he was the reason that I left her.

"So do you see your parents a lot?"

"I talk to my mother on the phone at least twice a week. She comes to visit every now and then. We always had a great relationship. My dad has been to my place once. I visit them when I can, but it will never be the same."

"I'm sorry, Becca."

"No biggie! The past can't be undone. If it could, I would have done things a lot differently and I would be sitting here *looking* at you instead of trying to figure out if I'm talking to the back of the taxi driver's head." She forced a smile.

"You have such determination. Such drive. You don't let it get you down. I admire that."

"Oh believe me.....I have my days where Satan himself wouldn't want to be around me."

We remained silent for the rest of the ride to the studio. She looked as if she was emotionally drained after talking about her father and I didn't want to make her more upset by continuing the subject. I helped her out of the taxi when we pulled up to the building and grabbed her hand, leading her inside.

"Can you please tell me what we are doing?" she giggled.

"You'll see!"

"Umm….no I won't."

"YEAH, you will!"

She sighed deeply and shook her head as I helped her up the steps. I took out my phone and pulled up the text message with the combination. I punched in the number on the door, and was relieved when it opened on the first try. I took Becca's hand and led her in, watching as she inhaled deeply.

"I smell paint." She tilted her head and her eyes were almost looking into mine.

"Come here, Becca." I took her and led her over to where the canvas was all set up and picked up one of the brushes. I placed it in her hand so she was touching the bristles.

She crinkled her eyebrows and shook her head. "Oh no. I can't –"

"Yes, you can. I want you to paint that beautiful sunset that you saw in your mind the other night."

"Mason, seeing it in my mind and painting it are two totally different things. I can't even see the paint colors."

"I will help you with that."

She sighed heavily. "I just don't think I can do this."

"Yeah, you can. Just tell me the colors that you need."

She bit her lip like she was deep in thought. "White, red, yellow, and blue."

I found the tubes of each color that she requested. "Okay, got them."

"Okay. Is there a palette or something where you can squirt just a little bit of each color onto?"

I looked down at the counter right by the easel and located the board that I was assuming was the palette. "Yup."

"Okay, squirt just a little bit of each color onto it."

I grabbed each tube and followed her instructions. "Okay, done."

"I need a two inch flat brush." I looked down at the array of paintbrushes sitting on the counter, picking up the one that looked closest to that description. I placed it in her hands and let her feel it to make sure that I had the right one. "Gently dip it in the white." I turned the brush around so the handle was in her hand as I guided it over to the paint and lightly dabbed the brush into it. "The whole canvas needs to be covered in white." Her hand was gripping tightly to the brush as I moved it over to the canvas. I stood behind her and held lightly to it as she began to sweep the brush over the entire area. "Is it all covered?"

"I guess. It was white to begin with so it's hard to tell."

She began to laugh. "I'm thinking the horizon should be yellow." My hand moved with hers to the yellow paint, gently dabbing it in. "We need to be in the very middle of the canvas."

"Okay, its right in the middle," I said. Our hands swept a thick straight line across the center with the yellow paint.

"Okay, mix some red in with the yellow," she directed. I mixed the colors together, letting her know when I was done. "Now we're going to put some orange above the yellow." I moved her hand and helped her guide it just above the yellow. "I think we should leave a little bit of the corner open for some blue. Kind of like a promise for a brighter day. What do you think?" She turned around and was so close that it was taking everything inside of me to not reach down and kiss her lips.

A smile was plastered across her face. I could see her confidence building and her body relaxing with each stroke of the brush. I was having just as much fun, as she taught me all about mixing the colors and blending them into the picture.

"Well, how's it look?" she asked once we were done. I stood back, taking it in. It really did turn out great and I was quite impressed with myself and my ability with helping her paint it.

"It came out awesome."

"Seriously?"

"Seriously, Becca. You did great."

"No.....*we* did great!"

"I had nothing to do with it, Becca. I was just your eyes. You're the one that painted it."

I took the brush from her hand and placed it on the counter. "Holding those brushes in my hand....that was the best feeling in the world. Thank you, Mason."

"Anytime, Becca."

She reached up and placed her hands on my cheeks. "That was really sweet of you. No one has done anything that nice for me in a very long time." She stood on her tiptoes and brushed her lips against my cheek. I inhaled the intoxicating clean scent of her perfume and I wanted more, but for the moment I would just settle with being with her and seeing the happiness in her eyes.

Chapter 36

"That was so much fun painting today. Thanks again, Mason. And I must say you are a pretty good cook, too," Becca said as we took a seat on the couch after dinner.

"Thanks. My mama taught me well."

She lifted the glass up to her lips and took a sip of her wine. "So have you always lived in Louisiana?" she asked.

"Yup, first time I ever left was when I was eighteen years old and left for basic training."

"So how long were you in the Marines?"

"Four years. My mom was diagnosed with cancer at the end of my enlistment. The doctors wanted to start her on chemo and she refused. They told her without it she could expect to live six months. She decided not to do it. She didn't want to put herself through it. So I didn't reenlist. I wanted to spend all my time with her."

"Oh, Mason, I'm so very sorry." Her hand reached for mine, finally finding it and interlocking her fingers with mine.

"Don't be. She found this really great Homeopathic doctor and took the holistic route. She's been Cancer free for seven years now."

A smile returned to her face. "That is awesome!"

"Sure is. I don't know what I would do without her."

"Do you have any brothers or sisters?"

"An older sister, Amy."

"So you and your family are close?"

"Yeah, we are."

"Well, your mother raised a fine southern gentleman, Mr. Boudreaux."

"Why thank you, Miss Keeton, and if you don't mind me saying, your mother and father made one beautiful woman." She began to blush, the same way she would way back then, whenever I would pay her a compliment. I placed my hand on her face and gently swept my thumb up her cheek. "No need to be embarrassed, Becca. I speak the truth."

"Well, I wouldn't know. I haven't seen what I look like in six years." Her eyes began to glass over. "I can't wear makeup unless someone else puts it on me. I have to let my hair dry whichever way it pleases. And I could be talking to you right now and have a giant piece of food stuck between my teeth and wouldn't even know it."

"Oh, is that what that green thing is between your two front teeth?" I teased. She giggled and shook her head. I moved closer to her and she took a deep breath. "Do you want to know what I see when I look at you?" The smile disappeared from her face and she nodded. I removed her hair clip, allowing her hair to fall down around her as I stared into her eyes. "I see a gorgeous woman with chestnut brown hair that falls to the middle of her back in natural, loose waves." I gently tucked the strand that was hanging in her face behind her ear. "Her face is so beautiful that she doesn't even need makeup. Her lips are a natural shade of red that no lipstick could ever match." I could see her blushing every now and then, trying to hold back both a smile and tears. "But my favorite part of her is…. her eyes. She has the most stunning eyes I have ever seen in my life. They remind me of the first really hot summer day and staring into a crystal clear swimming pool. The water looks so blue, so refreshing, and so inviting. You're dying to jump in and cool off but you want to test the water first to make sure it's okay." She swallowed hard as I leaned in and tasted her lips, unable to get enough of them. She opened her mouth, allowing my tongue access, and moved her hands down my back and I was instantly aching to be inside of her.

We were both breathing heavily as we ended our kiss. She placed her fingers on her bottom lip before sucking it in. "Is the water okay, Mason?"

"It's perfect. What about for you?"

She nodded. "But I'm a little afraid. I haven't swam in a while and the last time I did, I nearly drowned."

I took her hands in mine. "I promise you, Becca, I won't let you go under."

She grabbed my face and her lips were on mine once again. I gently laid her down on the couch, moving my lips to her neck. "Mason?" she whispered.

I lifted my head, staring down at her beneath me, trying to catch my breath. "I haven't been with anyone since my accident."

I bit my bottom lip and at that moment I was glad that she couldn't see the look on my face. *Was I the only man that she had ever been with?* I was instantly brought back to the very first night that we had slept together and that scared look that she had on her face. The same look that was on her face right now.

"I promise it will be okay," I gently whispered in her ear. Her warm, soft hands gripped the side of my face and she pulled my head down to hers as our tongues collided once again.

I picked her up and carried her into my bedroom before gently placing her down. She stood in front of me and lifted her arms, allowing me to remove her shirt with ease. I unhooked her bra and watched it drop to the floor. Placing my hands on her hips, I stood silently staring at her perfect body, remembering what it felt like to have my lips all over it. Our tongues began to clash as I lifted my shirt over my head and pulled her into me. She gently stroked my bare back and I could feel myself growing harder by the second. I undid her jeans and gave them a tug. She helped me out by pulling them down further and stepping out of them completely. I could feel her trembling as I laid her down on the bed. "Becca, don't be scared. I promise you, it will be fine," I whispered in her ear before placing a gentle kiss on her neck.

"I just have had my heart broken in half before and I'm afraid. Doing this for the first time in years and not being able to see…..it's just scary for me both emotionally and physically. But I do trust you, Mason."

"Why do you trust me, Becca?"

I turned on my side and pulled her close, feeling her heart beating a mile a minute against my chest. "I don't know. There's just something about your voice, your touch, that tells me you're a caring, gentle person. It's weird, but I can sense it inside of me almost like I've known you for years instead of just weeks."

I closed my eyes and rested my lips on the top of her head. If she only knew….would she be more at ease or would she be even more afraid? "We don't have to do anything, Becca. We can stay here just like this in each other's arms for the rest of the night until you feel one hundred percent comfortable."

She wrapped her arms tightly around me. "Thank you," she whispered, placing her warm soft lips on my chest while breathing in deeply. "Your cologne?" She lifted her head and stared off into space as if she was deep in thought. It was the same cologne that I had worn for years. The same cologne that I had used when I had first met her. I was filled with both hope and dread that maybe she was putting it together. She placed her head back on my chest. "I like it," she whispered.

Her lips trailed down my stomach as her fingers moved around, finally finding the button on my jeans. It was as if the scent of my cologne was all she needed to wash away her fear. Her hand reached under my boxers and began to stroke me, and I was instantly yearning to be inside of her. I pulled my jeans down some more, allowing her easier access. She moved her head further down until her tongue was sliding up and down my rock hard erection. I closed my eyes and ran my hands through her hair, basking in the familiarity of the moment as she wrapped her lips tightly around me.

"Oh fuck Becca!" I shouted.

It felt so damn good as I stared down at her taking me further in her mouth. She looked like that same girl from years ago, the one that I had restored confidence in. Not the scared one that was lying on my bed, trembling just moments ago. She was my Becca; the one that I had fallen in love with. The one that had trusted me enough years ago to be her first and was now placing that same trust in me again. And I, in turn, would make sure that I didn't let her down this time. She had made my body feel things that it had never felt before back then, the same way she was doing right now.

She moved up closer and whispered in my ear. "I'm ready to dive in completely, Mason. I'm ready to feel the water around me." I pushed her hair from her face, more than willing to obey her wishes. I removed her underwear and stared at her beautiful naked body. I couldn't resist placing tiny gentle kisses on her hips as my fingers moved in and out of her. "Mason, please. Don't make me wait," she begged, arching her back eagerly waiting in anticipation. She didn't need to ask me twice. I removed my jeans and boxers.

"Becca are you on birth control?"

She reached for my face and kissed me hard. "Yes, now please don't make me wait a second longer." I stood over top of her and slowly eased myself into her as she let out a loud cry of pleasure. I had to stop and catch my breath for a second as all of the memories of being with her so long ago came flashing through my mind. She felt so good, like her body was made just for me. I leaned down and kissed her hard as I moved in and out of her, getting in a slow and steady rhythm with her own movements.

"Is this okay for you?" I whispered in her ear.

She closed her eyes and nodded, swallowing hard. Her hands moved up and down my back and I was hoping that she sensed the same familiarity as I did with each move that I made. My tongue found its way to her hardened nipple as her breathing was becoming heavier. I could feel her heart beating faster as her body began to tighten up around me. She arched her back and screamed my name as I continued moving in and out of her. I kissed her on the lips as she tried to catch her breath, but I wasn't ready to let her just yet. I wanted to make up for all those years I had been without her. I turned her on her side so her back was pressing up against me as I entered her once again. My hands reached around her and cupped her breasts while my tongue cascaded her neck. I slid my fingers further down until I reached that spot between her legs, that spot that I knew could drive a woman crazy with one simple touch. I continued to move in and out of her as my fingers began to play with her, instantly causing her body to tremble.

"Oh my God, Mason!" she begged, but I wasn't letting up. I wanted her to enjoy every single second of this.

She threw her head back into my chest, screaming loudly as her entire body contracted. I could feel it building up inside of me. Six long years of dreaming of this moment, yearning to feel her touch and be inside of her again. I couldn't hold back any longer. I pulled her closer and with a few steady movements, I lost it completely inside of her. I wrapped my arms around her as we both tried to catch our breath.

"That was really great, Becca," I said, kissing her on her shoulder. I looked down at her, noticing the tears rolling down her face. "Are you okay?"

She nodded. "I don't know what my problem is. I'm just feeling so mixed up about all this right now. It's just been a while for me since I felt this way. I forgot what it was like. And then there's the whole mixing business with pleasure thing.....I mean, we're working together on this case. I just don't want it to get weird now between us with work. Not to mention if anyone finds out."

I turned her around so she was facing me and tilted her chin up to me. "Hey, how are they gonna find out? Unless, of course, you go bragging to everyone about how great I am in bed."

She let out a loud giggle that made me smile in return. "Your secret is safe with me."

"Well, you can still brag to me," I teased.

She laughed again and lifted her head, placing a gentle kiss on my cheek. "Thank you for making that so wonderful." I pushed her hair from her face and kissed her on her head. She moved in closer and nuzzled into my chest while I rubbed her back until she fell asleep, just like I always did after we would make love. I was unable to take my eyes from her as she slept. I wondered who she was seeing in her dreams. Was she making love to Drew Bryant or Mason Boudreaux? I pulled her closer and watched her breathe. She was so beautiful. So perfect, and for the moment, she was mine once again.

Chapter 37

I sat in Becca's office as she went over the last of the questions that were going to be presented to me today at the Grand Jury hearing. I had talked to her almost every day in the two weeks that had passed and we had gone out three more times, but sitting here in her office with her and Frank we acted as if we hardly even knew each other.

"Well, I think Becca has properly raked you over the coals and prepared you for this well," Frank teased.

"Yeah, she's good." I caught Becca's cheeks begin to redden as she looked down at her desk. Frank looked over at her and smiled.

"She's the best." *Yes, sir, she is.* "Well, I'm going to get another cup of coffee before we head in. Care for one?" he asked. I shook my head. "What about you, Becca?"

"Oh, no thanks, I'm good."

"Okay, I'll be back to get you in ten," he said.

"Sounds good."

"So, are you going to wow that jury and get us those indictments?" Becca asked.

"If I do, do I get a reward?"

She bit her bottom lip and giggled. "Agent Boudreaux, are you bribing me?" she whispered.

"Could be."

"Well, let's see what you get us and we'll see about the reward."

"Okay, sounds fair." My eyes burned into her, focusing my attention on the neckline of her shirt and how it accented her cleavage perfectly. I had to look away. The last thing I wanted to do was walk into that courtroom with a total hard-on because I was thinking about Becca's flawless body and having my lips all over it. "Will you be in the courtroom?"

"No, not unless I'm requested to be."

"Well, can I request you?"

"Now, why would a seasoned agent like yourself need me in the room with you?"

"So I can stare at your beautiful face the whole time."

She leaned over her desk and whispered, "Have you forgotten about our mixing business with pleasure deal?"

"No, I haven't. Have you?"

She creased her forehead. "No, I haven't."

"Well then, can I suggest that you stop wearing that perfume that makes me crazy and that top that shows off that beautiful body of yours?" She let out a giggle. "Oh and while we're at it, when you wear your hair up like that I can't stop staring at that sexy neck. So, I do believe that you, Miss Keeton, are the one that is breaching the terms of our agreement."

Her hair fell flawlessly around her shoulders and down her back as she reached behind her and removed her hair clip. "Is that better?"

"Nope. No matter how hard you try, you will never *not* be sexy."

I wanted to reach over her desk and kiss her warm, soft lips among other things that would totally break our business and pleasure agreement. I stood up and stared at her for a few seconds. She looked around the room, clearly still sensing my presence. "What are you doing?" she asked.

"Just memorizing your gorgeous face so I can think about it the whole time I'm in the courtroom."

She let out a loud laugh and shook her head. "Silly boy, go find Frank and get us those indictments."

"Congrats. I heard the Grand Jury handed down indictments on all sixteen charges," Liz said as she smacked me on the head with the file folder in her hand. "Drinks with me and Nat to celebrate?"

I looked down at my desk.

"Well, I'd love to, if you don't mind if Becca comes along."

She took a seat opposite my desk. *Shit, here we go!* "I don't mind at all. I told you before, I love Becca, but have you made any progress with what we had discussed previously?"

"Liz, you know I love you, but can you just butt out of this one?"

"So, I'm taking that as a 'no'." I looked at the computer screen, not wanting to respond to the question that she clearly already knew the answer to. "Okay, what time and where?" she finally relented.

"You tell me."

"Hmm….let me get back to you on that one. I'll text you later." She got up from her chair just as Agent Knox came walking into the office. "Agent Knox, sir, how are you?" Liz asked, standing at attention and removing the sarcasm that was normally second nature from her voice.

"I'm doing well, Agent Diaz."

She nodded and wasted no time making an exit.

I immediately stood up and extended my hand. "How are you, sir?"

"Well, that depends," he responded as he took Liz's now empty chair. "Have a seat please," he said, trying to be as informal as possible. "You know it's no secret that I want you for Johnson's job."

"I'm aware of that, sir."

"Well, I'm getting mixed stories through the channels. Do you want it or not?"

Talk about being put on the spot. "Well, to be honest, sir, I'm not sure. It's a lot to think about. I mean, you should know first-hand; you were an undercover for well over fifteen years before you came into the office. "

He raised his eyebrow and ran his hand over the side of his face. Crossing his leg and leaning back in his chair, he intertwined his fingers and rested them on top of his bald head as if he were deep in thought.

"I do know, very well, and you remind me so much of myself when I was your age, it's scary. You have the same drive that I had, the same ability to take charge and remain cool in any situation. I listened to many of the wires that you have worn and I have to say, I was quite impressed with how you handled some of those situations."

"Thank you, sir." I nodded.

"But the time to come out of the field is before you get burnt out. Don't be like me and have nothing left in your personal life when you do finally decide to take your life back." I furrowed my brows in confusion. "I'm fifty nine years old. I have an ex-wife who hates me. Two kids who are like complete strangers to me because I was never around to raise them, and three grandchildren who are even more foreign." I looked away for a minute, not knowing what to say. Agent Knox was a hard ass and to hear him spilling his heart and soul out to me made me feel a little awkward.

"I know you're still a young guy, but don't let this job dictate how you're going to live the rest of your life. This is a great opportunity for you and I think you would be a natural at it because you know everything that the people working under you are going through. Take time to think about it. Does a month sound fair?"

I nodded. "Yes sir, very fair."

I stood up at the same time as he did and shook his hand once again before he exited. I took a deep breath, knowing I was going to have a lot to think about throughout this next month. I was broken from my trance when I saw Becca's name flashing on the caller ID. If there was one person that could be the determining factor in this whole decision making process, it was the girl on the other end of that phone.

Chapter 38

Becca and I walked into the restaurant and I immediately spotted Liz and Natalie sitting in the bar area. I took Becca's hand and led her over.

"Hey Becca! How are you!?" Liz said in an overly friendly voice that was so unusual for her.

"Hi, Liz. How have you been?" Becca asked.

"Uh, okay I guess," she replied, sounding more like herself. Natalie stood up, waiting for an introduction. "Becca, this is Natalie, my partner, fiancé, girlfriend, take your pick."

Natalie took Becca's hand in hers and shook it. "It's so nice to meet you, Becca," Natalie said.

"And you as well." Becca smiled. I pulled out the bar stool for Becca and she sat down, immediately jumping into conversation with Natalie. She was so enthralled by Natalie's job as a social worker and the time that she spent volunteering at the women's shelters that I had to ask her three times what she wanted to drink before she finally answered.

"Well, it looks like Natalie's trying to steal away your girlfriend," Liz teased.

"Not a chance," I said.

"So what did Knox want today?" Liz asked as the two of us started up our own conversation while Becca and Natalie continued theirs.

"To talk about that promotion." I took a sip of my beer and looked straight ahead.

"And? What are you going to do?"

"I got a month to decide."

Liz nodded and looked over at Becca. "Or does *she* have a month to decide?" she asked, raising her eyebrow at me.

"Liz, don't start up with that again."

She held her hand up in defense. "I'm not. Just thinking out loud."

"Well, quit thinking, okay?"

I looked over at Becca. She was unable to wipe the smile from her face and every now and then I would hear that beautiful laugh of hers come from deep within. Liz was right in her assumption once again. This decision was going to be solely based on Becca. I knew I was going to have to tell her the truth by the time the month was up. If she would be able to accept it and want a life together as badly as I did, then I would take that job in a heartbeat. I just wanted her to realize who I was without me telling her. I wanted her to feel that connection to me, the same one we had all those years ago, even though I knew that once she did I could lose her forever.

"Oh Becca, if you would do it, that would be so awesome!" Natalie exclaimed. I stood up and wrapped my arm around Becca's waist.

"Do what?" I asked.

"I would love to have Becca be a guest speaker at one of our meetings for women of domestic violence. If these women could see how much she has achieved without her eyesight then maybe it would empower them to become stronger as well."

"Well, ummm…..that sounds like a great idea, but….." Becca said.

"But what?" I asked.

"Well, I'm just a little nervous about it."

"Becca, you have nothing at all to be nervous about. You'll do fine," I said.

Natalie shook her head and her smile became wider. Becca took a deep breath like she was deep in thought. "Well, I suppose I could."

"Ah! I love you!" Natalie screeched, throwing her arms around Becca.

"See that, the first pretty girl that comes around and she's already in love," Liz joked, lifting her drink up to her lips as we all began to laugh. I could just sit and watch Becca for hours as she talked to Liz and Natalie. Every time I was with her, I could see her becoming more and more comfortable with herself and with me. I was seeing so much of the old Becca tonight, the way she would throw her head back and laugh or move her hair completely to one side and twirl it around her finger. The way that her warm, soft skin felt underneath my fingertips as I stood by her and gently caressed the back of her neck. She leaned her head back into me and I breathed in her perfume, making me wish that we were all alone instead of a restaurant full of people. Liz ordered another round of drinks for everyone and held her glass up. "To Mason and Becca, for getting all sixteen indictments in the Mueller case."

"They're only indictments, Liz, he hasn't been found guilty yet," I said.

"Are you saying that you don't have faith in this beautiful prosecutor here to get the convictions?" Liz asked.

"Nope. I have all the faith in the world in Becca."

Becca smiled widely and Liz lifted her glass up once again. "Well then, like I said, to Mason and Becca….the perfect team!"

Liz looked at me and winked before we clinked our drinks together.

I leaned down and whispered in Becca's ear, "I forgot I have a reward I need to claim." She grabbed my hand and began to giggle loudly. Liz shook her head in defeat and chugged down her drink, but not before giving me a huge smile.

Becca unlocked her apartment door and wrapped her arms around my neck. "Now, about that reward…" She grinned.

"I'm listening."

Her hands swept down my face as she stood on her tiptoes and placed a gentle kiss on my lips. "Well, here's what I was thinking. Maybe it shouldn't be just one set prize. Maybe we should leave it up to our imagination and see what happens."

I bent down and moved her hair from her neck, unable to resist planting gentle kisses along it. "That sounds like a great plan," I whispered in her ear.

"On one condition."

"What's that?" I asked

"You have to spend the night."

"I agree to those terms." I smirked. She let out a loud laugh when I picked her up and carried her through the doorway, more than willing to take whatever reward that she wanted to give.

Chapter 39

The week was flying by and I was spending every single free minute that I had with Becca. I had just got off the phone with my sister, who informed me that she had planned a last minute party for my parents' fortieth wedding anniversary. I had been crazy busy at work with all of the drug busts that were going down, but I knew I had to try and get a few days off to fly down there or I would never hear the end of it. I waited for Becca to answer her door when a thought came to me.

"Well, hello gorgeous." I smiled upon seeing her standing there looking just as sexy as ever in her cut off shorts and tee shirt.

"I'm sorry, is there someone standing behind me to which you are speaking?" she joked.

"Nope, it's all you, Baby!" I pulled her close and stuck my tongue in her mouth as Lilly sat by my feet, waiting to be pet. Once I got done giving her owner the proper greeting, I bent down and gave Lilly some attention.

"She's trying to butter you up. She wants to go for a walk," Becca said.

"Well, then let's take her. It's a beautiful day out." I grabbed

BLIND SIDE OF LOVE

Lilly's leash from the hook and put it on her, taking Becca's hand in mine and heading out the door. I gave Becca the leash once we got outside and we began our walk, letting Lilly lead the way.

"That is just so amazing. How she is so well trained," I said, looking down at Lilly who was completely focused on the task at hand.

"She is my lifeline. I seriously don't know what I would do without her."

We stopped along the way and got ice cream and took a seat in the outside seating area to eat it. I tried my best to distract myself from getting totally turned on as Becca licked the side of her ice cream cone. "So Becca, have you ever been to Louisiana?"

"Nope. Can't say that I have!"

"Do you want to go?" I asked. She looked up from her ice cream, looking a little surprised. She shrugged her shoulders, clearly waiting for me to elaborate. "My sister planned a last minute anniversary party for my parents next weekend and I would love for you to come."

"Oh, umm....." It was too soon for her, and I instantly regretted asking her when I saw the look on her face.

"No big deal if you don't want to. I just thought maybe you would want to get away."

"No, I do and thank you so much for asking. It's just...I would have to make arrangements with Linda to see if she could take Lilly and –"

"Becca, really it's okay. I understand it's last minute. It's not a big deal. I just thought I'd put it out there."

She sighed heavily and nodded. "Well thanks for thinking of me." She forced a smile, staring off into space like she was deep in thought, before finally breaking her silence. "Mason?"

"Yeah."

"Did you tell your family about me?"

"Yes, I did."

"Do they know?"

I shook my head in confusion. "Do they know what?"

"That I'm blind."

"Of course." She looked down at the table and her eyes filled with tears. "What's wrong, Becca?"

"Nothing."

I reached over and grabbed her hand. "Becca, please tell me. What are you thinking?"

"Well, why would you want me?"

"What? Why wouldn't I?"

"You're so good to me, you have this great personality and I'm fairly certain that you're not bad to look at either, so why would you want to be stuck with someone who can't even walk down the street without a dog or holding someone's hand? You deserve so much better than that." The tears were now streaming down her face and I felt like I was taking a slow bullet to my chest.

I lifted her hand to my lips and placed a gentle kiss on her knuckles. "Because when I look at you I see so much more than just a blind girl. You make me happy, Becca. You make me feel things that I haven't felt in a very long time. So to me there is no one better; you're the best there is. I wish you could see what I do when I look at you. Please do not ever think that you are not good enough."

I took her ice cream cone that was melting all over the place and threw it in the garbage. I handed her a napkin and she wiped off her hands. I could still see so much doubt all over her face and I hated it. I stood up and grabbed her hand. As she got up, I took her face in my hands. "If I have to tell you all day, every day just how special you are until you finally believe it, I will. I will do whatever it takes for you to see yourself exactly how I see you." She began to reveal the slightest of smiles, which in turn made me smile. She wrapped her arm around me tightly and handed me Lilly's leash before we headed back off for our walk.

I wasn't sure if my body or brain was more exhausted as I sat in work, wrapping up the last of the reports from the epic week of arrests that had gone down. I was headed home tomorrow for a few days and wanted to get everything done before my time off. I tried not to think about not seeing Becca for the next few days. I knew I was going to miss her like hell. It was as if she had read my mind when I looked down at my phone and saw her name on the caller ID.

"Hey there, Gorgeous," I answered.

"Want to hear something funny?"

"After the day I had, it's going to take a lot to make me laugh, but shoot."

"Well, I just happen to be able to get off tomorrow and Friday and Lilly's going to be spending time with Linda and her husband. So I think I may be pretty lonely."

I could feel the smile stretching across my face, hoping I was deciphering her cryptic message correctly. "Oh well, that seems pretty sad to me, not funny." I played along.

"Hmmm...... I suppose. But maybe if there's still room on a certain flight to Louisiana I may have to take a trip down there. Assuming I'm still invited, of course."

I immediately pulled up the flight information on the computer and booked Becca a seat.

"Getting you on the flight as we speak," I said.

"Boy, Agent Boudreaux, you sure do work fast."

"Yes, I do! Well…..not all the time."

She let out a loud laugh and I couldn't hold mine back either. "Flight leaves at eight fifty seven in the morning. I'll be at your place to pick you up at six."

BETH RINYU

"I'll be ready and waiting."

"See ya tomorrow, Becca."

"See ya! Well, actually I won't, but you know what I mean." She giggled.

I shook my head and smiled as I hung up the phone. Becca was actually going to meet my *real family* instead of thinking they died in a car crash and I had no one. I knew that I should be happy; I was finally able to bring her into my world freely. But deep down inside, I felt like I was living a bigger lie than I was back then.

Chapter 40

It felt good to be pulling in my parent's driveway for the first time in two years. It had been too long since I had been home and I missed it. My mother loved New York City and her and my dad had been up to visit me quite a few times. Although, I loved seeing them, it still wasn't the same as being home. I took a moment and stared at the four bedroom brick colonial that I had lived in my whole life. Some of my best memories took place right in that house. Growing up, I loved spending my time running around my parents' six acres of land, riding horses, fishing, and hunting. I couldn't have asked for better parents than mine, they were so warm and caring. They accepted everyone for what they were and I knew that once they met Becca, they would fall in love with her the same way I had. I looked over at Becca, who had fallen asleep on our way from the airport.

"Hey, sleeping beauty," I whispered, gently tapping her on the shoulder.

Her eyes shot open. "Are we here?" she asked in a very groggy voice.

"Yes."

She reached for the elastic band that was around her wrist and pulled her hair back into a pony tail. Reaching into her purse, she grabbed a piece of gum, popped it in her mouth and put on a quick coat of lip gloss. "Okay, I'm ready."

I stared at her for a brief moment. She was so beautiful and she made it seem so effortless. She got out of the rental car and stood by the door, waiting for me to get the bags from the trunk. I threw each of our bags over my shoulder and grabbed Becca's hand. I could feel her tensing up. "Becca, don't be nervous. I'm telling you, my parents are the most welcoming people in the world."

She nodded, but I could tell I still hadn't completely convinced her of that. I opened the door and led her in. "Mason! Is that you?" I heard my mother's voice coming from the kitchen. She was grinning a mile wide when she saw me and Becca standing in the foyer. I put the bags down on the ground and let go of Becca's hand, allowing my mother to throw her arms around me. "Oh it's so nice to see you home, Sweetie."

"It's nice to be here. Mom, this is Becca."

My mother instantly focused on Becca, taking both her hands in hers. I could tell that she had fallen in love with Becca's beautiful eyes right away just by the way she was staring at them. "Becca, I cannot tell you how great it is to meet you."

"Thank you, Mrs. Boudreaux; it's nice to meet you as well."

"Please, call me Nadine."

Becca nodded and finally loosened up a little and smiled.

"Nadine! Where did you put the watering can?" my father shouted from the back door.

"Dennis, can you please come here? We have company."

The back door slammed and my father made his way down the hallway. A huge grin was plastered across his face when he saw me. I idolized my dad growing up and still did. He worked hard his whole life, allowing me to have the great childhood that I had.

"Well, hell, this isn't any company and you're not too old to give your old man a hug."

I placed my arm around him and he pulled me into his embrace. "You're looking good, son."

"Thanks, Dad."

"And who is this pretty lady here?" my father asked.

"Dad, this is Becca."

"Boy, Mason wasn't lying when he said you were beautiful."

"Thank you. It's very nice to meet you." Becca smiled.

My mother winked at me and gave an extra smile. "Mason, your old bedroom is all made up." She placed her hand on Becca's arm. "I'm with the times and I'm perfectly fine with the two of you sharing a room unless, of course, you would rather not."

Becca's cheeks began to turn red. "Umm....no, I'm okay with sharing a room." I grabbed her hand to try and ease her embarrassment.

"Well, go get settled. I'm just going to the market to grab some more things for dinner," my mother said.

I took Becca's hand and led her up the stairs and into my room. She stood in the doorway as I placed the bags down on the floor. I grabbed her hand and showed her around the room. "There's a bathroom right here." She nodded as I led her out the door and onto the veranda that overlooked the backyard. "And this right here was the best thing ever when I was a teenager. Do you know how many times I would sneak out of the house in the middle of the night down this?"

She let out a loud laugh. I pulled up a lounge chair and helped her sit down. "That warm sun feels so good," she said. I sat down next her and she rested her head on my shoulder. "It's so peaceful here. No horns honking or sirens. The air smells so fresh and clean."

"Yup, it's like being in a totally different world."

"What do you see when you look down?"

"Green. Everything is pretty much green. I can see my father's stable in the distance and the pond that I would fish in as a kid, but other than that not much else except for trees."

"Your dad has horses?" Her voice perked up.

"Yeah, he owns three and boards a few. He's an equine vet."

She lifted her head from my shoulder and smiled. "Really? That is so cool! So you grew up around horses?"

I began to laugh. "Yeah, I think if my dad could have had them eat dinner with us every night, he would."

"Wow! That is so awesome!" She rested her head back on my shoulder, but her smile remained. I kissed her on the top of her warm, strawberry scented head.

"Did you want to meet a few of them?"

"Who?" she asked.

"The horses."

"Yeah, that would be great!"

"Okay, in a little bit. But first I want to take a little rest." I pulled her close to me as we lay in the lounge chair. The warm summer breeze rustled the leaves on the trees along with the stray hair that was sticking out of Becca's ponytail. I looked down at her and pushed the hair out of her face. Her eyes were closed and her head was resting on my chest. "What are you thinking, Becca?"

"How happy I am right now. How I wish I could just freeze time and stay this content and relaxed forever." She wrapped her arms around me tighter. "What about you?"

"How happy I am that you agreed to come and how good it feels to have you in my arms."

"This would make a beautiful painting, you know?"

"Well then maybe when we get back you should paint it?"

She smiled and took a deep breath. "No, this is a moment that I want to keep all to myself, right in here." She placed her hand on her heart. "There are very few moments that I store in there, but I can tell you that each and every one that I do, I will never forget.

So, thank you for giving me another beautiful image to have inside my heart forever."

After a two hour nap, Becca and I were getting ready to head out to the stable. I sat on the bed, waiting for her to brush her teeth and wash her face.

"Hey, could you do me a favor and make sure I stuck my ID back in my wallet? I'm ninety nine percent sure I did," she shouted from the bathroom. I grabbed her wallet and looked through its contents, finally coming across her ID.

"Yup, it's there."

As I went to slide it back down into the slot, something was stopping it. Once I was finally able to get a grasp on it, I pulled it out and my stomach dropped as I stared at the picture of me and her taken on the night of the auction. She looked so happy. Her beautiful blue eyes that matched her dress perfectly sparkled for the camera. I knew that there was something different about her from the moment I had first saw her standing there that night all alone, looking so out of place. She wasn't a young typical girl whose beauty would fade along with her youth. There was something timeless about her and the fact that she was totally oblivious to just how beautiful she was made her even more attractive. I flipped the picture over and wished I hadn't when I saw what she had written on the back: *Best night ever....best guy ever.* I couldn't believe she carried around that photo after all of these years. I quickly shoved it back in her wallet when I heard the water turning off. I got up and went into the bathroom, handing her a towel to dry her face.

"Thank God it was there. That would have really sucked if I had forgotten to get it back after going through security." I watched as she patted her face with the towel and I couldn't resist hugging her. I wanted us to be that couple in that picture again so badly, and I would do whatever it took to try and make that a reality.

She smiled up at me. "What was that for?"

"No reason. Now, come on; we have to go see a man about a horse."

Chapter 41

"Hey there, where did you two run off to?" my dad asked as we walked into the stable.

"Fell asleep," I replied. "Becca wanted to meet your horses."

"Do you like horses, Becca?"

She nodded. "Love them!"

"Have you ever ridden?" my father asked.

"Yeah, a long time ago."

"Well, did you want to try again?" he asked.

She shook her head and the smile disappeared from her face. "Oh no, I really couldn't now."

"Why not?"

"Well, because I can't see."

He waved his hand in the air as if it were no big deal. "Oh, is that all?" He wrapped his arm around Becca's shoulder. "Do you think any of these horses know that?"

"No, but –"

"They can see just fine. They'll lead the way." I stood there quietly. I didn't want to pressure her into doing it. I remembered how nervous she was last time about getting back on and she was able to see back then, so I knew that this had to be a hundred times scarier for her now.

My father took her hand and led her over to a stall. "Herman, I want you to meet Becca. She's a little scared to get back on just because she's blind." I shook my head over my dad's frankness and I was happy when I heard Becca let out a little giggle instead of taking offense. He grabbed Becca's hand and placed it on the horse's forelock. "Becca, say hello to Herman."

The smile that stretched across her face when she touched that horse did something to my heart that I had never experienced before. It was so genuine and I knew she was having the same feeling that she did when she touched the paint brushes that day in the studio.

"What kind of horse is he?" she asked.

"He's an Arabian."

"Really?" Her head turned in my father's direction. "Is he brown?"

"Hey, I thought you said you couldn't see? I think she's lying to us, Herman," my father teased.

Becca let out a loud laugh and was still grinning from ear to ear. "I want to try and ride him," she blurted out.

I gave my dad an uneasy look. He held his hand up to me and nodded, his way of assuring me it would be fine. My dad knew these horses better than anyone and I knew that he wouldn't do anything to jeopardize Becca's safety. But I was still afraid of her getting in a panic once she got on it, and the horse in turn sensing that fear.

"Okay, let me get him saddled up and you can show us what ya got, kiddo."

I walked over to Becca and stood behind her. She couldn't wipe the smile off her face. It made me happy to see her so excited, so I did my best to try and hide my anxiety over her doing this. I wrapped my arms around her. "Are you sure you're going to be okay with this?"

"Yeah, I really do want to do it," she replied with a strong determination to her voice.

"Okay, Becca. You're date is all ready to go."

She took a deep breath and I led her out to the horse. My dad held on to the reigns as I helped Becca get on. I could feel her trembling. "Don't be scared, Becca."

She nodded as she swung her leg over its back like a pro.

"I did it!" she exclaimed as she proudly sat on top of the horse.

I nodded and smiled over her enthusiasm. "Yeah, you did!"

My dad took the line and walked the horse around the pen as Becca's smile grew bigger. "I think Herman really likes you, Becca!" my dad said. She looked totally relaxed and confident. If I hadn't known better, I wouldn't have even guessed that she was blind.

"Can I take him around by myself?"

"Do you feel comfortable enough doing that?" my dad asked.

Becca nodded. "I do! I really do!"

"Well then, let me remove this line and you can be on your way." My heart raced in anticipation as I watched him take the line off the horse. He moved out of the way and stood next to me.

"Dad, I don't think this is a really good idea. What if –"

"Hush, Son. She can do this. Just because she's blind doesn't mean she has to fear everything. She wants to do it, let her. Herman won't let her down."

"Okay Becca, take a deep breath," my dad shouted.

"Hey what's going on?" my mom asked, making her way out from the stable. "Oh no, Dennis. She shouldn't –"

My dad turned around and looked at both of us. "If you two are going to be sending off these bad vibes to Herman then please go back in the house. Becca wants to ride."

"Go ahead and pull on the reigns." Becca did as he said and the horse began to trot off. I was ready to run to her when I saw her entire body jerk once they started off, but my dad grabbed my arm to stop me. By the time they were halfway around, Becca's smile reappeared and it was her biggest one yet. "Just let Herman be your eyes, Becca! Trust him!" my father shouted. She nodded as they began on their second lap, this time going a little faster. My dad shook his head with his smile almost as big as Becca's.

"She is one brave girl," my mother said. I could see her eyes welling with tears from just watching the enjoyment that Becca was getting out of being up on that horse.

"Yeah, she is," I whispered.

"Okay Becca, pull on the reigns and start slowing him down."

She did as my father said and the horse slowed down before completely coming to a stop. She was so excited that she didn't even wait for me to help get her off. She dismounted him perfectly.

"Whoa, easy there," I teased.

"I did it, Mason! I did it! I rode a horse again!" She threw her arms around my neck. I picked her up and spun her around, placing her back down on the ground and wiping away the tears that were rolling down her face. "I never thought I would be able to do that again!"

"You did it, Baby, and you were great!"

I hugged her tightly and looked over at my mom and dad, looking just as proud as Becca with smiles plastered across their faces. My mother wiped a tear away and rested her head on my dad's shoulder.

Becca removed her arms from around my neck and reached over to the horse. She gently swept her hand up the side of his face. "Thank you, Herman," she whispered.

"You were like a pro out there, Becca!" my father shouted.

"Thank you so much for allowing me to do that."

"You are most welcome."

I took Becca's hand and headed out of the stable. "Where are you two headed off to?" my mother asked.

"I want to show Becca around."

"Okay, but don't disappear; dinner is going to be ready in a few hours and your sister will be here. I know she's dying to see you and she can't wait to meet Becca."

"Mom, relax; we're not going far."

I loved seeing my parents and spending time with them, but I loved being alone with Becca more. And right now, I wanted to be alone with her in one of my favorite places.

Chapter 42

We walked for some time before coming to a stop on the dock of the fishing pond. The sweat was pouring off both of us as we took a seat under the huge Weeping Willow that was blocking out the hot July sun.

"Well, it certainly is a lot more humid than back home," Becca said, fanning herself with her hand. "But it feels much better now. Are we in the shade?" she asked.

"Yup, there's a giant Weeping Willow over top of you and straight ahead was where I would catch some pretty big catfish back in the day. This has always been my best thinking spot."

"So, how many girls did you kiss in your *best thinking spot*?" she teased.

"Not a one!"

"Oh, you are such a liar. I can hear it in your voice."

"None that really mattered......until now." I reached over and planted a gentle kiss on her lips. She sucked in her bottom lip, looking like she was waiting for more.

"Okay, *Miss Prosecutor*, my turn to ask the questions now?"

"Okay, go right ahead." She smiled.

"How many boys have you kissed?"

Her face turned that adorable shade of red that I had grown so accustomed to. "Ummm…..I don't know. I never really kept track."

"Oh, that many?" I teased.

"No, actually. I was a good girl for a long time." The smile that was on her face suddenly shifted. "Until I met him."

My heart began to race. "Who?" I whispered.

She closed her eyes and shook her head. "Just some guy, who I thought was pretty special….turns out that he didn't feel the same way about me." God, this was killing me. I wanted to confess and tell her everything but I knew this wasn't the place or time. "I was just so stupid to think that the first guy I ever slept with would be the love of my life and want to be with me forever. But sometimes when you really want to believe something, your mind can manipulate you into really thinking it's true."

I cleared my throat and took a deep breath. "I'm sorry, Becca," I whispered.

"Don't be sorry, because if that were true then I would have never met you, so maybe everything does truly happen for a reason. Just wish the blind part didn't have to be part of it." She pulled herself together. "So what other kind of fish are in this pond?" she asked, totally changing the subject, but I could see the pain in her eyes.

"Oh…. um lots." I stopped talking and looked up at the sky when I heard thunder rumbling in the distance. Dark clouds were now winning out over the once sunny sky and the first drops of rain were beginning to fall. I took Becca's hand and helped her up as the rain became heavier. "Come on, I know a place we can go until it passes. Hop on!"

"What?"

"On my back."

She giggled as she climbed on my back. I walked a long way until we were inside one of my father's old barns that were on the property. The rain was coming down in sheets by the time we made it inside and both of us were soaked.

"Well, that was fun!" Becca laughed as she hopped off my back. "Do I look like I entered a wet tee shirt contest?"

"Just a little. And you would definitely be the winner," I teased. I moved in closer and kissed her on the lips. She placed her hands on my face and smiled. "Have you ever had sex in a barn, Becca?"

"No, can't say that I have."

"You want to check that off your list?"

"Hmmm….that depends. Who's the guy?"

I lifted her soaking wet shirt over her head and removed her bra, gently laying her down in the pile of hay. "Me," I whispered in her ear.

"Well, in that case….sure."

Her hands moved down my back and removed my shirt. I unbuttoned her shorts and removed them while she did the same for me. I reached under her panties and stuck my finger inside of her. She was so ready. She closed her eyes and a smile spread across her face as my fingers slid in and out of her. I could feel my erection growing more and more with each move my fingers made. My mouth found its way to her breast, teasing her with my tongue. I lifted my head and stared at her body. She was perfection. Everything and anything a guy could ask for.

"Becca, do you know how bad you make me want you, just by looking at you? You are so fuckin' gorgeous. You make me so hard just thinking about you."

She moved her hand under my boxers and began to stroke me up and down. "Well then, I guess you must be thinking of me a lot right now?" she teased.

"Oh yeah!"

"What are you thinking about, Mason?"

"You."

"I know that, silly, but what are you thinking about doing with me?"

I couldn't hold back my smile. "Do you really want to know?"

She nodded. "Well, right now I'm thinking about kissing this sexy neck." She giggled as I pushed her hair away and began to nibble on her neck. I glided my tongue down further. "And right now, I'm thinking about your beautiful naked body and how I can stare at it all day and never tire of it. It's the most perfect one I've ever seen."

She let out a loud laugh. "Oh, and just out of curiosity, how many have you seen in your lifetime?"

"Enough," I said as I took her nipple in my mouth. She closed her eyes and swallowed hard, running her hand through my hair.

My fingers trailed inside of her again. "And what are you thinking now?" she whispered.

"How I want to be inside of you. I want to feel your legs wrapped around my waist as I'm moving in and out of you, feeling your warmth and making you cry for more." I pulled down her panties and removed my boxers. She pulled me close when I eased myself into her. "I want to feel your body tighten up around me like it was made for only me, Becca." Her breathing became heavier and my thrusts became harder and deeper. She turned her head to the side and let out a gentle cry. I grabbed her face in my hands. "Open your eyes, Becca. I want you to see me in your mind and feel this in your heart. I want you to know what you do to me." Her eyelids slowly opened and those beautiful pools of crystal blue were staring into mine as if she could see everything. She skimmed her hand along the side of my face. "Do you see it, Becca?"

"I can," she whispered. I grabbed her leg, wrapping it tighter around my waist. "Becca, you are just too damn beautiful," I grazed her earlobe with my teeth just as her body began to contract. "Oh my God, Mason! Please don't stop!" she screamed. I moved quicker and harder. She dug her fingers into my back, looking right into my eyes as we lost it together. I was still inside of her as I tried to catch my breath while she ran her fingers through my hair.

"I love you, Becca." The words were out before I could even stop them. I knew it was too soon for her to be hearing this, but it had been six long years for me. Six years that I had been dying to say them to her and I just couldn't stop myself even if I tried.

"I – I –"

"It's okay, Becca. I know it's too soon for me to be saying that to you, but sometimes my heart starts talking before my mind can stop it. I didn't mean for it to come out."

"It's okay, Mason. Really, it is." She kissed me softly on the lips and I was hoping that she would say it back. I was hoping that maybe something about what we had just shared would have jogged her memory back to *us*. "It's just ….it's just that I've been hurt really bad in love before and I'm afraid." That wasn't what I wanted to hear. The same guy I was hoping she would remember was the same guy that broke her heart in pieces. "But I do know that I feel this strange connection when I'm with you. I feel safe. I feel beautiful. I don't feel like the blind girl that everyone pities. I feel normal."

I pushed her hair from her face and kissed her on the forehead. It's not what I wanted to hear, but I knew it was progress and that's all I could ask for. As she rested her head on my shoulder, I was instantly brought back to one of the hardest days of my life:

Becca laid in my arms after what I knew was the last time that I would ever make love to her. I had spoken with my supervisor earlier in the day and he had informed me that the busts were going to be going down in the next seventy two hours. I kissed her on the top of her head, wanting to tell her everything. Wishing that she would run away with me and we could start up a whole new life together. But I knew that would never happen. Becca had a bright future ahead of her and the last thing I wanted was for her to give up all of that to be with me.

"Can we just stay like this forever?" she whispered, finally breaking the long silence. My stomach dropped. It was as if she

was reading my mind. I pulled her closer and rested my lips on the top of her head.

"Becca?"

"Yeah?" She lifted her head.

"Promise me you will remember this forever."

"Of course I will. And I will remember all the times like this that are yet to come." Staring into those beautiful blue eyes was killing me. I gazed up at the ceiling before finally finding the courage to look at her once again. "Drew, is everything okay?"

No it's not. I'm not who you think I am. *That was all that I wanted to say, but instead all I could manage to get out was, "Yeah, I'm just tired I guess." She placed her head back on my chest and moved closer to me.*

"Then let's take a little nap."

I rubbed her back, and my eyelids began to give out. I was half asleep, but I could still feel her warm, soft lips all over my chest and hear her beautiful voice in my ear as she whispered, "I love you." Closing my eyes tighter helped to subside the burn that I was feeling inside of them, but nothing was stopping the pain in my heart.

I wanted her to know that I was finally answering her back from all those years ago. Those three little words that should have been said to her way back when had finally come out. I only hoped that one day, I would hear her say them to me once again.

Chapter 43

We headed down to dinner after we showered, and were immediately greeted by my six year old niece, Chelsea. "Uncle Mason!" she squealed.

"Hey there, gorgeous girl!" I lifted her up and kissed her on her forehead. "I can't believe how big you've gotten."

"Well, that's what happens when you only come to visit every few years," my sister, Amy, said as she appeared in the doorway.

She gave me a warm smile before approaching me and throwing her arms around me. "I've missed my bratty little brother."

"I missed you, too," I said, hugging her back. "Amy, this is Becca."

I grabbed Becca's hand and my sister reached for her free one to shake it. "It's so nice to meet you, Becca," Amy said.

"Thanks, you too."

Chelsea stared up at Becca in awe, tugging at the bottom of my sister's shirt. "Mommy, she looks like a Disney princess," she said in her best attempt at a whisper, causing us all to break out in laughter.

"Thank you, Chelsea." Becca smiled.

My sister shook her head and smiled as she and Chelsea walked back into the dining room. I leaned down and whispered in Becca's ear, "Told ya you were beautiful."

After dinner, we sat around talking. I was happy to see Becca looking totally relaxed and deep in conversation with my brother-in-law, who was also a lawyer.

"Mason, come into the kitchen and help me cleanup for Mom," Amy said. I got up from the couch and followed her in.

"So, Mom and Dad still have no clue about this party tomorrow night?" I asked.

"Nope, they just think that they're meeting me and Mickey for dinner. So don't let it slip."

"I promise. I won't."

"So, she must be really special."

"Who?" I asked.

"Who? Becca, silly."

"What makes you think that?"

"Well, let's see: for one, you never bring any of your girlfriends home for us to meet. She is absolutely beautiful and you have doted on her for the past hour at dinner."

I looked down at the dirty dishes in the sink. "She's beyond special, Amy."

"I'm happy for you, Mason. You deserve it. Is it hard with her being blind?"

I shook my head. "No, it's like when I'm with her I sometimes forget that she can't see. She's so independent and strong, it just absolutely amazes me. She went through her last year of college and law school, blind."

"Wow, that really is amazing. Well, I really do wish you both nothing but the best. She seems like a really sweet girl."

"Thanks." Amy's opinion meant a lot to me. She and I were always really close and I would still find myself calling her up for advice whenever I needed it.

After we finished cleaning up, we joined everyone in the living room once again. Chelsea was sitting next to Becca, playing with her hair, while Becca sat there looking totally relaxed and enjoying every minute of it. "Chelsea, Sweetie, what are you doing?" Amy asked.

"I'm playing beauty shop." Chelsea smiled.

"Well, I'm sure Becca doesn't want you messing up her hair."

"Oh no, it's fine. It's been a long time since I've been to a *beauty shop* so this actually feels nice," Becca said.

My sister looked at Becca with sadness in her eyes. "Well then, we're going to have to change that. I'm sure my girl can squeeze you in after my hair appointment tomorrow for a little well deserved pampering."

"Oh, that's very sweet of you, but —"

"I insist." She looked around to make sure that my mom and dad were out of earshot. "You have a party to go to tomorrow, so you have to look your best." I wrapped my arm around Becca's waist as I sat down next to her and she leaned her head into me. "Do you think you can manage to be without her for a few hours tomorrow, Mason?" Amy teased.

"Don't know about that," I teased back.

"Well, when you see how beautiful she looks, you'll realize that it's worth it."

I kissed Becca on the top of her head and closed my eyes, knowing it wasn't possible for her to be any more beautiful than she already was.

My sister called to let me know that she and Becca were running late and that Becca was going to get ready at her house. I patiently waited for them to arrive at the restaurant, hoping that my parents didn't get there first. I lifted my head and stood up when I saw Amy walk in the door. "Where's Becca?" I asked.

"Close your eyes," she said, grinning from ear to ear. She stood behind me and placed her hands over my eyes. "Okay, open them," she said as she uncovered them. Becca stood in front of me on my brother-in-law's arm and I was speechless. She was beyond beautiful tonight, wearing a short peach colored studded dress. Her hair was flowing around her face in big loose curls and her makeup was done up lightly to accent her natural beauty. "Just like Cinderella," Amy giggled.

I walked over to her and took her by the arm. "Do I look okay?" she asked.

"Becca, I can't stop smiling. You look gorgeous, Baby."

"The dress looks okay? Amy picked it out when we went shopping today. She said it's not too short, but –"

I placed my finger on her lips to stop her from talking. "Becca, it's perfect. You look perfect and I can't wait to show you off to everyone tonight." I leaned down and whispered in her ear, "There's only one problem."

"What's that?" I could hear her voice rise in panic.

"I'm gonna have a damn hard time keeping my hands off of you all night."

I gently rubbed Becca's back as she slept. Tonight was one of the best nights of my life. Just seeing how happy she was the entire night, holding her in my arms on the dance floor and finally making love to her after four long hours of staring at her perfect body in that dress that hugged her every curve. Even though it was pure sexual torture, it was totally worth the wait. Once I knew that she was in a deep sleep, I got out of bed and slipped on my shorts. I walked outside on the veranda and took a seat in the lounge chair. The full moon was trying to break through the overcast sky and I was hoping that maybe it was some kind of sign. I knew I had to tell her soon. I was hoping that maybe something from these past few months of being together would help her piece it together, but it didn't. Maybe she really did just want to completely erase Drew Bryant from her memory, but then why did she still carry that picture around in her wallet? I ran my hand through my hair, not wanting to think about what just may happen once she knew the truth. I didn't know if I could handle losing her again. The rumble of thunder broke me from my thoughts. I got up upon seeing the flash of lighting in the distance. When I walked inside, Becca was crying out in her sleep. I crept over to her.

"No, Drew please, please don't leave me!" I stood there frozen as the tears overflowed from her closed eyes and down her cheeks. I wanted to go to her and comfort her but something was stopping me. Her cries turned into sobs and I finally snapped out of it. I lay down next to her and held her in my arms, not saying a word. "Drew, please stay with me forever." She hugged me tightly and I hugged her back, feeling her warm tears falling on to my chest and seeping deep into my heart.

Part Three

Becca & Mason

Chapter 44

Becca

Two weeks later.....

The conductor helped Lilly and I off the train and I was immediately greeted by my mother. She threw her arms around me and held onto me for dear life. "Oh, Sweetie, it's so good to see you."

"You too, Mom."

She looped her arm in mine and we walked off to her car. I was already missing Mason, but I knew I was long overdue with visiting my parents. Plus, I had my yearly in depth eye exam which we were headed to. I didn't see the point; it was the same thing each year, my eyes were always the same with no sign of vision ever coming back. My mother helped me in the car and I heard Lilly jump in the back seat. I focused straight ahead when I heard her car door shut. "So, have you been busy with work? I haven't heard from you much these past few weeks," she asked as the car began to move.

"Yeah, I've got a few big cases going on." I wanted to tell her so badly about Mason, but I didn't want her running back and telling my dad. So I did my best to keep it inside and instead listened to her tell me all about the cruise that her and my dad had just gotten back from.

I took Lilly's leash and my mother's arm and we walked into the doctor's office. My mother signed me in as I grabbed my wallet from my purse. "Mom, can you please find my insurance card in this mess of a wallet of mine?"

She took my wallet from me.

"Here's her insurance card," she said to the receptionist. My purse slipped from my hand as we stood there waiting.

"Oh shoot!" I exclaimed.

"I got it," my mother said. The receptionist placed my insurance card back in my hand as I waited for my mother to finish picking up the contents of my purse.

She helped me over to the seating area and I could hear her putting everything back in my purse for me. "Honestly, Becca, do you really need half of this stuff that you carry around with you?" She was quiet for a minute as I heard the sound of papers rustling. "Who did you go to New Orleans with?" she asked. I knew right away that she must have been looking at my boarding pass from my trip with Mason.

"Huh? Oh… ummm… with a friend of mine."

"A friend?"

"Yeah."

"Do I know this friend?" she asked.

I shook my head and I could feel myself turning red. "Spill it, Becca!"

"I met him a few months ago. I've been working with him on a case. He's a DEA agent and just a really great guy."

"Oh, Sweetie, I'm so happy for you."

"He took me to meet his parents down in Louisiana a couple weeks ago. It was so wonderful, Mom." And just like that, I was divulging every last detail to her, exactly what I said I *wasn't* going to do. But I just had to tell someone about how wonderful he was, or I was going to bust. "Please, Mom, DO NOT say anything to Dad about this just yet."

"You have my word, Honey, but I would really love to meet him."

"I know, and you will."

She took my arm and led me into the exam room when the nurse called my name. Lilly circled around my feet and laid down, letting out a loud sigh once I was seated. I reached down and patted her on the head. "You had a busy day today, haven't you, girl?"

"She's such a sweetie," my mom said.

"Yes, she is."

The door began to squeak and the familiar sound of Dr. Jennson's voice followed after. "Well, hello Becca and Mom.....and Lilly."

"Hi Dr. Jennson," my mother and I said in unison.

He began to ask me all the standard questions that I now knew verbatim. Every year my answer to each would be the same. I let out a loud sigh, just wanting to get this over with.

I felt the cold metal of one of his machines pressing against the bridge of my nose and after years of this I knew that he was examining my eyes. "Well, everything looks good," he said after he had gotten done with his various tests.

"Well, of course it does. It couldn't get any worse, could it?" I joked.

"Actually, Becca, I've been working closely with Dr. Greenberg. The man is a brilliant ophthalmic surgeon. He's been performing this new exploratory surgery on several patients that have very similar cases as yours. You would be a prime candidate. It's not a guarantee but about fifty percent of the patients that he has done the surgery on have regained some form of vision back."

My mother let out a gasp. "Oh my goodness, that would be wonderful!"

I, on the other hand, wasn't feeling the excitement. "And fifty percent of them don't?"

"Well, yes, but some chance is better than no chance, Becca," Dr. Jennson responded.

I nodded. "I suppose, but I don't want to be a guinea pig unless I know it's a sure thing."

"Becca, it's a chance you would be taking. A chance to get your sight back," my mother interjected.

"And also a chance of getting my hopes up big time, only to be let down."

She let out a loud sigh and continued to discuss the procedure with Dr. Jennson as if I wasn't even in the room. I didn't want to think about this now. Being able to see again was what I wished for more than anything in this world, but now being faced with that possibility, I had mixed feelings. Not to mention the letdown of falling into the fifty percent that it didn't work for.

"His office is actually right in Manhattan, Becca. He has quite a lengthy waiting list to get into see him, but I'm sure if I give him a call he could get you in."

"Well, thank you, Dr. Jennson, but this is something I'd like to think about and research first."

"Becca, at least-"

"Mom, please. This has to be a decision that only I can make."

"I understand, Becca. I will give your mother his card and if you decide you want to go ahead with the appointment, just give me a call and I'll arrange it."

"Thank you, Dr. Jennson."

"Okay, your eyes are good for another year, but I do hope to hear from you sooner than that."

I stood up and felt Lilly immediately stand up as well. I reached down and grabbed her leash, saying my goodbyes to Dr. Jennson. My mother waited until we were a few minutes into the drive before she began her spiel. "Becca, I know it's a lot for you to think about, Honey, but why? If there's a chance that you may be able to see again, then why wouldn't you do it?"

"Mom, please. I just don't want to talk about it now."

"Becca, please, just-"

"Because I'm scared, Mom, okay?"

"What are you scared of?"

"What if it doesn't work?"

"Well, at least you will have tried."

"Do you have any idea of what a disappointment that would be for me? It's like waving a bone in front of a dog, maybe he can have it and maybe he can't. My world is darkness now. I've accepted that. I've learned how to live with it. I see things so much differently now. I'm able to visualize more than just the physical aspects of a person. I can see deep into their heart and soul, something I was never able to do when I had my sight. The sunsets in my mind are more beautiful than any that I've ever witnessed with my eyes and I don't have to wait until a certain time of day to see them; I could see them all day long if I choose to." I felt my throat lumping up and the familiar burn of tears. "I can see, Mom, just not in the way that most people do, and I'm afraid that if I do get my sight back, then all of those beautiful pictures in my mind and in my heart will disappear forever."

I felt the car pull over and come to a complete stop. She placed her hand on mine and squeezed it tightly. "I understand what you're saying, Becca, I really do. And I'm so happy that you are living your life to the fullest and not letting it hold you back. I'm not trying to push you into making a decision. I just want you to consider it."

"And I will, Mom, I just need some time to process it."

She lifted my hand to her lips and placed a gentle kiss on top. "Thank you," she whispered.

The car shifted back in drive and we were on our way again. "Where are we?" I asked, trying to change the subject.

"Right now, we're just passing by the Barretts' old house."

I still cringed, just thinking about Ashton Barrett all these years later. I hadn't spoken or heard anything about him since my accident. All that I knew was that his father was illegally dispensing prescription drugs. He was able to get himself a good lawyer and turn over some bigger names and his medical license in exchange for jail time. It was the big talk of the town for a while, but I was so wrapped up in my own problems and getting myself back on track that I didn't care to know.

"Do they still live around here?"

"Last I heard, they were living down in Florida. Your father doesn't talk much about anything that has to do with them. He totally wiped his hands clean of Edward and never really cared to say too much about it. But, I do know that Ashton still lives local." I closed my eyes and shuddered at the sound of his name. "Apparently, he's co-owner of the new restaurant that just opened up on Chadwick. There's been some talk about that place being a big front for drugs. Not sure if it's true, but I tend to believe it. Celeste Turner and her husband had gone there for dinner a few weeks ago and said Ashton looked like he was high on something."

"Doesn't surprise me one bit," I muttered. I couldn't believe how much I still despised him, even after all of these years.

"Yeah. Well, I think he had planned on living off his mother and father for the rest of his life and when everything happened, he finally had to work for a living."

"Wow, poor baby!"

My mother let out a light chuckle over my blatant sarcasm, just as the car made a quick right and she threw it in park.

"'We're home!" she exclaimed. To her, this would always be my home, but to me, this was now just a place that I came to visit only out of obligation. Still, I smiled while pretending that I wanted to be there.

My mom walked around to my side of the car and I waited for her to get Lilly from the back seat. She placed her leash in my hand and took my other hand in hers. We began to walk up the walkway when I heard someone shout. "Well, it's about time you show your face around here!"

I could feel the smile molding onto my face at the sound of Krista's voice. Krista and I still kept in touch, but not nearly as much as I would like to. She had been living in Maryland with her now ex-boyfriend and moved back with her parents until she could get herself settled with her own place. She was still the same old Krista from way back when, jumping from job to job and guy to guy. She had dropped out of college and ended up getting her cosmetology license, although the last time I had spoken to her, she wasn't working in a salon, she was waitressing instead.

"I thought this would be a nice surprise for you!" my mother exclaimed. I could hear the happiness in her voice.

Krista threw her arms around me and I felt all of my emotions coming up to the surface. It had been way too long since we had been together and quite a few months since we last spoke. We entered the house as my mother unlocked the door. "Girls, go have a seat on the patio and I'll bring out some snacks," my mother said.

I stood in place, waiting for Krista to take my arm and lead me out. "Oh, I'm such a scatter brain." She giggled, taking my hand in hers.

She pulled out a chair and I took a seat. The warm sunshine, the smell of my mother's rose bushes, and the humming of the pool filter brought back so many summertime memories of the countless hours spent out in this very backyard.

"So, what's going on, Krista? I haven't talked to you in forever!"

"Not much. I've got a job at RW Salon. So now maybe I can finally get a place of my own."

"Krista, that's great! I'm really happy for you."

"Said the successful lawyer to her loser friend."

"What?" I pinched my eyebrows in confusion.

"Look at you! You finished your last year of college, law school, and have a great job….and you're blind. Me, I couldn't even finish up my stinkin' last year of college."

"Krista, stop! Stop putting yourself down."

"I'm just speaking the truth."

I shook my head at her, trying my best to think of something to lighten the mood. "Hey, I want to show you something." I dug around in my purse for my phone. "I had my hair and make-up done for the first time in years!"

"Oh really and what was this for?" "Well…..I met a guy, and if I could ever find my darn phone I could show you a picture. And please tell me if I look hideous in this dress."

"What's his name and how'd you meet him?" I could hear the excitement in her voice.

"His name is Mason Boudreaux. He's a DEA agent and I met him through work."

"Oh, sounds exciting!"

I finally felt the side of my phone and pulled it from my purse. "Go into the pictures section. It should be the one and only picture in there." I giggled.

"Oh, I cannot wait to see what he looks like!" she exclaimed, taking the phone from my hand.

I waited to hear her reaction, but instead there was silence. "Did it come up?" I asked.

"What? Oh… umm….yeah," she said, sounding a little confused.

"Well, what do you think of the dress and more importantly what do you think of him?"

"The dress is beautiful. You look beautiful," she replied,

sounding like someone had stuck a needle into her and sucked all of the excitement that she had been conveying just a few moments ago.

"And? What about him? Is he as cute as I imagine him to be?"

"Umm….yeah, he's really nice looking. So what exactly does he do as a DEA agent?"

"He mainly works undercover and breaks up drug rings."

"Oh," she replied, sounding deep in thought.

"Okay girls, I got ice tea, chips and salsa, and some cheese and crackers." My mom's voice came closer as did the rattling of Lilly's dog tags.

"Krista, show my mom the picture," I said.

"Of what?" my mother asked.

"My new *friend,* Mason."

"Oh yes, hand it over!" my mother said.

"Oh darn!" Krista shouted. "I think I accidently deleted it. I'm so sorry, Becca."

"Oh really? Oh, well I can get his sister to send it to me again."

"Aww, I wanted to see!" my mother pouted.

"I promise I'll have pictures next time, Mom."

"Oh my God. I cannot believe what an airhead I am. I actually have a three o'clock appointment that I just totally remembered. I'm so sorry, Becca. I promise we'll catch up the next time you come and visit." I heard the chair move and felt Krista's lips grazing my cheek.

We said our goodbyes and my mother got up to walk her to the door. I was feeling a little saddened, wishing that Krista and I could have hung out for a little while longer. I jumped when my phone began to beep and the voice on the speaker said, "Call from Mason." Suddenly, I wasn't feeling so down anymore.

Chapter 45

Mason

I said my goodbyes to Becca and slipped my phone back in my pocket just as Liz got back into the car. "Well, did I miss anything?" she asked. We had been waiting on a bust for the past hour and a half and something told me it wasn't going to happen today.

"Not a thing. I think Ortiz got stood up."

"Since when are dealers on time?" she asked.

"True." I remained focused on Agent Ortiz as he stood out on the corner, waiting for the deal to go down.

"So, I haven't talked to you in a while. How was your trip home?"

"It was really nice."

"Did Becca have a good time?"

"Yeah, I think she did."

"Guess she still doesn't know?"

"I'm working on it, Liz." She raised her eyebrows and nodded. "What's that look for?" I asked.

"Nothing. Nothing at all."

"What fuckin' ever!"

"Boy, someone is cranky. Is it because his girlfriend isn't around?" she taunted.

Maybe it did have a little to do with Becca not being around and a lot to do with knowing that my time was coming closer and I had to tell her the truth. Every time I thought about it, I got a sick feeling in my stomach, and I didn't need Liz reminding me of that fact and making me feel worse.

"How do you know she's away?"

"Natalie was talking to her the other day. She wanted to get together with her this weekend to go over the details of the meeting Becca's going to be speaking at."

My eyes shifted to the guy talking to Ortiz, trying not to look conspicuous. I watched as the money exchanged hands. "Can I do the honors?" Liz asked.

"Be my guest." *If it will get you off my case about Becca, do whatever you please.*

"Hey gorgeous girl," I shouted as the conductor helped Becca off the train. I took her bag from her hand and pressed my lips against hers.

"Well, that was a very nice greeting."

I looped my arm in hers and we began to walk. "Are you hungry?" I asked.

"Actually, I am starving."

"Good, so am I." We decided on a place and were on our way.

Lilly lay under the table as we sat in the outside seating area and ate our dinner. Becca told me all about her doctor's visit and the new surgery that he had told her about. "I don't get it. Why wouldn't you want to go for it if there's a chance that you may be able to see again?"

"It's a fifty percent chance," she said very nonchalantly as she took a bite of her fry.

"Okay? And that's fifty percent more of a chance than you would have without it."

"I-I just don't want to talk about it right now." She shook her head and ran her hand through her hair. "So, my friend said you pass the cuteness test."

"What?" I asked in confusion.

"I asked your sister to send me a picture that she had taken of you and I at your parents' party and I showed it to my friend, Krista. She said you were very nice looking. I wanted to show my mom, but Krista accidently deleted it." I felt my insides twisting. *What the fuck?* There was no way in hell that her friend Krista didn't know who I was and then to delete the picture? Clearly, she didn't want Becca's mother knowing, but why? I tried my best to focus on Becca's conversation, but I couldn't turn off the million thoughts racing through my mind. I knew I had no choice but to come clean right away. The last thing I wanted was for her to find out from someone else.

After Dinner, I took Becca back to her apartment. I sat on the couch, battling with my nerves and the fact that this may be the last time we spent together. After tonight she may never want to talk to me again. I took a deep breath and prepared myself for one of the hardest things I was ever going to have to do.

Chapter 46

Becca

It felt so good to have Mason's arms wrapped around me as I cuddled up with him on my couch. Even though it had only been two days since I had last seen him, I missed him like crazy. "Is everything okay?" I asked. "You seem like something is on your mind."

He let out a deep breath and I felt my stomach begin to drop. I could just sense that something wasn't right. "I have one more week to make a choice about this promotion."

"What promotion?" I asked.

"It's a supervisor job. I wouldn't be doing undercover work anymore."

I could feel the happiness building inside of me, but I wasn't going to let it show to him. I didn't want him basing his decision just on how I was feeling. But I was hoping that he would take it. I worried about him every day. At least with this job he would be a lot safer. "Well, what do you want to do?"

"I don't know. I'm just so used to doing undercover work it's like it's a part of who I am."

I nodded, trying desperately to not show my disappointment, but I knew where he was coming from. I was fighting the same battle in my head with this surgery. I had been blind for so long now, it was kind of who I was. "Well, then -"

"But since you've come into my life, everything has changed."

"Mason, I don't want you basing your decision on what I want or because of me. I want you to be happy, and if working undercover makes you happy then please don't let me stop you."

"You know what makes me happy, Becca?" I shook my head. "You."

I closed my eyes, holding back the tears. I didn't deserve this man; he was too good to me. I reached for his hand and wrapped my fingers around it. "Thank you, Mason. That makes me really happy, but will I be enough?"

"What do you mean?"

"Do you really want to be stuck in an office job because you feel like you have to be around to take care of your blind girlfriend? I don't want you to resent me for feeling like I was the reason you took it. I want you to base this solely on how you are feeling. Take me totally out of the equation."

"Why would I do that? You are part of my life now and I don't want to lose you again."

I lifted my head from his shoulder. "Again? What do you mean by again, Mason?" He let out a deep exhausting breath. "What do you mean by again?" I repeated, this time raising my voice a little louder.

He grabbed the back of my neck and pulled me into a kiss. I struggled to break free but he wouldn't let me. I was breathing heavily as our lips finally disengaged. "Becca, tell me who you're seeing when I kiss you."

My head was spinning and I was praying that what my heart had been telling me for a while wasn't true. "I-I don't know."

"Damn it, Becca, tell me!" All the signs were there and I chose to ignore them because I didn't want to believe it. "Say it, Becca!" he shouted.

The tears began to spill. How could this be happening again? "Drew," I whispered.

I backed away when he went to touch me again. "Becca, I wanted to tell you but-"

"But what? You just figured you would use me like you did back then and leave me again?"

"No, that's not what I did back then and that is not what I'm doing now."

"You are a sick bastard, you know that!?"

"Becca, I had no choice back then. My cover was going to be blown. They had you running drugs to some pretty dangerous people and I had to do everything I could to protect you." I shook my head. None of this was making sense to me. "That Simms guy; he is in prison right now for human trafficking. Becca, don't you see? The Barretts' had you doing all of their dirty work and were going to use you as an added bonus for this guy." I covered my ears with my hands. I couldn't listen to any more of it. How could I have been so naïve back then and still be so naïve now? "I may have lied to you about who I was, but I never lied about my feelings for you. I would have given up everything to be with you back then."

"Then why didn't you? Why did you make me feel like I did something wrong?! Why did you make me run off and sleep with someone I hated so badly that I needed to go out and try and kill myself to forget what I had done?" I tried to catch my breath in between my sobs.

"Becca, what are you-?" He stopped himself as if he finally got what I was saying. "Why?"

"Because all I wanted to do was hurt you the same way you had hurt me. I wanted the memory of you gone!"

"Becca, I am so sorry." He placed his hand on my face and I smacked it away.

"Don't touch me ever again! You lied to me now, the same way that you lied to me back then. Everything I thought we had was a lie and I can't believe I was stupid enough to fall for it again! I hate you and I will never ever forgive you for doing this to me again! How dare you use my blindness to your advantage!?"

"Becca, please don't do this! Why the fuck can't you see how much I love you? I never stopped loving you. I wanted to tell you, but I was afraid of losing you again."

"So you just strung me along again and made me feel like I had something special that would make you actually fall in love with a blind girl when the whole time it was just your guilt over what you did to me?"

"I swear to God that's not true. You are special; you always were and you always will be. Don't you see I don't give a fuck that you're blind? To me you are still that same girl that made me fall in love with her all those years ago."

I couldn't listen to it anymore. My heart couldn't handle it. "Leave now!" I shouted.

"Becca."

I pulled my legs up onto the couch and wrapped my arms around them. I buried my head into my knees, completely ignoring him, finally letting out the loud sob I was holding back once I heard the door close. My head was spinning. Was I really that clueless? The smell of his cologne, the way he knew exactly how I took my coffee and my love of sunsets. Why did I choose to ignore all of those signs? I knew the answer to that better than anyone. For the first time since my accident, I had been happy and I knew that admitting to what my extra sense was telling me would take that happiness away, so I chose to ignore it. Yes, he lied to me, but I was partly to blame as well for disregarding that little voice deep inside of me. Then there was Krista… Why didn't she tell me who was really in that picture when I showed it to her yesterday? Lilly jumped up on the couch and whimpered. Her cold nose touched my face and she nuzzled into me, trying her best to comfort me. I wrapped my arms around her and kissed her on top of her head.

"Oh Lilly, you are the only one I can trust." I buried my face into her, letting it all out. Her fur was soaked in tears, but she didn't seem to mind. She stayed by my side the entire night—just like any true friend would do.

Chapter 47

Mason

It had been three days since Becca found out, and it was killing me not seeing her and not talking to her. I missed her so much and I just wished that she understood *why* I did what I did. But I knew I hurt her bad and in her mind it was unforgivable. I had been fooling myself the same way that I had been fooling her by actually thinking that maybe she would have been able to overlook it and move on.

"What's going on with you? You look like shit!" Liz asked when I walked into her office.

"I told her."

Her jaw dropped and an honest to goodness look of concern washed over her face. "Oh no. That bad?" she asked.

I nodded. "Yup, she hates me."

"Well, did you try and explain yourself?"

I ran my hand through my hair and looked out her office

window. "Yeah. She didn't want to hear it. Can't say I blame her." I turned around and faced her once again. "Just don't say 'I told you so'."

She sighed heavily. "I won't. Well, maybe she'll come around once she has some time to digest it all. I mean, she fell in love with you once and it seems as if she was beginning to fall in love with you again, that has to account for something."

"I seriously doubt it. You didn't see the look on her face when I told her."

"What made you decide to finally come clean?"

"This whole promotion thing. I was so up in the air about what I wanted to do and I was hoping that Becca would help me make that final choice. Guess she did now; it just wasn't the choice that I was hoping it would be."

"Well, you still have a few more days to ponder that. Don't give your answer until the last possible second." She stood up and walked over to me, placing her hand on my shoulder. "I have to run. I'll be around later tonight if you need to talk."

I nodded and watched her walk out the door. I remained seated and my mind wondered once again to her friend Krista and why she wouldn't have jumped on the opportunity to tell Becca who was in that picture. It wasn't as if she exactly liked me—far from it. I stared off into space and was immediately brought back to that day that I found out exactly what a bitch that girl really was:

We had just finished up kayaking as I sat around, trying my hardest to seem interested in Ashton's juvenile conversation. Krista was making a complete spectacle of herself, hanging all over Ashton. I couldn't believe that she and Becca were best friends. They were complete opposites.

"So, where's Becca?" Krista asked in a very condescending manner.

"I guess she's home," I replied. She rolled her eyes. "And she's allowing you out without her?" Ashton gave her a high five and they both began to laugh. This girl was a total bitch. Clearly, she wasn't as loyal to Becca as Becca was to her.

"Why wouldn't she?" I snapped back.

"Well, it just seems like the two of you are inseparable. I mean, little Miss Studious is usually so caught up in her school work and her little goody good volunteer work that she doesn't have much time for anyone else. You must be really special or really good at something." She raised her eyebrow and sucked in her bottom lip. I was really hoping that she was acting this way because she was drunk, but something told me that she had some deep seeded jealousy issues with Becca. "She'd better watch out, all this time that she's spending with you may cause her GPA to slip and Daddy won't be very happy about that!" She and Ashton began to laugh once again.

I couldn't stand there and listen to this jealous little bitch rip Becca apart anymore. "Wow! And you call yourself her friend?"

She narrowed her eyes and took another sip of beer. "Oh I'm sorry, did I upset you?"

"You know, jealously is a terrible thing, Krista."

"Oh damn, guess he told you!" Ashton shouted.

"Whatever! Sorry we can't all be perfect like your precious little Becca!" she shouted as I walked off, not wanting to listen to any more of what she had to say.

I spent the rest of the afternoon listening to Ashton and Troy talk about when their next deal was going down and who it was with. When I was satisfied that I had enough information and could no longer take hanging out with these arrogant assholes, I decided to pack it up. As I made my way to my car, I heard Krista calling my name. I reluctantly turned around, not even wanting to acknowledge her. I remained silent as she approached me, looking all disheveled. "You know that wasn't cool; the way you dissed me in front of everyone earlier!"

"Yeah and it wasn't cool the way that you were talking about your so called best friend."

"I'm sorry if I offended you by the things I said. But Becca always had everything that I ever wanted. She's pretty, gets good grades, and now she's got a hot guy." She moved closer to me. "I

for one happen to know one thing that I am better at than Becca. So, I won't tell if you don't." In a matter of seconds her arms were wrapped around my neck and her lips were on mine.

"What the fuck!?" I shouted as I pushed her away, but not before Ashton saw what was going on.

"Damn, Drew, save some of these chicks for the rest of us, bro!" Ashton shouted.

"You are trash that doesn't even deserve a friend like Becca," I whispered to Krista.

"Oh fuck you! Go home and fuck your little goody two shoes then. She's probably like having sex with a rock."

I shook my head and watched her walk away, wrapping her arm around Ashton and throwing her head back and laughing.

Becca had trusted that girl so much as her friend. The same way she had trusted me. I ran my hand through my hair and let out a deep breath. I was no better than Krista. In fact, I was beginning to feel like I was actually worse.

Chapter 48

Becca

"Are you going to be okay?" Linda asked as she helped me take a seat on the couch.

I nodded, still in shock over hearing the words *you're pregnant* come from my doctor's mouth. I had been on birth control since I was seventeen. I took them every day, faithfully even when there wasn't a reason to, except to regulate my cycle. Unbeknownst to me that the migraine medicine my neurologist had switched me to a few months ago would weaken the effects. I had thrown up three times at work in the past week, had been feeling light headed for the past few days, and all I wanted to do was sleep. As much as I kept telling myself it was just a stomach bug, something else was telling me otherwise, and that something else was confirmed today. This couldn't be happening. I felt like most days it was a struggle just to take care of myself. How on earth was I going to be able to take care of a baby?

Linda placed her hand on my shoulder. "Becca, if you need

anything, you know Steve and I are here for you, Honey."

Linda and Steve were the best neighbors that I could ask for and I was so grateful to her for being there for me today. The last thing I wanted was to ask my mother to come with me. I felt as if I had overwhelmed her and my father with enough drama after their visit yesterday when I dropped the whole Drew and Mason story on them. My mother was in shock, but my father, surprisingly, didn't have much to say. I figured that would be the perfect opportunity for him to prove to me that he had been right all along, but instead he just told me how sorry he was to hear it. I, in turn, apologized to him for placing the blame on him all those years for Drew's departure. My parents were just as baffled as I was by Krista's behavior that day when she saw the picture. I had called her several times and left messages asking her *why,* but hadn't received a call back. The knock on my door broke me from my thoughts.

"I'll get it," Linda said.

"Hi Becca." I briefly closed my eyes upon hearing Liz's voice. I knew she was here to plead Mason's case and I just couldn't deal with that right now.

"I'm going to get going, Becca. If you need me, just call," Linda said.

I nodded as I felt Liz taking the seat next to me on the couch. "Liz, I really got a lot on my mind."

"Becca, please just hear me out and then I will be on my way."

I let out an exhausting breath. "Fine."

"I am not going to make excuses for him because I will be the first one to tell you that it was an asshole move on his part. He knows how I feel about it, but in his defense—"

"I don't want to hear it, Liz. I don't! He deceived me not once but twice!"

"And you have every right in the world to be pissed at him for it. But Becca, the first time he had no choice. I pulled up the case that he had been working on back then. You should have seen some of the information that Barrett confessed to the police. That son of a bitch should have been thrown in jail, too. If it weren't for Mason, you might have been in some foreign sex trade. Simms wanted you as a form of payment for expanding the Barretts' drug business. Mason knew this and went above and beyond to make sure that didn't happen."

I shook my head, not wanting to listen to any of it. "Okay, so he just felt like it was okay to continue that same façade six years later and use my blindness to his advantage?" I snapped.

"I will be the first to tell you, he was dead wrong with that. But if he had told you who he was right from the beginning, would you have even given him another chance?" I stared into space, already knowing the answer to that question. "It seems to me that these past few months have been pretty special to you. Just think what you would have missed if he *had* told you. You would have denied yourself the pleasure of falling in love again." I sucked in my bottom lip, trying to hold back the tears. "Despite the bonehead move that he made, he really is a great guy, but I think you already know that. And I can tell you, from someone who knows him very well….he never lied about his feelings for you. He is completely in love with you." I felt her warm hand on mine as I held back my tears with everything I had. I was so angry at him that I didn't want to admit it to anyone that I was in love with him, especially not myself. I felt her stand up and heard her footsteps on the hardwood floor. "This picture?"

"Which one?" I asked.

"The one of the moon and the stars hanging over your loveseat. Did Mason give this to you?"

"No," I whispered. I had wanted to forget about that picture and part of me had wondered why I had even kept it after everything that had happened.

"Mason has the same one hanging in his apartment."

And with that, I could no longer hold back the tears. He had kept that picture with him after all these years? "I painted one for him and one for me when we had first met. I told him that he was the one half of the moon in his and I was the other half in mine. I can't believe he kept it." I let out a loud sob. Liz sat down and placed a tissue in my hands. I dabbed my eyes and pulled it together as best as I could.

"I didn't come here to plead Mason's case. He's a big boy. He doesn't need me to do that for him. I came here to try and make you realize that despite what he did, he really does love you. In two days, he has to give his answer about this job. You were the only thing that was going to make him say yes. I just don't want both of you to pass up the life that you can finally have together."

I sat there silently. I knew I was going to have to tell Mason about my pregnancy and as angry as I was at myself for admitting it, I knew that I wanted to be with him. I just wasn't ready to let go of the anger yet. "Mason needs to do what's best for him. And if working undercover is what he wants to do then that's what he should do." I remained stone faced, not wanting to show my true feelings to her.

She was silent for a moment before letting out a deep sigh and placing her hand on my shoulder. "You take care of yourself, Becca." I nodded and felt her weight lift off the couch. Her footsteps began to fade away and I heard my apartment door open. "Everyone makes mistakes. Just don't let one turn into another one that's going to affect the rest of your life."

I closed my eyes and chased away another bout of tears. "Been there, done that, six years ago, Liz, and I am paying the price every day for the rest of my life."

Chapter 49

Mason

I was miserable with my whole existence. I hated being home and I hated being at work. Everything reminded me of her and how stupid I was for not being honest right from the beginning. I just got done with my run and sat down on the couch, flicking through the channels for about the hundredth time, totally zoned out and not paying attention to what was even on. I knew now more than ever that going back undercover would be the best possible thing for me. Becoming a new person for a while would create the perfect diversion from thinking about her every single second of the day. The knock on my door broke me from my depressive state.

"Hung over?" Liz asked as I opened the door wider and let her in.

"I wish." At least if I was hung over, the way I was feeling would only be temporary, instead of the slow torturous ache in my heart every time I thought of Becca.

"Here's some coffee, maybe that will help."

"Thanks," I mumbled, throwing myself back on the couch.

"Well, tomorrow's the day. Have you decided?" Liz asked.

"Yeah, I have."

She gave me a slight rise of her eyebrow and nodded. I was just about to tell her to spare me the lecture, but I was too late. "Well, before you go into that office and tell Knox one way or the other, there's something I think you need to know."

"What's that?"

"Becca's pregnant."

I choked on the sip of coffee that I had just taken. "How do you know that?"

"Well, I stopped over to see her yesterday and she had a prescription for prenatal vitamins and a bunch of paperwork on her coffee table from an OBGYN....that's a baby doctor in case you didn't know." I ran my hand through my hair, still in shock. "You're gonna be a daddy, Mason, just in case that has any bearing on your decision." I felt a smile instantly conform to my face. The girl I loved more than anything was going to have my baby. I needed to try and make things right with her. Even if she didn't want me in her life, I wanted her to know that I would be there for our baby. "She was still pretty bitter when I spoke to her yesterday, not that I blame her at all, but I think if you talked to her again, maybe, just maybe she can start to forgive." I nodded. "Mason, can I just give one more suggestion and then I will butt out.....I promise?"

"I don't think it's possible for you to ever butt out, but what's that?"

"Us women get very hormonal when it's certain times of the month and especially during pregnancy. So I'm thinking you have a double edged sword to face here. Not only does Becca have raging pregnancy hormones, she's extremely angry with you at present. Just handle her like a very fragile piece of glass and don't get offended or walk away in defeat if she snaps at you. Keep at her. I could see from the look on her face yesterday that she really does love you. You hurt her bad and you deserved to be punished by her silence for what you did. If it were me, I woulda'-"

"Alright Liz, I get it! I know, you would have resorted to violence."

"You got that right!" I stood up and looked at the clock. I had to be at work in a few hours for some arrests that were going down, but I needed to go see Becca right away. I was going to do whatever it took to get her back. I didn't care if it meant camping out in her hallway until she had no choice but to talk to me. I wasn't going to let her go this easy this time. I wasn't going to let her go at all. "Where are you going?" Liz asked.

"I have to go talk to Becca."

"Umm….Mason, just one more thing."

"You said you were going to butt out, remember?"

"Yeah, I know, but since you're going to need all the help you can get with this one, maybe you should take a shower first, instead of going over there all sweaty and gross."

I looked down at my tee shirt still drenched in sweat, silently admitting to myself that Liz was right. I did need a shower….bad! "Now, get yourself looking all handsome and go get your girl back. My work is done here," she said as she stood up from the couch.

I leaned in and placed a quick kiss on her cheek. "Thanks, Liz."

"Anytime, that's what friends are for." She flashed me a quick smile before heading out the door.

I took a deep breath and headed into the bathroom to shower with a new found confidence. I was going to get Becca back, no matter what it took. I was going to prove to her just how much I loved her.

Chapter 50

Becca

Lilly and I were just returning from our walk. It seemed to be just thing I needed to clear my head. I couldn't keep this from Mason any longer and I knew I had to talk to him. After getting some fresh air, I felt like I could finally tackle that. Today had been a good day so far; I hadn't thrown up at all, which was a rarity these days, and I was starting to feel like I had a bit more energy.

"Let's go inside and get you some water, girl," I said to Lilly as she led me down my hallway. She began to growl as I placed the key into the lock. "What's the matter, Lilly?" I asked as her growls suddenly turned into a deep angry bark. "Lilly?" She was starting to freak me out as I felt the presence of someone standing in the hallway.

"Who's there?" I shouted.

My heart started beating faster. I knew that Linda and Steve weren't home, which was only adding to my fear. My hands were trembling as I turned the key and Lilly continued to bark. Relief swept over me when the lock finally opened and I hurriedly made my way in. Just as I walked in and began to close the door, I suddenly felt the force of someone pushing it behind me. Lilly let out a loud snarling growl and then yelped loudly. "Lilly, Lilly are you okay?" I bent down, trying to find her on the ground as she whimpered, when suddenly I felt a hand gripped tightly around my arm, roughly lifting me up. "Who are you?" I cried. They were silent, clearly toying with me, knowing that I couldn't see. I had never been so scared in my life as I stood there in total darkness, clueless as to what was going on. Not knowing what had happened to Lilly and not knowing what was going to happen to me.

"You want to know who I am, Becca?" I froze and was instantly overcome with nausea. I knew that voice; even after all these years, I couldn't erase it from my head. "I'm the guy that helped you fuck away your precious Drew's memory. Well, I see it didn't work too well since you're still with him, so maybe I need to do it again."

"Ashton. What are you doing here? You have no reason to do this to me."

"Oh but I do, sweet little *Becca*. You see, your boyfriend, *Drew, Mason* whatever the fuck his name is, is the reason my family lost everything, which means I have a score to settle with him and what better way to get back at him than to get to you?"

"We're not even seeing each other anymore so you wouldn't be getting to him by doing this."

He gripped his arm around my neck. "Liar! Krista told me how you were going on and on about how great *Mason* is. We had a really good laugh at how stupid you were."

"Krista wouldn't do that to me." I played along, trying to find out why Krista would do such a thing.

"Oh Becca, you really are dumb. Krista isn't your friend, she never was."

I tried to break free when I heard Lilly whimpering once again. "Please just let me see if she's okay."

"What are you going to *see,* Becca? Remember, you're blind. You and I have some business to take care of first and then I'm going to let Mason know exactly how it felt to fuck his girlfriend all over again." He lifted my hair and kissed the side of my neck. "Oh you are just as sweet as always."

"Please, I'm begging you, don't do this." I struggled to break free and he yanked on my arm.

"Becca, don't even think about it. I didn't want this to get ugly, but if I have to, it will." He still had one hand gripped tightly around me while he reached into his pocket. "You feel this, Becca?" he asked, pressing the cold metal against my head. "I don't want to use it, but I will if I have to."

I felt the bile rising up in my throat when his lips touched my neck once again. His free hand moved up my shirt while his other hand held the gun that was pressed up to my head.

I let out a loud gasp when I heard a knock on my door. He covered my mouth with his hand just as I was about to scream for help.

"Becca, it's Mason. Open up. I need to talk to you and I'm not leaving until I do!" he shouted from the other side of the door.

A golf ball sized lump formed in my throat just from hearing his voice and not knowing what Ashton was going to do. He bent down and whispered in my ear, now pointing the gun into my back. "I'm going to walk you to that door. Answer it and get rid of him. I will deal with him *after* we are done having our fun."

The tears were now streaming down my face. I was useless to do anything. All I kept thinking about was my baby. I had to keep him, or her, safe and if doing exactly what Ashton said to do was the only way, then so be it.

BETH RINYU

Chapter 51

Mason

My head was pressed against Becca's doorframe, waiting for her to answer. I was in shock when I heard the door knob finally turning and the door slowly opening. She didn't look herself; her eyes were filled with tears and her hands were trembling. "Mason, I'm really tired. Can....can it wait?" Her eyes widened. Something was definitely wrong. Lilly didn't bark like she normally would when she heard me knocking.

"Becca, what's going on?"

She let out a loud gasp and shook her head. I immediately pushed my way in. I was speechless as I stared into Ashton Barrett's glassy eyes. "Nice to see you again, *Drew*. I wondered what had happened to you and now I know." He pressed the gun that he was holding further into Becca's back while gripping tightly to her neck. "Now, if you are as smart as you think you are, you will hand over that gun that I know you have in your holster and put it right there on that table."

276

"Ashton, let her go. This has nothing to do with her!"

"Put the fuckin' gun on the table!" he shouted. I carefully reached for my gun and placed it on the table, never taking my eyes off Becca.

"There. Now let her go. This is between me and you."

His eyes were dilated and his foot was nervously tapping up and down. I knew he was totally amped up on something, which was going to make reasoning with him even harder.

"No, Drew, Mason, or whatever the fuck your name is today. This does have to do with her. Because I happen to know that *she* is something you care about and what better way to get back at you for fucking up my life than to fuck up something in your life?"

"Ashton, you're really going to sink that low? Taking your frustrations out on a blind, innocent girl?"

"If it will get back at what you took away from me, then I have no problem with that."

"I didn't take anything away from you, Ashton."

"You stupid mother fucker! I have to work my ass off now just to afford the one bedroom condo that I'm living in. My parents were loaded and I was set for life and then *you* had to go and fuck everything up."

I looked at Becca, trembling as he gripped her tighter. I needed to do something. I could see in his eyes that he was desperate and not caring about the repercussions of his actions. "Mason, is Lilly okay?" Becca cried.

"Shut the fuck up about that fuckin' dog already! Do you want me to shoot it and put it out of its misery?" Ashton shouted.

"No!" Becca sobbed.

I looked over at Lilly lying on the floor. Her breathing was labored and I could tell she was in pain. "Don't even fuckin' think about it!" Ashton said through clenched teeth as I took a step forward to check on Lilly. I wished that Becca could see me so I could send her some kind of signal. She looked so helpless

277

standing there. He lifted her hair up and moved his mouth to her ear. "Tell Drew how you begged me to fuck you that night." I watched as she cringed at his words, feeling my own stomach churning in the process. She bit her bottom lip and held back a cry. "Tell him, Becca!" He gripped her tighter.

"No! I won't!" she shouted.

I could see the fury building in his eyes and I knew that I had no choice but to make my move now as he moved the gun up to her head. He looked down at her for one brief second and I knew that was my chance. I lunged at him, knocking the gun out of his hand as Becca broke free from his grip. "Becca, find the door and get out of here!" I shouted. As I went to grab the gun from the floor I felt the weight of him on top of me, tackling me down to the ground. His fist met the side of my face but not before I gave him a good right hook. I looked up at Becca, who was standing there frozen in fear. "Becca, go!" I shouted again as Ashton struggled to get the gun from my hand. I gave him another swift punch in the face with my free hand, still keeping my eye on Becca who was still in the same spot, looking terrified. I just wanted her out of there in case the gun went off, but I could tell she was paralyzed in fear. I held tightly to the gun, getting in jabs, trying to get him off me. He got in one good punch, knocking the gun from my hand as he quickly scooped it off the floor. I looked up at the barrel of his gun and his piercing eyes, which were showing no mercy, immediately feeling the burn of the bullet ripping into my flesh.

"No!" Becca screamed. "Mason! Mason!" she shouted.

I wanted to answer her, but I couldn't. It hurt to breathe and all I wanted to do was close my eyes, but I couldn't yet. I couldn't leave her again until I knew that both she and my baby were safe. I was going in and out of consciousness as I watched Ashton inching toward her. I willed myself to find the strength to grab my gun. I painfully reached up on the table just as he cocked the trigger and aimed it at Becca. The last ounce of strength that I had was exhausted as I shot off two rounds, and watched Ashton fall to the ground. She was safe now….. I could finally close my eyes.

"Mason! Mason!" I could hear Becca's faint screams.

She looked so beautiful as we danced under the star filled sky.

"That moon is beautiful tonight."

"Yeah, it is."

"I prefer half-moons, though."

"And why is that?"

"There's just something about it, you know... kind of like it's looking for its other half to make it whole, but still beautiful just the same."

Her beautiful eyes flashed in front of me. You're safe, Becca; that's all that matters. That's all that ever mattered.

"Mason!" Becca cried.

I was just too tired. I couldn't fight it anymore. Becca was safe and this time I was able to make sure of it before I left her. "I love you, Becca," I whispered, not knowing if my words were even audible, but hoping that this time she heard them loud and clear. A sense of calmness overtook me as I finally gave in to the darkness.

Chapter 52

Becca

"Mason! Please answer me!" I crawled around on the floor and followed his labored breathing. "No, no, no!" I cried as I moved my hand down his body, feeling the warm liquid seeping from his shoulder. "Somebody help me!" I screamed. "Mason, hang on, Baby. Please hang on! I'm going to get you help."

I was so turned around that I didn't know where to begin to look for the door. I moved over to the wall and felt around until I finally located the door knob and ran out into the hallway. "Somebody please!" I shouted at the top of my lungs just as I heard footsteps and Linda and Steve's voices coming up the stairs. "Help me!" I screamed once again.

"Oh my God, Becca!" Linda exclaimed. I could hear the panic in her voice.

"Becca! What's going on? You're covered in blood," Steve said.

I shook my head, trying my hardest to get the words out. "Call nine one one. Mason…." I broke down in tears and felt Linda's arms around me while Steve rattled off the address to the person on the other end of the phone.

I was sobbing uncontrollably as Linda did her best to calm me down. "It's okay, Sweetie. The ambulance is on their way. Steve has EMT experience. He's with him now." I could feel my entire body trembling. I moved my shaking hands down to my belly and all I could think about was our baby. Mason couldn't leave me again. He couldn't. I needed him too much and so did our baby.

"Becca, what happened?" Linda asked.

I tried my best to speak, but my sobs wouldn't allow it. I took a deep breath, hoping that the sounds that I heard coming off the elevator were the paramedics.

"Right in there!" Linda shouted. I stood there, feeling so helpless. I wanted to go to him. I wanted to tell him that he had to pull through this. Linda grabbed my hand and led me into her apartment, guiding me over to the couch. "Just sit down and try and calm down. The ambulance is here and so are the police."

"He can't die on me, Linda. He can't." I broke down completely.

She pushed my hair from my face and I rested my head on her shoulder. "Just calm down and breathe, Becca."

I jumped when I heard a knock on the door. "Come in," Linda shouted.

"Hi, I'm Detective Reynolds. Are you Miss Keeton?" I tried my best to focus on the gruff male voice that was coming closer to me.

"My dog? Where's my dog?"

"She's fine. I'll give you the information of the vet that they took her to. The EMT that tended to her seems to think she may have a broken rib, but that's it," Detective Reynolds said. I nodded and swallowed hard. "Miss Keeton, I'm going to need you to tell me exactly what happened. Do you think you can do that right now?"

I nodded. Linda placed a tissue in my hand and I wiped away my tears. "Detective Reynolds, she's blind," Linda interjected.

"Okay. Just please explain to me what happened." The sound of police radios and voices filled the hallway as I took a deep breath and pulled it together, recounting every last detail as well as giving him the history that Mason had with Ashton Barrett. "Is Mason going to be okay?" I asked.

"I'm not aware of his medical condition. He's at the hospital now, so he's at the best possible place he could be," Detective Reynolds said, trying to put my mind at ease but failing miserably.

"This can't be happening. It just can't!" I cried.

"Shh…" Linda consoled me, rubbing gentle circles on my back.

"Becca!" I lifted my head at the sound of Liz's voice and began to cry even harder.

She took a seat on the other side of me and wrapped her arms around me. "Liz, don't let him leave me again. Please tell him that he can't. I love him. I love him so much and I never got to tell him."

"Mason won't go down without a fight; especially when he knows he's got you and the baby to wake up to." I moved my head from her shoulder and looked up in confusion. "I saw the prenatal vitamins on your table yesterday and all of your paperwork from your doctor and I kind of told Mason today. I'm sorry, but he had to make a decision about that promotion and I thought that maybe that was the push that he needed. That's why he came to see you. He was so happy, Becca."

I buried my face in my hands and began to sob uncontrollably. I had lost him once and lost my sight. I knew if I lost him this time so much more was at stake. I closed my eyes, hoping that this baby was enough to give him the will to pull through this.

After three long days, I didn't think I had any more tears left inside of me. It hurt to breathe. Why did this have to happen? I rubbed my belly and the tears began to flow once again. All I could think of was raising this baby alone and how he, or she, would never know what a wonderful man their dad was. I couldn't do this without him.

"Becca, are you ready?" Mason's mother asked. I nodded and wiped away the tears. She took my hand as I stood up and I walked beside her in a straight line for what seemed like eternity before turning off. She guided me over to the chair and I sat down. "Okay, I'll give you your privacy. Talk to him. He's here. He can hear you."

I reached down and felt around for his hand and wrapped my fingers around it. "Mason, there are so many things I need to tell you, but most of all; I love you. I fell in love with you all those years ago and you made me fall in love with you again. You and I, we're that perfect full moon that shines among the stars. I will not let you leave me this time. You have too much to live for. We still have so many sunsets together, and I can only see them with you, through your eyes, with your heart." I leaned my head on his chest and listened to his heart beating. As I stood back up, I took his hand and placed it on my belly. "Do you see what I do, Mason? Can you see our unborn baby? I can see him so clearly. Call me crazy, but I just know it's a boy." I bit my bottom lip and smiled, wiping my tears with the back of my hand. "He has your boyish charm and good looks. He's the most beautiful little boy in the world, Mason, and he needs you. He needs his Daddy. Don't leave us. I'm begging you." I gasped when I felt his hand move up my stomach. "Mason? Are you awake? Can you hear me?" I grabbed onto his hand and he gripped it tighter. Leaning over, I whispered in his ear. "We need you, Mason. Please wake up." He grasped my hand tighter and I felt a smile rush across my face. "Wake up, Baby. Wake up." I kissed him over and over again on the top of his head.

"Becca?" His voice sounded so weak.

"Yes?" I couldn't wipe the teardrops quick enough as they spilled from my eyes.

"Who needs me?" he asked.

"I need you, and our baby needs you."

I swept my hand across the scruff of his face. "Say it again, Becca."

"Our baby, Mason; our beautiful little baby needs you."

"I love you, Becca."

"I love you, too. More than you will ever know." I ran my hand through his hair and rested my lips on his forehead. He came back to me after six long years and now he had come back again after the three longest days of my life and I would never let him leave me again. He was here and he was mine—this time forever.

Chapter 53

Mason

After two long weeks of being in the hospital, I was finally home. I knew that I wouldn't have been doing as well if it weren't for Becca. She gave me a reason to wake up that day. Having her love was enough, but knowing that she was going to have my baby only added to my reason to survive.

From what I had heard from Liz, Ashton was released from the hospital last week and was now facing a slew of charges. My mother and father had just gone back to Louisiana and I was climbing the walls to get back to work. I had made my decision and took the promotion and I knew now that it was the best decision ever. I had called Becca's father earlier in the week and asked if I could meet with him. Since I was still unable to drive, he agreed to come into the city and meet me for a drink. I was surprised by his willingness to do so and was hoping he was as amiable to what I had to say. As I walked into the restaurant, I spotted him right away sitting at the mostly empty bar.

I took a deep breath as I approached him. "Dr. Keeton."

He looked from his drink and stood up to shake my hand.

"How are you feeling?" he asked.

"Pretty good," I responded.

He nodded as he looked me up and down the same way he always did when Becca and I were first together. "I—umm… I wanted to tell you thank you for saving her." I could see the emotion building in his eyes.

"No need to thank me, Dr. Keeton. I love Becca with all my heart and I would have gladly died for her that day."

He closed his eyes and nodded. "I'm not just talking about what happened a few weeks ago. I'm talking about six years ago, too." I stared into his eyes and nodded. "I spoke with one of the agents on that case. When I found out how Barrett had intended to use my daughter, I swear to God I wanted to kill him and I realized if it weren't for you, something much worse could have happened to Becca."

"You never told her about the case or about me? Why?"

"Because I gave you my word that I wouldn't and I did realize how much you truly did care for her."

"She means everything to me and that's the reason I asked you to meet me, sir. I want to ask her to marry me and I would like to have your blessing." His eyes widened in surprise. "I know it may be a little old fashioned, but that's the way I was raised."

He stared straight ahead like he was deep in thought. "You weren't lying when you told me that you really did love her all those years ago."

"No, sir, I wasn't. And I promise to be the best husband and father–" I stopped myself, knowing that I had just said too much. Becca and I hadn't told anyone that news yet.

His eyes filled with emotion and I knew right away that he caught on to my slip up. "Becca's pregnant?" I hesitantly nodded.

He formed the slightest of smiles. "My little girl is going to have a baby? I'm going to be a grandpa?" His smile broadened.

"Becca is probably going to be really pissed at me for letting that slip because I'm sure she wanted to be the one to tell you, but yeah, she is."

He shook his head and tapped his hand on the bar. "Bartender, get my future son-in-law a drink. He's going to be a dad!" He looked into my eyes and extended his hand to me. "You have my blessing, Mason."

Lilly and I took a walk to Becca's office to pick her up from work, stopping along the way to pick her up some roses. Tomorrow was her birthday and I wanted to start celebrating tonight. She was deep in thought as she sat there listening to a recording. I stood in the doorway just smiling at her. She was glowing and just knowing that in seven months she would be having my baby made my grin grow even wider. Lilly began to whine, causing Becca to take out her earplugs. I walked over quietly to her and stuck the roses under her nose.

She smiled. "Roses!"

"But can you guess what color?"

"Hmm….I'm thinking red."

"Nope." She furrowed her eyebrows in confusion. "What's your favorite color?"

"Oh…. pink!" She inhaled their fragrance once again and smiled.

"Early birthday present for the birthday girl."

"Wow, beautiful roses!" Stephanie, Becca's assistant, said as she walked in the door.

"Thank you. They're a present from this guy here." She giggled.

"Want me to get them in some water for you?" Stephanie asked.

"Yeah, that'd be great," Becca replied. I waited for Stephanie to exit before bending down by the side of Becca's desk, kissing her on the lips and then her belly.

"How are you feeling today?" I asked.

"Great, actually. Didn't throw up once, so I'm hoping that the worst of it is over."

"It is, Becca, and it will only get better going forward." She placed her hands on my face and smiled, clearly knowing that I wasn't just referring to her pregnancy.

"What about you? You haven't been overdoing it today, have you?"

"Nope!"

"Mason, don't lie. You know the doctor said he wants you taking it easy until you go back to see him for your follow up visit."

How could I forget? *Taking it easy* meant no sex, and Becca wasn't caving on bending the doctor's orders. "Cross my heart. Lilly and I had an uneventful day." She didn't need to know that this afternoon consisted of meeting up with her Dad and picking up her ring from the jewelers.

"Here you go, Becca!" Stephanie said as she brought the vase full of roses back in and placed them on Becca's desk.

"I'm going to leave them here. That way when I'm sitting at my desk, I can smell them and think of you."

"Sounds good to me."

She reached around for her bag on the floor and stood up. I took her arm in mine and we were on our way.

We went back to my place and ordered Chinese takeout. Becca had been staying with me since my parents left to go back home. She said that it was because she wanted to make sure I wasn't doing anything that the doctor told me not to do, but I knew part of it was because she was freaked out about staying in her apartment after everything that happened. Ashton was being held in prison without bail, which put my mind at ease a little bit. And I was hoping with any luck that he would be staying there for a very long time. I hated the fact that Becca was going to have to be put through the stress of testifying and I hoped that wouldn't happen until after she had the baby.

"I'm so excited that you are coming to my parents' with me this weekend for my birthday!" Becca beamed. "Having you there and my brother, it's just gonna be great!"

"Hey, I wanted to give you another early birthday present."

"Mason, you're spoiling me.....but I'll allow it." She laughed.

"Well, this is actually something old." I grabbed her wrist and clasped the bracelet that I had given her all those years ago for her birthday.

She reached down with her other hand and felt around. "My bracelet," she whispered. "You kept it all this time?"

"I did."

She threw her arms around me and placed a gentle kiss on my cheek. "This means more to me than anything. Thank you so much."

"Well, *you* mean more to me than anything, so *thank you*, Becca." She placed her head on my shoulder and let out a deep breath. "What's wrong?" I asked.

"I just never thought that I'd be this happy again. When I lost my sight, I thought my life was over. I never imagined that I would find someone to love me and actually have a baby someday. They were all dreams that I let fade away because I thought they were impossible. But you made those dreams a reality for me."

"I never stopped loving you, Becca, and I'm just so happy that I found you again."

"Me too!" She smiled and gave me a tight squeeze before rubbing her belly which wasn't showing any signs of pregnancy yet. "But I'd be lying if I said I wasn't a little scared."

I moved her hair from her face and stared down at her. "Why

are you scared?"

"Because I want to be the best mother that I can be and I'm just afraid that I won't be able to without my vision."

"Becca, Baby, you have so much love in your heart, and that's the most important thing you can give to our baby."

"I know, but what if –"

I placed my lips on hers to stop her from talking. "Becca, we're in this together and I promise you our baby is going to have the best life ever and you are going to be the best mom ever."

She let out a deep breath. "I can't wait until *he* gets here."

"Well, what makes you so sure it's going to be a he? It could be a beautiful little girl, just like her mommy."

"Nope, I have a strange feeling that *he's* going to be all you."

I reached over to the table for the bag of fortune cookies. "Maybe one of these fortune cookies has the answer," I teased.

"Oh yeah! Maybe!" She laughed. "Read it to me." I cracked open the cookie and was silent for a moment. "Well, I'm waiting!"

"The person reading this fortune to you loves you very much."

She giggled. "Really, silly, what does it say?"

"You really want to know?"

"Yes!"

I took a deep breath and prepared myself. "Will you marry me?"

The smile that was on her face instantly disappeared and I wasn't sure if that was a good or bad thing. She gasped and covered her mouth with her hand as she sat there speechless.

"Umm…. Becca. Can you kind of tell me which way you're leaning here?" Her smile returned, followed by tears.

She nodded. "Yes," she whispered. I took her left hand in mine and slid the ring down her finger. It was a perfect fit, looking like it was made just for her. She wrapped her arms around my neck and pressed her forehead to mine. "I do believe that I am the happiest woman alive right this very second."

I placed my lips on hers and her tongue found its way into my mouth. She pushed me down on the couch and her hands began to wander. "Hey Becca?" I whispered.

"Hmm?" she replied as she continued planting tiny kisses along my neck.

"You are making it very hard for me to follow my doctor's orders right now."

"I promise I'll be very gentle." She giggled.

"Feel free to break that promise," I said, grabbing her face and meeting her lips once again.

Chapter 54

Becca

Seven months later……

Mason and I married two months after our engagement in a small intimate ceremony at his parents' house. It was truly the happiest day of my life. He was settling in nicely with his new job and I decided to take a leave of absence from mine once the baby was born. I was scared to death, every time I thought about taking care of a baby without my sight. We had hired Linda's sister to help me out once the baby arrived. I hated feeling like I couldn't care for my own baby. Every time I would begin to doubt myself, Mason would help me chase those feelings away. I had fully popped with only two weeks to go. I was actually glad that I couldn't see what I looked like because I felt like I had a giant watermelon growing inside of me. We had found out at my three month ultrasound that my suspicions were correct; we were having a boy and we had decided on the perfect name for him – Drew.

Ashton was sentenced to twenty five years, which to me still wasn't long enough. Krista tried to feign innocence in the whole matter, but once she saw that I wasn't falling for it, she begged me to forgive her without any success. What she had done to Mason and I was unforgivable and I totally wiped my hands clean of her. I was putting the past behind me and now focusing on my new life with Mason and our baby.

Liz and Natalie had finally gotten married and Mason and I were having a great time at their wedding. I was just wrapping up my conversation with Liz's sister when Mason came up behind me and wrapped his arm around me. "Come outside with me," he whispered. I excused myself and took his hand as he led me out the door.

"Is there a reason that you made me come outside on this chilly April night?" I asked.

"Yeah, there is." I felt myself warming up a bit when he placed his suit jacket around my bare arms. "Becca Boudreaux, can I please have this dance with you?"

"Well, sure, but couldn't we have done that inside where it's a lot warmer?"

"You're right; we could have, but inside doesn't have the right kind of music."

I creased my eyebrows in confusion until I heard the familiar tune of *Moonlight Serenade*. My heart was smiling along with my face as he pulled me close and we began to dance. I rested my head against his chest and closed my eyes, remembering that night on the beach from so long ago, never imagining the long journey that I would have to take to be back in his arms again in this way. My humongous belly was pressed up against him when I felt the familiar flutter of our baby, letting us know that he was there.

"Boy, I think he's trying to tell us something." Mason laughed.

"That is the best feeling in the world."

"Just think, in two more weeks this guy is going to be coming out screaming."

"Are you scared?" I asked.

"Hell, no. I want this more than anything in this world."

"Mason, I called Dr. Jennson this afternoon. I want to have the surgery done after the baby is born."

"Really?" I could hear the excitement in his voice as he pulled me closer and hugged me tightly.

I nodded. "If there's a chance that I will be able to see my baby, then I'm going to take it."

"And you will, Becca. I just have a feeling that you will."

"Well, even if it doesn't work, I know that I will still be seeing him with my heart. You will help me do that, right?"

"Of course I will." I rested my head back on his chest, not wanting the music to end. "Hey Becca?"

"Yeah?"

"Do you see all the stars that are out tonight?"

I lifted my head toward the sky before turning my attention back to him, tracing the outline of his face. "I do and it's beautiful." I stood on my tiptoes and whispered in his ear, "And you know what?"

"What's that?" he whispered back, grazing his lips against my earlobe.

"There's going to be a full moon tonight, tomorrow..... and forever."

I knew that no matter what the future held, I could deal with it. I was still seeing that beautiful star filled sky so clearly even without my sight. As long as I had Mason by my side, I wouldn't be missing out on any of the beautiful moments in life. They would be forever captured in my heart.

Epilogue

Seven Months Later

I was completely out of it, not knowing where I was. The light was unbearable. I quickly shot up in bed. After seven years of darkness, I was finally seeing light. My eyes were slowly focusing in on shapes. The big square outline on the wall was a television. The smaller squares with pops of color were pictures. My heart was racing with excitement. "Becca, you're awake." I heard the familiar voice of Dr. Greenberg as the shadow of him moved closer. He sat down on my bed and shined a bright light in my eyes, causing me to close them. I opened them back up once he took the light away and a smile stretched across my face. "You have a moustache and wear glasses."

"Becca, you can see that?" I could hear the happiness in his voice. I nodded. "Do you have any idea how great this is? Most patients that have made a full recovery from this surgery haven't been able to see any type of light until after the first few months once the optic nerve gets stronger and then they can start making out shapes." I couldn't stop smiling. "I'm going to let your husband know you're awake and that he can come and see you. I won't share your good news. I'll leave that up to you."

"Thank you." I smiled and pulled my blanket over me. My *white blanket*. I could see colors; something that I would never take for granted again. My vision was nowhere near where it was before my accident, but it was a start.

"Becca." Mason's voice inched closer to me. He took a seat on my bed and I placed my hands on his cheeks as my eyes focused on that beautiful face that I had remembered from so long ago. He sat there quietly, almost as if he was afraid to know the results of the surgery.

"I always loved the way you looked in blue," I said as my eyes drifted down to the pale blue shirt he was wearing.

"Becca! You can see that!" his voice cried out in sheer joy.

"Yeah, I can!" I nodded, trying my best to blink away the tears.

"Oh Baby! I knew it! I knew that it would work." He kissed me on the head over and over again. "I've been dying to do something since the day I first walked into your office."

"What's that?"

He took my face in his hands. "Look at me, Becca." The teardrops blurred my vision a little more as I stared into his eyes for the very first time in seven years, and they were more beautiful than I ever remembered.

"My handsome, handsome husband," I whispered.

"I love you so much, Becca."

"I love you, too."

He hugged me tightly and I melted in his arms. "Where are you going?" I asked when he stood up from my bed.

"I'll be right back. I have a surprise for you."

I was unable to wipe the smile from my face. I couldn't wait to get home and *see* my baby for the first time. I closed my eyes and opened them quickly, making sure this wasn't just a dream.

My eyes focused on Mason as he walked back in the room holding Drew. I was speechless. "Becca, this is Drew." He placed him in my arms and my heart melted. Tears streamed down my face as I laid eyes on my beautiful little boy for the first time ever. I ran my hand through his baby fine hair that was almost as white as my blanket, focusing on his perfectly round face, his rosy cheeks, and his bright blue eyes. The same eyes that I always remembered staring back at me in the mirror for the first twenty one years of my life. "He's so beautiful, Mason; just how I imagined him."

"Yeah, he is." The familiar butterflies that he had always brought to my stomach from so long ago were unleashed when I saw his face turn up into a huge smile.

"I thought he was with my mom and dad?"

"He was. I asked your parents to come here. I thought you would want to *see* him as soon as you woke up."

"Thank you, Mason." I choked back a sob. "I will remember this moment forever," I whispered.

"I want the painting," he said, kissing me on the forehead.

"Well, I don't know about that just yet."

"If it's in your heart, you can paint it."

"My heart is overflowing with it." I smiled.

He moved in closer and pressed his lips against mine as he wiped the tears from my eyes.

I leaned my head on his shoulder and squeezed his hand tightly as I watched Drew finally give into his sleepiness and close his eyes. I rested my lips on his head, breathing in the familiar scent of his baby shampoo, and closed my eyes, wanting to seep every ounce of this moment into my heart forever. I was instantly bought back to that day on the beach and the blind man that I had made the drawing for:

"If you ask me, everyone should be blind before they can see. People would view the world much differently."

Truer words had never been spoken. My world was dark until Mason came back into it, allowing me to see once again, the same way he had allowed me to see before my accident and neither time with my eyes. Drew allowed me to see a life that I always dreamed of but was afraid of living. Mason allowed me to have that life through the visions in my mind, the feelings in my heart, and his love. I was fortunate enough to be blessed not once, but twice by the man sitting by my side and the beautiful baby sound asleep in my arms.

Mason and Drew—the two greatest loves of my life.

The End

Made in the USA
Columbia, SC
17 May 2018